Always a Weaver

by

Maija DeRoche

sequel to Forever Chrysalis

Always a Weaver

Cover Art by *The Wild Rose Press, Inc.*

The Wild Rose Press, Inc.
PO Box 708
Adams Basin, NY 14410-0708
Visit us at www.thewildrosepress.com

Publishing History
First Edition, 2025
Trade Paperback ISBN 978-1-5092-5982-3
Digital ISBN 978-1-5092-5983-0

sequel to *Forever Chrysalis*
Published in the United States of America

Dedication

This book is dedicated
to generations before, now, and after…

Acknowledgments

A great deal of gratitude, first of all, goes to my editor Nan Swanson of TWRP. Throughout the process, she has been a wonderful sounding board and, with her eagle eye, a guru of catching my "Finnishisms."

A big thank you also to Martha Horton. She would see an oddity in my writing and gently mention that "Here in the USA, we would probably say it this way…"

Without my 12-year old granddaughter's input, the book might still be without a title. Thank you, Edie.

Thanks to Mackenzie Bristow, who kept me on the right track on how an American might view things Finnish. I am grateful for that ever since *Forever Chrysalis* days.

Thank you also to my husband, who kept cooking, and the Canandaigua Writers Group, who kept listening.

Chapter 1

It's scary, when you forget your own name. I had to verify it on the bracelet they wrapped around my wrist prior to surgery: Kaisa Weston 6/6/1949. God, I'm older than dirt! Reaching for my phone to check the time, I hit the guard rail of the bed with the hard, plastic venous port on my hand, making a hollow, metallic sound. No phone. No expected bedside table.

"How are we doing, sweetie?" The nurse appeared to be addressing me. "We are fine, honeybun," I said, annoyed at yet another patronizing person in a helping profession. "I may have lived longer than you, but I am not your sweetie."

The blood pressure cuff squeezed my arm. I realized I was still in the recovery room. Oh, crap, Alice will kill me! She had me swear a solemn promise never to use the stairs to the lakeside. Why does she always have to manage my life? I moved into a small condominium from my beloved house because Alice said it was a good idea. I started driving again because Alice thought I should try to hold onto all skills and abilities as long as possible. I listen when Alice speaks. She can't help but offer me solutions to my problems. She even has answers to issues that are not problematic—at least, not to me. Once a teacher, always a teacher. Of course, she bosses her kids around, too. The only one she leaves alone is Tom, but he is almost non-human with his sweet disposition and a

1

way with people, all people. He knows exactly how to handle Alice. Who is Alice to control her mother's life anyway? So I have Parkinson's. That doesn't make me an invalid. In valid. Void of relevance. Without importance.

Besides, I do need to get to the bottom of the mystery of who moved next door. You can only get a glimpse of the condominium next to mine from the dock. The balcony may give some hints. It bothers me that the woman stays to herself. Who moves in and pays no attention to her neighbors?

I'll work on that when I get out of here.

My eternal curiosity! It probably wasn't worth the broken hip this time around.

****

Alice shut off her computer and took off her glasses sporting leopard print frames. Her students had grasped the opportunity to give her the nickname "Cougar," although the description was a far cry from Alice's character and possibly not fully understood by some of the more sheltered high schoolers. Alice allowed the slip, as she knew it was well meant. She tilted back her head and closed her eyes. She loved teaching history. When she was a little girl, she had preferred bedtime stories that took you to different times. The present was too mundane, and the future too intangible, but the past was fascinating. Stories with people dressed in old-fashioned garb transported her back in time to the Egyptian pyramids, the Silk Road to and from China, the court of King Louis XVI.

She also loved teaching in general. Her Chrysalis sisters—Christine, Crystal, and Lisa—had been dutiful pupils in her game of school in their childhood years, where Alice was always the teacher. Alice's choice for a career had been clear. Little did she know then that teaching is not a nine-to-five job. Alice spent countless hours after school correcting tests and reading papers. Luckily, today, it's all accomplished by computers, so there was no need to lug reams of paper from the classroom to her house and back.

Alice got up and called her mother, an established daily habit. This routine was partly her daughterly duty, partly an action expected by Kaisa. Either way, left ignored, it would cause inordinately large pangs of guilt for Alice. When the task was accomplished, Alice could move on in her life each day.

Kaisa had emerged from her hip surgery surprisingly well and had been able to return home after a short rehabilitation period. According to Kaisa, the success was due to her innate *sisu*, a dogged determination to go through a hard rock when necessary, a quality Finns are known to possess. Kaisa was a proud Finn.

Yet Alice worried about her stubborn, almost pig-headed mother. When Kaisa had finally decided to sell her house and move into a worry-free condominium, Alice had imagined Kaisa's life to be rather uneventful, and to become more and more so with her advancing Parkinson's disease. However, Kaisa had a habit of taking the reins into her own hands without considering consequences for herself or for the loved ones in her life.

Alice's husband Tom's real estate business was showing signs of revitalization with people in the bigger cities, New York City in particular, wanting country homes for their virtual work life, and the Finger Lakes with its slower pace of life and natural beauty was a frequently chosen area to move into.

Today, Tom came home earlier than usual.

"Hi, how are you?" Tom tipped back Alice's office chair to kiss her on the forehead. "And, how is Kaisa today?" The ever-so-polite Tom! Alice knew Kaisa wasn't the most important topic on his mind.

"She's fine. You know, as fine as a cantankerous queen bee can be."

With both of the children busy—Bobby getting ready for a long bike ride and Pam in her room waiting for her friend Stephanie to arrive, Alice grabbed the opportunity and suggested a walk. Tom eagerly agreed.

They drove a couple of miles to the beginning of an old dirt road. It had rained most of the day, and the numerous potholes were filled with muddy water.

Alice was quiet. Tom sensed apprehension and discomfort in her.

"Okay. What's on your mind?"

"What makes you think I have something on my mind?" Alice lifted her head at Tom, tilting it in a coquettish fashion.

"I know. A twenty-year marriage teaches you a thing or two. Really, what's bothering you?"

Alice sighed.

"You know how Pam and Stephanie have spent a lot of time together in recent weeks…" Alice walked around a large pothole filled with dirty water.

"Uh-huh."

"I don't know if you knew, but Stephanie was dating Michael Albright since before Christmas."

"Well, I don't much pay attention to those things." Tom smiled sheepishly. "That's the orthopedic surgeon's son, right?"

"Right." Alice hesitated for a minute and jumped over a pothole. Tom followed and simply took a big step with his long legs.

Alice was quiet. She was calculating her next navigation.

"And?' asked Tom, knowing this could not be the main point of the discussion, for which Alice seemed to have a definite purpose.

"Well," Alice skipped and hopped between the small holes on the road as she spoke. "Turns out Stephanie is pregnant and her parents threw her out of the house, can you imagine? And her aunt, although she took her in, isn't too keen on keeping her either, and Stephie has no place to go, and she is, and you can see this, totally distraught. She wants to keep the baby, and this is not about whether or not to have an abortion, she's decided not to, and that's her thing, but this is an awful situation, and I think we should take her in."

There! She had poured it out in one long string! Alice stood breathlessly between a deep puddle and a budding bush that somehow had managed to survive in the middle of the dirt road through the rough winter months. Alice waited for Tom's response.

"Whoa!" Tom was shaking his head as if to shake off cobwebs. "Can we slow down a bit? Us? Take her in? This is a lot to digest. Can we think about this for a while? You know, you are asking quite a bit of us as a couple, as a family?"

"Of course." Alice sniffled. "I just think it's awful of her parents, well, her mother, to do this to her daughter when she needs her support the most."

Tom put his arm around Alice as they continued their walk in silence. Alice started to leap over a large puddle, miscalculated the distance, and stepped smack in the middle of the muddy hole with her right foot, soaking her new sneaker. Tom pulled his annoyed wife into his arms.

"Before we talk more about Stephanie, please, think about your already full plate: Your mother is demanding, your job is challenging and tiring, our kids are having issues of their own, your husband is being a pain in the butt…"

Alice hugged Tom with all the warmth she could muster. She had just heard Tom say "yes" without saying so.

Chapter 2

Alice's heart was light. On the drive home from their walk, she leaned her body toward Tom and rested her head on his shoulder. How had she lucked out in nabbing this treasure of a man for her husband years ago?

In the driveway, they noticed large, transparent, plastic bins neatly piled on top of each other in front of the garage door. Her forehead in a quizzical wrinkle, Alice studied the contents: fashionable teen girl clothing, stuffed animals, books and magazines. It appeared that Stephanie's parents were clairvoyants who anticipated the Fitzpatricks' next move regarding the girl.

Pam and Stephanie sat in the den, almost hidden among the various throws and pillows on the gigantic couch built for easy living and lazy entertainment emanating from one type of screen or another. They had large bowls of ice cream in their hands. Stephanie's eyes were bloodshot and her face swollen. She looked up at Alice with red blotches on her pale throat and chest.

"I'm sorry." The words were coming out laboriously. "My mother just called. She told me I should never even think of coming home again, and…" Her voice trailed off.

Pam reached over and saved the bowl of ice cream that had started to slide off Stephanie's lap.

"I don't know what to do," Stephanie whispered almost inaudibly.

Pam directed a desperate look toward her mother.

"Let's talk," said Alice calmly. "Tom and I agree that you should stay with us until your life is a bit more settled."

Pam's delight was evident. She hugged her mother, almost making her lose her balance, and jumped onto the couch, grabbing Stephanie into her embrace. Her joy was almost overly enthusiastic.

"You mean I could stay with you guys? You mean I could, like, live here?" Stephanie's eyes were large.

Alice nodded. Stephanie burst into tears again. Alice continued, "There's one thing, Stephanie, since you'll be living here. As you know, Pam takes care of Niles and his litter box until my friend Dr. Hughes returns from Afghanistan. Make sure you don't touch the litter. Cats can spread toxoplasmosis through their feces. That is dangerous to fetuses. Chances are small that an indoor cat would be infected, but you should be careful." Alice imagined unforeseen health problems that were easily prevented.

Alice left the room, leaving the girls to chat about the future, from the minute, insignificant details to the life-changing event waiting for Stephanie.

Later, Alice returned to the room. "Okay, girls, before dinner, let's get the stuff."

"What stuff?" the two girls recited together.

"The bins of your things outside." Alice was confused.

The girls jumped up and went outside. Stephanie looked at Alice.

"Did you and my mom have this all figured out between the two of you? She must have dropped the bins off."

"No, Stephanie, I haven't talked to your mom."

"Then it's even worse," Stephanie said bitterly. "You know, she really is a bitch."

Stephanie's belongings safely in the house, Alice made a cup of coffee and called her mother. She believed there's no point in postponing experiences you know will be unpleasant. After the call, she could not decide whether her suddenly developed heartburn was caused by Kaisa or the strong coffee.

****

I need to talk some sense into Alice! What is that girl thinking? As if she didn't already do too much for everybody, including me. To take in a pregnant teenager is trouble, if you ask me, especially a teenager with a mom and a dad. There are also the parents of the Albright boy, who got her pregnant. Albright! Not too bright this time! Were they consulted? Both sets of parents have the means to help, but I can just imagine what this does to the image, the public picture of the high-class families with all skeletons neatly stashed in their closets. Alice is sticking her nose into a mess, I tell you! Tom couldn't even talk her out of it. I love him, but sometimes he's milquetoast.

Chapter 3

When Kaisa downsized from her large home to the cozy lakeside condominium over a year ago, certain items were "stored" at Alice's house, "stored" being a misnomer in that Kaisa knew she would never again have the items in her place of residence. Today, the mahogany grand piano stood in Alice's living room taking up half the room space. The piano and the bobbin lace with bobbins on the pillow in the front and completed lace slowly coming off the roller in the back were items Kaisa insisted on keeping. The two women's opinions on what was worth saving and what could be sold, donated or trashed were very different.

The small condominium felt restricting to Kaisa, and she welcomed any outing as temporary relief from boredom. She had done a good job following Alice's advice for getting rid of extraneous things. She had even discarded items of great emotional importance to her, items from Finland including inherited valuable glassware: internationally acknowledged, prize winning vases and bowls by famous designers, and a large steaming system for making juice from berries, a gadget honoring the old thought of using everything from the earth in all forms. Among the discarded items were also famous fish fileting knives with carved reindeer bone handles and blades signed by the designer. Kaisa envisioned few chances to clean fish or to hold large dinner parties in her future. Therefore, as usual, she eagerly accepted an invitation to have dinner with Alice's family on a beautiful April Sunday. The dinner visit with Alice's family also gave her an opportunity to play a couple of her favorite tunes on her old piano, as out of tune as it was. The other beloved item of her past, the bobbin lace pillow, Kaisa would have been willing to part with, had it not been for Alice, who all of a sudden showed interest in the old art.

After dinner and Kaisa's rendition of Oskar Merikanto's "Summer Night's Waltz," the mother and daughter sat down for a lesson in bobbin lace weaving. The piano piece had been lovely, even with Kaisa's difficulties reaching a full octave. Kaisa accepted that hindrance as a result of the natural progression of Parkinson's. Alice chose to look at it as a sign of a lack of practice. Both were, most likely, correct. Maybe the bobbin lace would be a smoother activity.

Alice held in her hand a smooth bobbin with natural linen thread wound around it. The bobbin had snapped loose from among forty-eight bobbins spread in a seemingly haphazard order on the firm pillow.

"Tension! You have to be aware of the tension!" Kaisa demonstrated how to reattach the thread to the rest of the lace. "If you leave the thread too loose, you get flimsy-looking lace, and if you pull too tight, this is what happens. Snap!"

"This is trickier than I thought." Alice shook her head.

"Now, try again. Remember that you always work with pairs, two bobbins in your right hand, two in your left. You move them in a basic pattern: the second from the left between the two on the right, then the two move to the left, each over one bobbin, and repeat. You do this once, twice, or one and a half times with the two pairs, then move on to the next pair, depending on the pattern. Go ahead."

"Right… What?" Alice was confused. She started to remember why she had not been enthused about picking up the hobby from her mother before.

Alice moved the bobbins as instructed.

"I made a knot. What now?"

"You are supposed to make a knot. Now you have to stabilize it. You put a pin on the pattern on the roller. You make another knot on this side of the pin, and, the important part, tighten it with the right tension."

"How do I know which hole out of hundreds I put the pin in?"

"That you'll learn as you go along. The pattern is on the roller but it's also in your head."

"Not in my head!"

"Not yet. You're a quick study. You'll get it."

Alice started to wonder whether trying to please her mother by picking up her hobby was a good idea.

Kaisa sensed her apprehension and said, "I have a feeling this will be a long-term project…" She looked at Alice from under her brow testing the air for perhaps having hurt Alice's feelings. When Alice laughed, Kaisa added: "Why don't you keep this pillow. I will order myself a new one." Kaisa looked lovingly at the old pillow on the wooden frame her father had made for her when she was preschool age. She started to smile, then let out a soft giggle. "This way, you'll have a piece of history with you. You know, I hadn't thought of this for decades, but the soft cloth under the cardboard pattern on the roller is actually strips of my father's long underwear from the fifties. Perfect stretchy fabric allowing for easy placement of straight pins into the pattern. Wouldn't he be surprised to know that his long johns made it from Finland to America!"

After Kaisa left, Alice thought to herself: *What did I do? This may mean that Mom will spend a lot of time at my house, first playing the piano and now... Sometimes I'm a masochistic ditz...*

Alice had no particular emotional attachment to the tools of Kaisa's hobbies. She had an ulterior motive: Kaisa's Parkinson's was advancing and any fine motor activity would keep her fingers limber and functioning as long as possible. This arrangement also necessitated Kaisa's visits to Alice's house, if she wanted to enjoy playing the piano or weaving lace again.

Chapter 4

After Pam had driven her grandmother back to her condominium, she decided that, although it was late, tonight was the night for her to talk to her mother about Stephanie. She hoped Alice would still be up when she got home. She felt eager, yet slightly apprehensive.

Pam opened the front door to a quiet house. Stepping in, she heard a sound of her mother's hair dryer from the master bedroom wing. Good, her mom was still up. She grabbed a soft drink from the refrigerator and took a swig, with the carbonation traveling swiftly up to her sinuses. When her knock on the master bedroom door did not produce a response, Pam felt safe to open it. She saw her father sound asleep with his CPAP machine whirring like a purring cat. She walked to the master bathroom door and rapped on it as softly as she could. A good thing her mother didn't have the need to have the radio or any other sound-producing gadget on like her dad always did, or she never would have heard her knock.

Alice hesitantly stuck her head out the door and mimed Pam to come in.

"What's up, cookie?" said Alice, applying a night-time cream to her face.

"Can we talk about Stephanie for a second?"

"Sure. What's on your mind?"

"Well," Pam took a sip of her soda. "I have some

questions, but if this is a bad time, we…"

"Not at all, Pam. Tell me."

Pamela felt trapped now. She had been anxious and excited to talk to her mom, but now the moment was at hand, her confidence waned.

"I was just wondering…" Pam leaned on the towel rack. "How could it be that Stephanie got pregnant, when she said that she used birth control?" Pam's voice was hushed but forceful.

"Honey, no birth control outside of surgical methods is a hundred percent guaranteed. What did Stephanie tell you?"

"She said he used a condom."

Alice felt out of her field of expertise. She weighed the information given in health classes against the seldom-discussed emotional component of sex in young people's lives.

"Like I said, nothing is a hundred percent certain. Condoms have been known to break or possibly not be used correctly."

"Yeah… I asked her why she even did it, and she got really mad at me. She said I didn't understand anything and that I had all the good things in life, especially a family that loves me. You know what I think? I think she was not being careful on purpose. She said that having a baby will give her someone who will love her unconditionally, someone who will be only hers."

"I know. I've heard that before. There are some issues she needs to work on. Do you feel all right about being her sounding board?"

"I don't know. I'm afraid I don't have the right answers. How could I? I'm a teenager myself! Can you talk to her, Mom?"

"What do you think I should talk to her about in particular?"

"Well, about this big responsibility she is putting on her baby that hasn't even been born yet."

Alice was taken aback at Pam's mature thoughts.

"I'll see. I don't want her to put you in a bad spot. It's getting late. Let's sleep on it and we'll deal with it tomorrow." Alice began to feel protective of her kind, old-soul daughter.

"Thanks, Mom!"

Pam gave her mom a hug, left the bathroom quietly, and tiptoed through the master bedroom where her father had now grabbed all the covers from her mother's side of the bed.

"Poor Mom," thought Pam.

"Poor Pam," thought Alice. *"She's taken on a great deal without having the resources for the issue. Must be an inherited trait."*

Alice sat on the edge of the bathtub. By helping someone in need, she had created a problem for a loved one.

Is this always the case, being in the middle? Can there be a winner? She knew it would be a sleepless night.

As Alice stepped out of the bathroom, the whirring of the CPAP machine attached to the man in the cocoon of blankets wafted into her ears. Alice settled herself on her side of the bed and stared at the ceiling. It really could use a fresh coat of paint.

Chapter 5

Kaisa looked out the window. Although fall with its richness of colors was her favorite season, she delighted in the coming to life of nature all around her in the spring and early summer. She regretted not having been being able to dig up some of her favorite plants at the old house and bring them to the yard of her current home. The condominium only had common areas between the building and the lake. There were other plants growing there, but no lilac bushes, peonies, or Finland's national flower, the lily of the valley. She decided to contact Abdul Nazari, the nice, recently widowed professor from Afghanistan, who had bought her house. With five children to take care of, he probably didn't have a whole lot of time for gardening and wouldn't mind if she removed some of the plants. Of course, that would mean Alice and Tom would have to help her, now that she had a strict directive from her daughter to stay away from the steps leading to the back of the building.

The waves on the lake had foamy crests. With the great depth and its location in a deep valley, the lake could, at times, become dangerous for boaters and especially kayakers, in strong winds. Her thoughts turned to the scenery of her childhood in Finland, where water surrounded her. When she and her friend Lola had visited her old summer cottage by the Baltic Sea a couple of years ago, she'd looked at the experience as perhaps her last chance to travel. There was no way to predict how and with what speed her Parkinson's would progress. She was pleased and surprised that Lola fell in love with Finland and with the little old cottage in particular. While there, Lola started to paint again and claimed to be happier than she had imagined possible. When at the end of their three-week trip Lola asked to stay on, Kaisa was pleased. In a way, she internalized the compliment, homage, and endorsement on behalf of her birth country. Kaisa also felt jealous. Lola returned to the States after the allowed ninety days in Finland, but had promptly left to go back to the island about a year ago. Kaisa found it interesting that, although Lola and she both had daughters in Haudenosaunee Hills, Lola found it easy to leave her daughter Crystal behind, while Kaisa couldn't imagine living so far away from Alice and her grandchildren. "Motherhood is a different entity for different women," she thought.

As Kaisa watched the waves and listened to the wind, she saw something move on the balcony next to hers. She opened her door and stuck out her head to bring the neighboring balcony into full view. There appeared to be two mink coats hanging on hooks on the outside wall.

"Odd," thought Kaisa. "Fur coats this time of the year! Maybe she is airing them out before storing them for summer. Nice coats." She decided to take a closer look.

The coats were two mink, one full-length mahogany and the other "car length" silvery pearl.

"Well!" Kaisa exclaimed out loud. It was clear that the long coat had what appeared to be dried blood on the front of it. It looked like someone had taken the wearer by the lapels with bloody hands.

With her heart pounding, Kaisa quickly withdrew to her living room. She dialed Alice's number. No answer.

"Of course, Alice is at work. What was I thinking?"

Kaisa left a message.

****

Alice waited till Pam, Stephanie, and Bobby had left the dinner table before addressing Tom.

"Do you remember when I told you that Mom thinks some woman has moved into the condo next to her?"

"Yes. And I told you that the condominium is empty. Has been for a while. I checked with other realtors, and I got the same info from everybody. What's Kaisa saying now?"

"Mom left me a voice message. She says there is obviously a woman living in the unit, a woman who has two mink coats, and, get this—the minks are airing out on the balcony with blood on the lapels of one of them!"

Tom snickered. "Wow, her imagination is getting the best of her!"

"Don't laugh. I've been doing a lot of reading about Parkinson's. In some cases, the disease can cause hallucinations. You know that medication ad on TV where the older man sees a cat where there isn't anything there."

"I guess so. Do you want to go over and check out this bloody fur?"

"I am super tired. Let's just wait and see."

"Sounds good. Go read your book. I'll take care of the dishes."

Tom collected the plates, glasses, and flatware from the table and carried them to the kitchen sink with Alice's adoring eyes caressing his broad back.

Chapter 6

Tom folded his legs into his large SUV. Pam had obviously driven it last and, as usual, had forgotten to readjust the seat to meet her father's requirements. As an unusually tall person, Tom needed the leg space. Pam and Bobby affectionately called their father "Lighthouse," emphasizing his 6'7" frame and the shiny, shaved, bald head. He adjusted the height of the seat, the distance to the steering wheel, and the slant of the seat back for an optimal view of all mirrors.

Tom's first appointment was scheduled for the afternoon, which gave him a chance to stop in to check on the progress of Magnus's house renovations.

Magnus Lindqvist had bought his childhood home, an old, handsome colonial structure in need of serious help. Magnus didn't only want to renovate the rooms in need of work. He had his heart set on restoring the old place to its original glory. This was also his sister Christine's dream. For a few confused moments, Christine had entertained the idea of buying the house herself. She had come to her senses realizing that restoring a house in the Finger Lakes while living in Seattle was close to insanity. Both siblings were realistic about the condition of the building, which had, most recently, served as the sleeping quarters and a party den for a college fraternity. The pair romanticized the home of their youth and looked forward to recreating the feeling of their carefree days with each step of the restoration—finding the authentic light fixtures, refinishing the stair railing back to its rich sheen, and choosing paint colors to cover the graffiti created by the latest occupants.

Magnus opened the heavy door. He was dressed in worn out jeans and a red T-shirt with a simple line-drawn map of the local area. Tom read the text: "IAC Championships 1999."

Interesting that a millionaire has a twenty-two-year-old T-shirt, Tom thought but said nothing, concluding that Magnus perhaps was emotionally attached to the shirt from his high school swim team days, or that he truly was frugal and wore his clothes till they were threadbare.

"Hey!" said Magnus. "Come in. I'm just starting on the master bath restoration. I don't really know what I'm doing, but come see."

The newly restored stairway led them to a landing with doors opening to bedrooms in all directions. Magnus proceeded to the large bedroom extending from the front to the back of the house. Tom followed him, noting new improvements. Everything had been removed from the bathroom, which gave the room a spacious feel. Boxes of tiles were stacked on the bedroom floor and cans of paint sat on what looked to be an antique dining room sideboard, or maybe the bottom part of a hutch. Styles of furniture had always confused Tom. To him, function came first, appearance and style a distant second.

Magnus noticed Tom eyeing the sideboard, a piece of furniture obviously out of place.

"I'm going to use that as the vanity and put an old

wash basin on it as the sink."

Tom nodded.

"I'm keeping this the master bath, with the only entrance from the master bedroom." Magnus indicated the direction by tilting his head back.

"That's why it's called a master bath, after all," said Tom.

Magnus let out a small chuckle. "I found the plans for the last renovation my parents did, in the '80s. The original plan had the door open into the bathroom from the hallway and the master bedroom was two rooms. Anyway, I'm playing plumber, big-time. I'm changing the set-up for all of it—the toilet, the shower, and the sink.

"A shower? So, you're not keeping the tub?"

"Well, I'm installing the deep old clawfoot tub in the other upstairs bathroom. Christine told me to keep one tub in the house for bathing babies and toddlers."

Tom nodded. "Absolutely. A tub is great to have. Also, for the same reason, it's a good move for the resale value of the house."

"Yeah. You know it! Not that I'll be selling this place any time soon."

Tom had to hand it to Magnus. The brilliant metallurgical engineer with patents to his name appeared to be just as brilliant when it came to building or restoring a house.

"Especially now," Magnus continued.

Tom raised his eyebrows.

"I don't know if you heard through Christine or Alice, but I have found a mother for my baby. She's a newcomer to the Finger Lakes, and she has many qualities I would want my child's mother to have. She also has a job she loves and won't be moving any time soon. Partner parenting works well if you live near each other."

"So..." Tom tilted his head and looked at Magnus quizzically. "What does this mean? Are you, like, courting?" Tom smirked.

"Courting! Right!" Magnus let out a big laugh. "A gay man does not court women. This is purely a business arrangement with some emotional investment added into the mix. We have communicated on FaceTime, mostly, but we've been meeting in person more recently."

"But, the whole thing... how..." Tom started, then stopped. "None of my business. I'm glad you found someone."

Magnus grabbed a tile-removing tool and squatted on the floor covered by small black and white hexagon tiles.

"I'll share some more with you later, but now I've got to get at this monster job," said Magnus.

"No, no. We're fine. I'll see you soon."

Walking back downstairs, Tom admired the wallpaper in the hallway. Being independently wealthy had allowed Magnus to concentrate on his project full force. It looked like he'd attacked the job from bottom up, and the downstairs spaces appeared completed, with only a few details missing. Tom decided to google the parent partnering—or was it partner parenting?—later. Tom did not consider himself old or off course from modern ideas, but some struck him as uncomfortably different. "One should never judge anything without at least some detailed knowledge about the issue at hand," Tom convinced himself.

It was 10:45 according to his phone. There was

enough time to make a detour to the lake and his mother-in-law's condo.

Kaisa's condominium was ideal. It had great access from the street level and a gorgeous view of the lake from the balcony and the large windows. Tom parked his car and descended the steps to the lakeside. He admired the view with the water and the light green hillsides of early spring. He turned around to look at Kaisa's balcony. She had already brought out some of her house plants. He moved his gaze to the balcony next door on the right. Nothing there. Typical sight of an empty condominium, just as he had anticipated. Wrought iron railing showing beginning signs of rusting, dirty sliding glass doors with spider webs in the corners, shriveled up bugs still caught in one of them, and a lonely flower pot with dead plants hanging from a wall bracket by the door.

Kaisa appeared through the sliding glass doors of her balcony.

"You all think I'm nuts, don't you?"

Chapter 7

Stephanie jumped up from the large, sectional couch where she and Pam had been resting cozily with soft fleece throws around them, their eyes and thumbs dancing on their cell phones.

"What's wrong?" The unusually sudden movement alarmed Pam.

"Nothing," said Stephanie, and dashed out of the room.

Returning shortly, she announced, "Man, I have gas, but nothing comes out!"

"Thank you for sharing that," Pam said. "What do you expect? We had cabbage casserole for dinner."

"But I can't get rid of the gas!" Stephanie insisted.

"Well, isn't this a delicate conversation!" Pam rolled her eyes.

Stephanie usually liked Alice's cooking, even all the dishes using Grandma Kaisa's Finnish recipes. All, that is, except the liver casserole with barley and raisins. Stephanie would endlessly push a small forkful of it on her plate like a hockey puck on ice. And then there were the blood pancakes, which she had mistaken for dessert due to their chocolaty color and the lingonberry jam on the side. Alice was understanding and never expected people who were unfamiliar with the more ethnic dinner offerings to like them on the first try. After all, she remembered well the time when Tom's mother had served tripe for dinner during her first visit to her future in-laws' house. At the time, Alice had thought of it as a test of her sense of adventure or as a colossal joke. She never did learn to like tripe.

Stephanie was careful not to wrinkle her nose at anything that was offered to her. She was painfully conscious that Pam's family had taken her in when she was at her most vulnerable, and she truly was grateful. At one time, she had casually said to Pam, "Beggers can't be choosers," which both infuriated and saddened Pam.

"Don't be an idiot!" she had snapped at Stephanie. "You're here because we care. This is not the nineteenth century, where you were brought in because of your "unfortunate situation" and need to toil and grovel for your keep." Pam provided air quotes for the "unfortunate situation" term while rolling her eyes straight up as if sending a subtle message to the heavens.

Stephanie resettled into her comfortable chair, only to jump up quickly again and leave the room. When she returned, Pam asked her: "What does it feel like?"

"What does what feel like?"

"Well, the gas that doesn't come out. Does it hurt?"

Stephanie thought for a moment. "No, it does not hurt. Why?"

Pam put down her cell phone and assumed a motherly stance by leaning forward and taking both of Stephanie's hands into hers.

"Hey, you goof, you don't have gas. You're quickening!" Pam seemed to be truly delighted.

"I'm what?" Stephanie was baffled.

"You know, quickening," Pam repeated.

Stephanie sat motionless with no sign of

26

understanding Pam's words.

"Quickening!" Pam's voice got louder and more impatient. "You are feeling your baby moving."

Stephanie's hands went to her lower belly automatically.

"Really? Already?"

"What are you now? About sixteen weeks?" Pam knew precisely, but let Stephanie answer.

"Yeah, I guess…"

"What do you mean you guess? You're the one having the baby! You're the one who had sex! Don't tell me you don't know for sure!"

"How sure can I be of the weeks? I didn't have sex just once, you know." Stephanie's tone of voice conveyed an insecurity, yet also a strange sense of pride.

"What did the obstetrician say?" asked Pam.

"It's all written down in the report. I didn't think I would need to think about this stuff so soon."

"Girl, you're gonna be a mom. You're gonna be responsible for another human being. You'd better start thinking!"

Stephanie's eyes moistened. Pam reached over and hugged her.

"It'll be okay."

Later, in bed, Pam thought about her reaction to her friend. Stephanie didn't need her criticism. She had had enough of harsh treatment from her mother. Pam vowed to make sure that Stephanie learned about pregnancy and childbirth, that the baby had the best possible chances to enter this world as a healthy new human. Pam realized that, once again, she was taking on more responsibility, taking charge of a situation.

"Just like Grandma Kaisa and Mom, always in

charge."

She reached for the book on her night table: *Guide to Pregnancy and Childbirth.*

Chapter 8

Alice tried to settle in her bed, arranging the pillows for the best possible position for reading. For years, reading in bed had been the most successful method for falling asleep for Alice, even if the book's plot was designed to keep the reader riveted to the task.

Now, Alice would read a few paragraphs and, invariably, her thoughts would wander to the issues of her daily life. Turning the page, Alice had no idea what the printed symbols on the pages had spelled out, and she had to reread the material over and over again. She gave up, turned out the light, and nestled herself into a cave of blankets and sheets with only her eyes and nose showing.

Tom lay on his back with his fingers neatly crossed on the top sheet, the blanket carefully half folded for easy access during the night.

Listening to the muffled giggles of Pam and Stephanie in the next room, Alice shifted her eyes to Tom on her right without moving her head.

"So, what do you think so far?"

"About?"

"About the girls? About Stephanie?"

"Seems like things are going quite well. Under the circumstances, I mean."

"I'm just worried about the next step. She needs the support right now, but what happens when the baby is born? Stephanie is so needy and immature. She looks at the pregnancy as something that passes."

"Well—" started Tom.

"I know, I know, it does pass, but it also continues. Right now, she is sharing her womb with her baby, but does she have any idea that she'll need to share her whole life with her child for years to come? To be a parent, a guide, a support, and an example to a vulnerable new person?"

"Well, what young—"

"And," Alice interrupted again, "to think that there is no help coming from her parents! Imagine that! Could you just put your daughter out of your mind, if she took a wrong step, did something you didn't approve of?"

"I'm sure I—"

"Besides, can you imagine being so judgmental? Haven't her parents ever done anything wrong? I should actually check on that."

"And you'll find out prim and proper Mrs. Smith used marijuana as a teenager. Then what? Who's being judgmental now?"

"I suppose the Smiths' past has no bearing on Stephanie's situation, and even if it does, I can't do anything about it. This is so frustrating!" Alice let out a loud sigh.

"Mmm," Tom sympathized, but didn't add anything more, slowly drifting off to sleep.

"But, you know…" Alice enthused.

Tom's body jerked slightly in half stupor.

Alice sat up.

"We can't be the only people to support Stephanie. We really should get a meeting together. She's entitled to some support from official sources—you know, Social Services, et cetera, don't you think?"

"Most likely. Let's think about this in the morning when we're more alert. Go to sleep."

When *you're* more alert, thought Alice to herself, but she said: "You're right."

Tom was right. Tom was always right.

Alice stared out the window with wide eyes. The budding tree branches swayed gently in front of the almost full moon. Alice stayed awake until the moon moved beyond the window frame, rendering the room completely dark.

Chapter 9

Kaisa stormed out through the sliding glass doors onto the balcony. After a time of procrastination, she had been struck with a robust determination to clean the outdoor space, to bring it back from the winter's doldrums and non-use. She juggled a telescoping duster, a broom, and a bucket with rags and sudsy, warm water. She closed the door behind her and saw in the door a reflection of the cleaning lady portrayed by a TV comedienne so often seen years ago on television.

As her mother had taught her sixty-some years ago, you always start cleaning at the top and proceed downward. Kaisa had proven the theory to be true through trial and error. She remembered the time she had deep-cleaned the large bathroom in her parents' home. She had failed to attack the light fixture above the mirror first, and when returning to the task, dropped a heavy cover of dust in pieces onto the shining vanity fixtures and countertop, causing herself extra work.

"Always be economical in everything you do. It's better in the long run," her mother had said.

In the long run? I am lucky if I can do a short sprint these days, and that one slowly.

Kaisa followed her mother's advice and looked at the spiderweb glittering in the sun. She stopped and stared at the woven net carefully constructed in the triangle-shaped space between the wall and the horizontal part of a metal plant hanger. A close study of the sparkling web made her think of nature in general as well as the exquisite design of the work by the tiny weaver. She grabbed the duster and reached up with it. In the middle of the action, she stopped abruptly and interrupted her thoughts in order to carry on a vivid debate with herself.

How can I do this to the diligent worker and artist? How would I feel, if someone had no appreciation for my woven bobbin lace, my rug on the loom, my knitting and crocheting?

Well, your weavings are for fun, art work created for art's sake, not out of necessity. The bobbin lace, most like a spider's web, is an intricate construction of threads leading in varying directions, forming imaginative designs, only to please your imagination. It's not a death trap.

But the sweaters and mittens I knit are certainly useful, warm, and comforting.

They are, but to think practically, you can just as easily buy one in a store and for a whole lot less money.

I know, but I can eat without weaving.

What?

This clever creature weaves the web in order to catch a meal: an unsuspecting fly, mosquito, or any bug with wings and a poor sense of danger.

Kaisa thought of the web as a necessary tool for the spider and decided to leave it alone and move down to the next level in the cleaning order: wiping down the wrought iron railings showing signs of burgeoning rust.

The sliding door opened with a scratchy squeal. Alice stepped out onto the balcony.

"I'm sorry. I let myself in with my key. I knew you

were here, and I got scared when you didn't answer the doorbell."

"What do you mean 'scared'?"

"Well, you know. You could have fallen again, broken something or worse, and you are barely over your last mishap."

"I could have fallen or worse, but I didn't. You worry entirely too much! Want some coffee?"

Kaisa stepped into the condominium, while Alice looked around, recognized Kaisa's cleaning efforts, and said, "You missed something."

And with a haphazard whisk of the hand, she swiped away the spiderweb, only to have it shrivel into a sticky glob in her fingers. Alice had no inkling that the web had survived after Kaisa's painful consideration of its value.

Inside, Kaisa poured coffee into cups and sat with Alice at the table.

"Mom, I need to talk to you." Alice stirred her black coffee for no reason.

"Why aren't you teaching today?" Kaisa asked.

"Mom, it's Saturday."

"Oh, that's right. It is."

A look of worry swept across Alice's face. Her mom was shaking, she was seeing things, and now she couldn't remember what day of the week it was.

"Mom, can I ask you something?"

"You will anyway." Kaisa winked at Alice.

"It's Stephanie. She's now about a third of the way into her pregnancy, and it seems Pam is more interested and prepared than Stephanie. How is she going to be a mother? She doesn't even understand the meaning of the word."

"I said you didn't need to step into this quagmire,

but did you listen? No. You can't be everything to everybody."

"Well, you always have been. I come by it naturally. But, really, Mom, what can I do? I can't be the one to set her straight, nor should I be. Stephanie is taking so much time. She's not really contributing her share to the household. I mean, she's not used to helping in the kitchen, doing her own laundry, or otherwise taking care of her own life. She does things when asked to, but she lacks initiative. Bobby is starting to resent the concentration on her within the family. Pam acts like a pregnancy coach, mother, and friend all at once, reading everything she can get her hands on about pregnancy, delivery, and child rearing. But that's not her job at seventeen."

"That's her choice." Kaisa lifted her head. "You know, in the olden days, a girl got in trouble, she had her baby, the child was brought up by the whole family, and nobody talked about it. Nobody read books about it."

"Oh, yeah?" Alice became irritated. "Or they sent the girl away for a long visit with the relatives, to give birth and return home a little less pudgy a few months later. Nobody talked about it?" Her voice had a definite cynical tone. "Give me a break! Nobody but all the gossip mongers."

Kaisa felt defeated and too tired to continue.

"It sounds to me like the girl needs to see a counselor, and you are not it. We talked about this before, but you haven't done anything about it. You need to stop taking on these causes."

Chapter 10

Haudenosaunee Hills truly is a lovely spot on the map. Alice got into her car in the condominium's parking lot along the lake. *Where else can you find all this beauty created by the glimmering lakes, the sloping hillsides covered by vineyards, a relatively slow pace of life, and a rich, unique history going back to the days of the Iroquois Nation? The people who live here are either members of families whose roots reach deep into the past and would not even entertain the idea of leaving, or they are newcomers who have discovered the spot on their vacation trip and have developed a plan to settle in the Hills for good.*

Alice drove past the familiar sights of her high school—her alma mater and current employer. The school building gave her nothing but pleasant memories from both her student and her teacher days.

She passed the entrance to a state park with ravines and waterfalls, and the hospital with its architectural design combining characteristics of styles popular in decades past, each contributing to the final result of a mishmash of red brick and stone, Victorian and modern, a mix of styles that both comforted and disturbed her.

She drove by a gym she had joined as a New Year's resolution effort in January a year ago. It had closed its doors shortly thereafter due to problems found in the annual building inspection, and it showed no signs of reopening. Secretly, Alice did not mind. She knew she carried around a few extra pounds, but her self-image did not depend on her physical appearance. Of course, she wanted to be slender and fit like her high school quartet sisters, but not necessarily *thin*. She wondered how Christine was doing in Seattle in her high-powered job, and how Lisa was faring in Afghanistan. Lisa would have her hands full as an obstetrician with Doctors Without Borders. Crystal, the other Chrysalis quartet member, who lived in town, was doing well. Crystal had married Gavin a year and a half ago and they still acted like newlyweds.

Crystal! Crystal could shed some light on Stephanie's situation. Although Crystal and Stephanie are light-years apart in every way, Crystal, an OB nurse, must have some experience with teenaged girls pregnant out of wedlock. "Wedlock." What an odd word. Locked into what? The connotation of locking, stripping someone of their freedom and isolating the person into an inescapable state struck her as frightening. The term had certainly outlived its time.

Alice called Crystal on her speed dial. The two women had developed a closeness after the quartet sang at Alice's father's funeral two years earlier, and their friendship had strengthened after their mothers became traveling companions on a trip to Finland. They were now each other's confidantes and created situations where they were able to see each other and talk face to face, a practice preferred by both of them. Similar to and different from each other, both were only children and had definite ideas they relentlessly held onto, both had had lonely childhoods and had developed a need for friendship and closeness, and both had chosen socially responsible careers to help others, teaching and nursing.

However, the structure of their families had been different, almost the opposite of each other. Alice grew up in a safe, steady environment of the upper middle class, with a judge as a father and an alien as a mother, as Kaisa often said, tongue in cheek. Kaisa's Finnish roots were forever present in the household with the language, the customs, and the foods—especially the foods. Kaisa had a degree in home economics, and she didn't shy away from proudly displaying her culinary skills. Alice was a happy beneficiary of the products Kaisa turned out in the kitchen.

Crystal, on the other hand, grew up without a father around, and, as far as Alice knew, she still didn't know who her father was. Crystal's mother, Lola, was an adventurous world traveler, not fond of ties of any kind, the opposite of everyone else in her large Italian family. She had a boisterous, artistic personality and was ready to take risks and accept a challenge. Lola's travels had increased as soon as she saw Crystal as an independent, capable individual, which happened immediately after Crystal's high school graduation.

As Crystal responded, to Alice's inquiry, that she had nothing to do and Gavin was occupied elsewhere on their huge organic farm, Alice invited herself over for a visit and a talk.

The Koladziejskis' border collie Rufus met Alice at her car. Crystal, for a number of reasons, had kept her maiden name Giordano. Although not Johnson or Smith, it was still easier to spell and pronounce than Koladziejski.

With cups of coffee in their hands, the two women sat on the patio furniture recently brought out of winter storage.

"Okay, out with it," said Crystal in a rather brash manner uncharacteristic of her.

"Right." Alice readjusted herself in the wicker arm chair. "Things aren't going great with Stephanie, or rather with Stephanie and us... I mean the family... Mostly, I mean between Stephanie and me. She's hard work. She just doesn't seem to be interested. She decided to keep the baby but doesn't do anything to assure that the child has a good beginning in life. I mean, she doesn't eat right, doesn't get enough sleep, et cetera. I took her in and I feel responsible. Also, she seems to be oblivious to what the near future looks like. She has a delivery to prepare for and she's clueless about that, too. Once I heard her tell Pam that she is going to choose a Caesarean section because it would hurt less! Can you imagine? Major abdominal surgery instead of a natural experience you recuperate from rather quickly in most cases."

Alice got up and paced back and forth on the patio with her coffee cup. "Whoever made childbirth a medical issue? It's not an illness, it's an experience of health." Alice flailed her right arm and with it the coffee cup, spilling coffee on the slate of the patio floor.

"Oh, I am so sorry! How do you clean rock or stone? I'll go get some paper towels." Alice started for the kitchen door. Crystal reached for Alice.

"Stop, please." Crystal calmed Alice with a hand on Alice's arm. "Let's talk about this. The floor can wait. Have a seat."

Alice obeyed. "I just get so riled up, but you can see why, can't you?"

"I can, I've seen my share of teenaged girls who come to the delivery suite completely unprepared. On the basis of their level of knowledge, I've expected to hear about cabbage patches and storks. It's not a good scene. We try to do the best we can and go through an instant short course, but their ability to listen at that time is nonexistent. Somehow, we need to have Stephanie open up to the information she needs. Then, maybe, her attitude will change. Tell me you are not responsible for Stephanie financially."

"Well, that's another thing. It's been such a short time, and I've been meaning to look into that. She is under age and her parents are still responsible, I think. I'm assuming she's still in her family's health insurance plan."

"You can't leave this to assumptions. You should contact Social Services as soon as possible to get some information."

"I know, I know. Tom's been telling me this. You see how dysfunctional I am. I can't do anything right."

"Alice, sometimes your heart is too big for your own good."

Alice wiped her eyes. "Crystal, a couple of minutes ago you said 'we' need to help Stephanie. Do you mean you will help me in a concrete way?"

"Yes. I will. I am pregnant, too, and maybe I can talk to her as one expectant mother to another."

"You are pregnant? Really? How wonderful! I am so happy for you. For Gavin, too." Alice's mood changed from sadness and self-pity to total euphoria in a couple of seconds, and she enveloped Crystal in the warm blanket of a hug.

"I'm at the same stage in my pregnancy as Stephanie, so that will give a nice comparison point for us. Of course, a pregnancy for a teen and for a woman in her forties are sometimes two very different things…"

"You are pregnant! I had no idea." Alice shook her head slowly. "Why didn't you tell me?"

"I wanted to be sure. You never know about these things. Like I said, I am in my forties, an old woman to be having my first child, but so far, so good."

Alice gave Crystal another hug.

Chapter 11

"Was that Alice's car I saw drive out?" Gavin came into the kitchen and gave Crystal a kiss.

"Yeah, she's all upset. Hey, take off your muddy boots!"

"I just came in to get a cup of coffee. What's bothering Alice this time?"

"You know she and Tom have the Smith girl living with them now, Pam's friend. Things aren't going as smoothly as they had hoped, and Stephanie's presence is causing some trouble in the family constellation. You knew Stephanie is pregnant, didn't you?"

"Stephanie, right. Really? Why is she living with the Fitzpatricks?"

"The parents pretty much threw her out in the street. Can you imagine? In this day and age."

"Aren't the Smiths the rich couple who always have the biggest and the newest of everything? I hear the missus is not a very pleasant person."

Crystal chuckled. "The missus is called the Dragon Lady by Alice's kids. With the Fitzpatricks, Stephanie has a chance to experience a normal, everyday life with caring people, but Stephanie doesn't seem to be adjusting."

"Maybe the drastic change in the home environment is too much for her. You know how even the most positive things in your life can be stressful. I remember her from my teaching days. She was in my history class—a quiet girl, kind of a teacher's ideal pupil, never caused trouble, did her homework, handed in her assignments on time, paid attention in class. Then, again, she was, how should I say, forgettable, a kid who disappeared into the woodwork. I always wondered if there were issues with the parents' health or other family concerns. She could have used someone to talk to back then, I'm sure."

Crystal bit on her lip. "There *is* something missing there. She's pregnant, as far along as I am." Crystal's hand traveled almost unintentionally to her lower belly. Gavin's eyes followed her hand and he smiled gently.

"Yet," Crystal continued, "Alice says she doesn't seem to show any interest in her pregnancy or her future as a mother. Alice is worried about what will happen to that little mother-baby twosome in the years to come if something isn't done now. I always wondered how Pam and Stephanie could be close friends. They are completely different from each other, Stephanie an immature, almost shy yet sexually active girl, and Pam a take-charge young woman to whom nothing is impossible. I guess they found something in each other that makes them friends. Alice has such a big heart, always on the side of the have-nots, but with her emotions all over the place, she's not able to handle the sometimes tough issues that come her way."

"And she also has her own mother…" said Gavin.

"Yeah, there's that, too. Those two have always had their issues, but what mothers and daughters don't?"

"Speaking of mothers, did you hear anything from your mother this week?"

"Mom and I spoke on FaceTime on my day off on

Thursday. She's doing famously. Right now, she's building a new boathouse at the water's edge. Well, she and Mauno. You know, ever since I told her that she was going to be a grandmother, she's been in contact with me much more frequently. She's finally accepted the fact that she's getting older and will be a grandma, but she made me promise she won't be called that. The word would make her feel too old. She wants to wait till after the baby is born and see whether she'll feel like a Nana, Mimi, Gammy, or Nanny, et cetera, and decide at that point."

"Okay. Whatever." Gavin shook his head.

"I don't expect her to be like *her* mom. Nonna was the epitome of a mother and a grandma. She loved children, and the more there was happy noise in the house, the better. Mom told me her memories of childhood were that Nonna always had a baby in her arms, even when cooking. A picture of a woman wearing an apron while holding a baby is the opposite of the picture I have of my own mother. I know she loves me and loved me as a baby, but she had no great desire to hold a baby, to engage in baby talk or cooing, or to take part in games I played as a child. Mom has always preferred adult company and conversation. Come to think of it, my mom and Alice's mom are a lot alike. No wonder they ended up traveling to Finland together."

"Right. A trip that changed your mom's life—or was it Kaisa that did the changing? Well, I'd better get back to my job." Gavin turned on his heels, grinding in the dirt he had brought to the kitchen floor.

"See you later." Crystal poured coffee into the thermal cup and ran after him. "You forgot something…"

Chapter 12

Two years earlier, Lola, who had traveled the world over, made a snap decision to invite herself to join Kaisa on a trip to Finland. Lola's good friend Margaret had just died, and it had been revealed that John Lindqvist, a married man, whom Lola had loved with all her heart—and who was Crystal's father—had also been Margaret's lover. Lola had been heartbroken. With her best friend gone in more ways than one, Lola had no outlet for her rage and disappointment. To make things unbearable, John's sweet widow Carol still lived in town, and even worse, their son Magnus had just bought his old childhood home on Maple Avenue. Carol's dementia had advanced rather rapidly. After living in a vacuum-like state for a time, not recognizing even her children, she had passed away peacefully. Whether she knew about her husband's indiscretions remained a mystery.

Dealing with the truth about Crystal's paternity had been difficult but liberating. For decades, Lola had lived with the secret, which was painfully stressful. In addition to Lola and Crystal, Kaisa was the only one who now knew the truth of John Lindqvist, the handsome Swede, a pillar of the community. Sitting on the bench outside the sauna on the Baltic, Lola, in a moment's weakness, had blurted out the facts to Kaisa. Kaisa was loyal and would not divulge the secret. Or would she? Lola had heard that Kaisa's Parkinson's could affect her thinking.

Who knew what she might tell her daughter and others? If the truth were known more widely, what harm would there be? Her reputation could be ruined? She could be shunned? John's reputation would definitely be tarnished, but who cared? Lola chuckled at her thoughts.

Although the trip to Finland was supposed to have been an escape of sorts, a change of scenery, Lola had quickly and thoroughly fallen in love with the countryside, its beauty, variety of weather, the food and the people of the small island where she and Kaisa settled for three weeks. When Kaisa returned home, Lola stayed until the allowable ninety days were up. She had made a trip to the United States and another one back to Finland as soon as it was possible.

Lola was conveniently isolated on the island. She spent her days painting, taking walks, skiing in the woods. In the dark winter nights, she meditated and read by candlelight. Kaisa's cottage was the summer place of her youth. Kaisa had wanted to keep it as it was in her childhood in the 1950s, which meant no amenities such as electricity, heat, running water, or indoor toilet. All this suited Lola's adventurous spirit, although walking through the snowdrifts to the outhouse under a tall pine tree was a bit much, as was waking up a couple of times a night to add chopped pieces of birch to the wood-burning stove. When the neighbors heard of her return to the island, they unobtrusively took care of her. Lola would receive moose meat from a hunter neighbor, whose wife also sent along boxes of frozen bilberries, lingonberries, and cloudberries with a gentle note attached asking her to return the plastic boxes when she was finished with them.

Mauno, Kaisa's classmate from years ago, took a

special interest in Lola, as he had done the moment he met her the summer before. Lola, in response, was interested in the silver-haired, bearded banker-turned-ferryboat captain with a brilliant smile.

Lola's allowable time in Finland was coming to an end again in March. For a world traveler, it was awkward that she didn't look forward to traveling back home and actually found it objectionable to be part of the huge crowds corralled through the airports dictated by their itineraries.

More and more, Lola was spending time at Mauno's place: an ultra-modern house with huge windows from floor to ceiling facing the Baltic Sea. The house had geothermal heat and all conveniences possible. Lola felt guilty. She had begged Kaisa to allow her to stay at her cottage, but here she was, a traitor to the beautiful little red house with white trim. It had also become increasingly obvious that Mauno's charm had defeated Lola's resolve to have no men in her life. All the old captain with silver hair and beard had to do was flash his gorgeous smile and Lola weakened at the knees.

By the glow of the fireplace fire, they had discussed Lola's mandatory upcoming exit to the United States.

"I really have…not a fear, but a dislike of flying. By the way, did you read Erica Jong's book *Fear of Flying* way back when? It's a feminist work."

"Yes, I did. Where do you think a man can learn most about women and their psyche? I was only twenty or so. A guy would not necessarily buy a book like that or even take it out of the library. Even some girls were reticent to reveal that they owned a copy or that they had read it. There was one circulating among my friends. I think a buddy of mine had stolen it from his sister's bookcase."

"I think Crystal has my copy now. It was considered quite racy in its day. Of course, compared to today's literature, it was nothing. And, to make this clear, I do have a fear of sitting in a plane with coughing, sneezing, sniffling idiots and screaming children. Other than that, I love to fly!" Lola looked at Mauno with a devilish smile on her lips.

"It's funny," she continued, "I've always been a restless sort and have had a need to scoot as soon as things became familiar and routine. Finland has had the opposite effect on me—I want to slow down and rest, stay put."

"Then do that," said Mauno.

"But I can't. My time is going to be up."

"There is a way, you know." Mauno looked into Lola's brown eyes with a steady gaze. "We can get married."

"What?" Lola burst out laughing. "Are you serious?" She became quiet after studying Mauno's face. He had meant what he said.

"Isn't that making a mockery of marriage?" Lola got up from the comfort of the sofa and walked to the window. She touched her forehead to the glass and tried to look out into the dark, seeing only indefinite forms against the snow along the shore. Juniper bushes and small spruce trees, covered by whiteness. Like her future, everything looked undefined and fuzzy.

Mauno stood behind Lola, holding onto her shoulders. He pointed to the reflection in the window. They saw a mature couple: a tall, handsome man with an athlete's build, a carefully shaped beard, and bright blue eyes, and a tiny woman with unruly salt-and-pepper hair, deep brown eyes, and beautiful teeth revealed by a smile gradually growing wider.

"If marriage allows me to keep you here, it works for me," Mauno whispered in Lola's ear. "If it's only a legal arrangement to solve a big problem, that works for me, too." He turned Lola around.

Lola moved slowly as if in a fog. She looked Mauno in the eyes and whispered back, "Me, too."

They'd had a short time to get to know each other, but both their emotional connection and their physical chemistry were strong. *What is the use of waiting?* Mauno thought, and he took her by the hand and led her to the bedroom. As their kisses became more and more passionate, the seriousness of their intent was disturbed only by Lola's giggles at the tickling of his beard on her face.

His fingers tangled in Lola's long, curly hair, he egged her on. "Prove to me that you have no fear of flying."

"Flying to the States might give me a virus, but I doubt that I'll get one from you, or that you'll give me a disease of one type or another. Are you saying we need protection?" Lola smirked.

Mauno laughed. "Hardly."

They undressed each other slowly and deliberately, accepting every wrinkle and crease, every droop and sag.

"You know, I may need some help," said Lola.

"Oh?" He winked. "I'll help you in every way I can. What would you like me to do?"

"Things may not glide as well as they did before. Do you have some sort of lubricant?"

"I don't think I do, but I may have some in my workshop."

She laughed heartily.

Mauno continued, "Let me see what I can come up with…or if anything comes up at all." He winked again.

Both were aware of a tension, an urgency that led them to the bed before any of their so-called concerns had been taken care of. Their lovemaking was slow and relaxed. Afterwards, they spent a long time in each other's arms, conscious of the ways in which sex was a great deal better now than in their youth or even a few years ago. There was no pressure to perform, to show your skill or superiority, as if in a competition. There was a desire to concentrate on the needs and sensations of your partner rather than those of your own body. They slowly fell asleep, and the next morning woke up to a bright winter morning. To those who were able to read nature's signs, the sense of spring was in the air, although still far in the future. Lola looked at the sea and the recently finished sauna building with the dock leading into the water.

"A great erection, huh?" asked Mauno behind her.

Lola smiled. "Well, I've seen bigger, but maybe not better. You are talking about the sauna, right?"

"Of co—" He stopped. "This is where English gets me. It should be against the law to have more than one meaning for a word. But I won't take back my words."

"I won't, either."

Chapter 13

Lola had returned to the cottage the next day confused and baffled. She had just accepted a man's proposal of marriage—she, Lola, the epitome of independence, a preacher for women's rights and individual freedom, and a firm believer in the theory that marriage was an outdated institution and unnecessary for a woman.

Guilt was strangling her. Was she doing this solely to be able to stay in Finland? To avoid a flight with numerous passengers? Was she brazenly taking advantage of a country's law allowing a legal stay in the case of being married to a citizen? Had she turned into a conniving, manipulating female who used any method to get her way?

She thought of Mauno. He was kind and gentle, full of life, and funny. And, she had to admit, he was completely enamored with her. She forced herself to evaluate her own feelings toward him:

Am I in love with this man? I know that, were I to leave, I would miss him desperately. Isn't that what happened before? If I'm truthful, I returned to Finland because of Mauno, not the allure of the country, although that too is undeniable. Do I find him attractive because of his feelings towards me? Would I marry Mauno if I had met him in the States?

Lola struggled with her guilt. Guilt was a waste as a

feeling, a useless, ugly sensibility, disturbing in its meaning and purpose. If yellow was the color for joy and green for envy and jealousy, then guilt, in Lola's imagination, shone as a muddy, undecipherable mixture of colors, rendering it a dirty, grayish, faded dullness.

Lola grappled with her conflicting thoughts. She needed to come to terms with her confusion. She had accepted Mauno's proposal. It was time to move on...or to cancel. She looked up into the ceiling, clenched her jaw, and gasped out loud, "Why am I doing this? Why can't I decide? Why on earth did I say yes if I have doubts?"

With the morning sun bright on the snow-covered paths, trees and bushes around the cottage offered an unbelievable brightness, enough to cause snow-blindness. Lola shoveled a narrow path to the outdoor privy—and yelled out loud when she sat on the seat, the edges slightly covered with frost. She laughed. Some people would find the situation intolerable. She had experienced a great deal in her travels and was used to circumstances and conditions only the most daring individuals would find comfortable. Yet here she was, not wanting to fly with other passengers. What a wimp she was!

She made herself a cup of strong coffee and spent the day looking out into the winter wonderland. She vacillated between marriage and staying single. After a while, she came to a decision, wondering why it had taken her so long. Marriage and independence don't have to be mutually exclusive. The old format for marriage still lived strong in some people's lives, however: The man was the head of the household, the head being the site for brains, the thinking organ, the place for decision-making. The wife was the rest of the body, making sure that all decisions the brain made were promptly and effectively executed. Lola laughed. Such unconditional black-and-white thinking was never healthy. However, the roles in a marriage were fairly clearly defined. Her parents had lived in those roles. If a woman wanted to keep her independence, and her identity, she didn't get married.

My marriage will be a union between people from two cultures with both parties relishing and respecting the differences. Lola had made her final decision.

As the sun started to set in late afternoon, Lola looked for her cell phone. She had fought against having one, but had given in for the sake of safety in a cottage without neighbors within shouting distance. She found the phone in the kitchen, carelessly thrown in what appeared to be a junk drawer. Dead. She untangled the phone cord from a variety of household items—string, rubber bands, safety pins, and match books.

Lola dressed warmly and walked to her rental car, left close to the road, a secondary one at best. With the cell phone charging in the still-cold car, Lola entered Crystal's number and got an almost immediate answer.

"Hello?" Crystal put down her hair drier.

"Hi, am I calling at a bad time?" With the seven-hour time difference, and Crystal's ever-changing work schedule, it was difficult to keep track from the other side of the globe.

"I am just getting ready to go to work," said Crystal. "Are you all right?"

"Sure. Everything is fine. I won't keep you. I'm just calling to tell you that I have to get married."

"You have to get married? What? To whom? Don't

tell me you're pregnant!" Crystal laughed with great hilarity, "That would be one for the records!"

Crystal had been surprised but not shocked at the news, which now seemed to have come a lifetime ago. Crystal had been convinced her mother would not forfeit her independence in any way, least of all by getting married. After thinking of her mother's decision, Crystal came to the conclusion that either Mauno must be an extraordinary man or else Lola had softened in her recent years, to adopt an idea of sharing and compromise.

Chapter 14

Looking up at the cupola on top of the Social Services building on Main Street, Alice tripped on a crushed beer can on the massive steps. She had never before had a need to step foot into the building, which, to her, meant one of two things—either she was very lucky in life and had never needed aid of any kind from Social Services, or she was entitled and uncaring, not even making contact in order to help someone else.

The building itself was colossal, a large structure with tall, thick Roman columns at the top of what appeared to be countless steps, intimidating and almost threatening when viewed from the street level, a building whose original purpose and function were far from aiding those in need.

As a native of the small city, Alice had driven by the establishment almost daily, first on her way to school and later to work. She knew the history of the court house turned post office turned social services complex.

Alice opened the heavy door to the lobby and, seeing the uniformed officer, realized security measures were in place. She had known it but was surprised by it, nevertheless.

She handed her purse to the security guard, feverishly trying to recall what the bottomless bag held inside. She was relieved she had already delivered the hemorrhoid ointment picked up for Kaisa at the drugstore.

After being directed to a room down the long, gloomy hallway and through a welcoming, open door, Alice was greeted by a beautiful, dark-complected young woman. Alice stared at the deep brown eyes and the waist-length black hair.

"Am I in the right place?"

"Yes, you are. Please, come in. I'm Denise DuBois."

"Alice Fitzpatrick."

They shook hands.

"How can I help you?"

"Well, as you know from my phone message, I have a situation. Or, I don't really, but my daughter's friend does, but I guess I do, too. The whole family kind of does. She lives with us. She's only seventeen, she's pregnant, and her parents threw her out of the house—actually, her mother did—and she doesn't understand her situation, and she's causing trouble with my family, not deliberately, but, you know, just by being there. At first it was okay, but now she doesn't really help around the house or seem to be interested in her pregnancy or what happens when…"

"Mrs. Fitzpatrick," Denise interrupted, "let's slow down and go through this calmly and in detail. We have time."

"Oh, I am sorry. I babble. I tend to get excited about this. I want to help so badly, but how do you do it, when you hit a wall time after time?"

"How long has this girl lived with you?"

"A couple of months now. She moved in right after she found out she was pregnant, informed her parents about it, and was told to leave. Of course, Stephanie, that's her name, has spent a lot of time at our house starting from the time the girls were in kindergarten. They are best friends."

"What is it that you are looking for? Counseling services? Financial resources? Legal advice? By the way, what has been the role of the father of the baby so far? Do you know who the father is?"

"The father? That's another story, another teenaged child of well-to-do parents. I would like to know where Stephanie's parents stand in this situation. With her being under eighteen, aren't they still legally responsible for her? She has an obstetrician's appointment coming up. Does the parental permission to treat need to be obtained for every appointment, or is it a one-time document?"

"Are you in contact with the parents at all?" Denise asked. "If you are, you could get a consent from them. If not, in New York State, there is a stipulation that a child under the age of eighteen can give consent in circumstances like…Stephanie's, is it? In circumstances like hers."

"That's great! If I ask, the parents may cooperate. After all, we have prevented their child from becoming homeless. Financial help at this point? We are not asking for that for us, but what about the baby? All the paraphernalia that goes with bringing a baby home?"

"That's where we can be of assistance, and with counseling services, of course. How acute is the need, in your estimation?"

"Our whole family could use help, I'm sure. Adding a pregnant teen who's not even a relative into the household has its problems."

"Yes," said Denise matter-of-factly. "Let me work on some contacts. I would recommend that you try to touch base with Stephanie's parents. Chances are, they are well aware of their responsibilities but are waiting for an opening from your direction. They may also be a little ashamed and regretful. Or have you thought of the possibility that you only have the child's side of the story? You have seen yourself that she has some problems dealing with things. There may be more to what happened to cause her homelessness."

Alice rolled her eyes. " 'Ashamed' and 'regretful' are not in the mother's vocabulary as far as I know, but I am willing to try. There's been no contact from the parents after they dropped bins of Stephanie's clothing on our driveway while we were out. Of course, we have not attempted to contact them, either. I thought all this would be easier, but I guess I always jump into action without thinking."

"You have been very thoughtful and helpful. No need to regret your generosity. We'll sort this out."

Denise stood, announcing by her action that the meeting was over.

Alice walked to her car, contemplating the interaction. *It was all very nice, but will it lead to something? Is there real help available, or was this just bureaucratic lip service? Denise seems competent enough, but how much power does she really have to make things happen?* Alice promised herself to give Mrs. Smith a call in the next couple of days.

It started to rain. Alice looked through her bag for her car key—attached to a key chain holding Alice's entire life—but without luck. She walked back to the Social Services Office, only to find out her keys had not been noticed. Alice called Tom.

"Hi, honey. You aren't at a showing, are you? Could

you come and bring me my spare car key, please? I seem to have lost mine, along with all the other keys."

Tom was quiet for a moment or two. "Sure, where are you?"

"It's raining. I am going into the coffee shop across the street."

"What street? Where?"

"Oh, yes. Across from Social Services, on Main." Alice realized she had failed to mention to Tom that she had an appointment today.

"Okay. I'll see you there. It'll be a few minutes. I have to go home to get your key. Is that in its regular spot? I don't want to make the trip for nothing."

Alice sensed annoyance in Tom's tone of voice. "Yes. It's there. See you later. Thanks."

After ordering a cup of latte at the counter of the coffee shop, Alice walked to a booth by the window. She took off her coat and her long sweater. Her heavy key chain fell out of the sweater pocket to the floor.

Chapter 15

"Hello."

"Mrs. Smith?"

"Yes. Who's this?"

"This is Alice Fitzpatrick." Alice had gathered all the courage she could find to make the phone call. "I'm calling about Stephanie. This is really difficult, so bear with me—"

"Is everything all right?" Mrs. Smith interrupted.

"Yes. Stephanie is fine. It's just that… Mrs. Smith, we are having some problems communicating with her about, you know, her pregnancy."

"You're telling me nothing new, and, call me Melinda. I have a feeling that we'll be talking a lot in the near future, and we might as well be on first-name basis."

Alice was taken aback. She did not expect the swift openness Mrs. Smith exhibited, nor was she ready for Melinda's practically inviting her to communicate with her more.

Melinda continued, "I have left Stephanie alone, and I wanted to give you time, as well, before contacting you. I suppose she told you that we kicked her out of the house and that we hate her."

"I'm sure she doesn't think you hate her, but she definitely feels that she's a big disappointment to you and your husband. She did tell us that she was asked to leave. When you delivered her clothes to our driveway, we took it as an indication that the door had been closed and locked."

"I didn't deliver anything. My sister did. Stephanie lived with her for a couple of weeks, but my sister found her to be too difficult to deal with, especially when she tried to talk to her about her issues. That's when Stephanie announced that she was going to Pam's house and that since she's not wanted she wouldn't be coming back. If she imagined she could just move in with you, it was completely presumptuous. And, by the way, when Stephanie left our house, she left of her own volition."

Alice's thoughts whirled in circles. She realized this issue might just be another occasion when she had jumped to conclusions, taken one side of a story and run with it, without a more careful study of the situation.

"Alice, my husband and I only have one child, and we've done all we can do to make her life a good one. Both Craig and I built our lives from ground up. Craig's father died when Craig was in kindergarten, and his mother struggled to make enough money to support her four children. My parents were alcoholics and, I think, drug users, but I can't prove it. We were called trailer trash. When my husband and I met, we both had a burning desire to get out of the miserable existence and our barely minimum-wage jobs. Both of us cut all ties to our parents. And, here we sit, with our daughter wanting nothing to do with us, and this after all we have done for her." Alice heard sniffles at the other end of the phone connection.

"Mrs. Smith—I mean Melinda—I had no idea."

"How much do we really ever know about other people? I don't fool myself. I know that people look at us as *nouveau riche* tight-lipped social climbers. They have no idea I am basically a very shy person and that causes me to come across as aloof and quiet. I know some kids call me 'Dragon Lady.' I've probably earned that name, since I don't tolerate a lot of nonsense. Kids today don't understand that you should try to maintain what you own in good condition. That's why I lose it when Stephanie's friends come over and put their dirty shoes on my white couch or drop a snack on the floor without making the smallest effort to pick it up or clean up after themselves. Yes, I become Dragon Lady!"

Alice chuckled to herself. No one ever had a chance to put their shoes on the couch in her house, as there was an ingrained rule at the Fitzpatricks—No outside shoes allowed in the house. Kaisa had made sure her daughter knew the Finnish custom and practiced it. Due to that habit, Alice knew immediately that Melinda was not talking about Pam or Bobby.

"I get it," said Alice, amused. "Just so you know, Tom and I told Stephanie she could stay with us. So…" Alice sighed. "Where do we go from here? I'm pretty sure she doesn't want to talk to you, so I can try reaching her. I feel she's having a struggle within herself and doesn't know which way to turn. There's one more thing: What about Michael? He's the father of Stephanie's baby for sure, right?"

"Yes. Well, as far as I know. I'm pretty sure there was no one else. They were really close and let their hormones take them for a ride. Michael is a wonderful kid, every mother's potential dream son-in-law. You know, valedictorian, class president, captain of the football team, and from a great family to boot."

"So…is Michael involved in any way? I haven't heard Stephanie—or Pam, for that matter—talk about him at all."

"I don't know, and of course, Stephanie hasn't talked to me for weeks now."

Alice felt helpless. "How do you feel about this? Do Michael's parents know?"

"Craig left a voicemail message at Doctor Albright's practice, but there has been no return call. I will encourage him to try again. Craig and I are trying to be reasonable about this. This is not Michael's fault or Stephanie's fault. We just want to help them. One thing is certain—and correct me if I am wrong—Stephanie definitely wants to keep the baby. That's still the case, right?"

"Yes. The odd thing is, though, that she looks at her pregnancy as something that's happening to someone else, on a tangent, not in her body. I think she's pushing it aside out of guilt. She feels guilty for having done something unacceptable, guilty for disappointing you and your husband, guilty for ruining her future."

"Poor child. We are used to a go-getter daughter, a smart girl who can do any task presented to her—you know, like Pam. We need to get that girl back."

"I agree."

The two women were quiet for a moment or two.

"Oh, and Alice, thank you for all you are doing for our daughter."

After they ended the call, Alice sat quietly staring at the pudgy little daffodil and tulip shoots pushing themselves through soil by the patio.

Interesting, she thought. *For a quiet and shy woman, Melinda certainly talked a lot on the phone. She's completely different from what I imagined her to be. Or, is she a master at conniving, giving an impression that she is the one to be understood better? Maybe she appears shy to people because she doesn't allow anyone to get close to her. I could become her friend, now that we share a concern.*

Alice shook her head. What was she thinking! Her life was already full of challenges and troubles. She could help Stephanie. Melinda would need to find a different therapist.

Chapter 16

Having spent the day dealing with the intricacies of the American Civil War, Alice needed a break before dinner. She drove to the park by the lake and walked briskly from one end of the parking lot to the other and continued on, following the shoreline. She ended up at her mother's condo and rang the doorbell.

Kaisa opened the door. "Well, where is your key?" she said with sarcasm.

"Geez, Mom. Nice to see you, too. I didn't have my key with me. You know I now always ring the doorbell first."

As they walked into the kitchen, Kaisa asked, "Do you ever think that I might like my privacy undisturbed? What if I walked around here in my skivvies? Or left the bathroom door open? Or…" she hesitated for a moment, "what if I was entertaining a gentleman friend?"

Alice burst out in boisterous laughter. "Right, Mom."

"Why is that so unbelievable? Lola married Mauno over a year ago, and we are about the same age."

"Mom, you are not serious." Alice felt the slightest chance of a possibility that she could be wrong.

"Not about the gentleman part, but I do wish you'd consider my privacy a bit more. I am not disabled to such a degree that I need someone to worry about me or to require instant access to me."

Alice thought of her slender, youthful mother. She was attractive, intelligent, and interesting, and handled her ailments with a light sense of humor. On the other hand, she was independent, stubborn to the point of being pig-headed, a complete know-it-all, and often unwilling to accept others' points of view. There was no man on this great earth who would put up with her, Alice was sure. She was thankful Kaisa had never taken on a martyr's role overtly. It cropped up in well-disguised ways—a request cloaked in a compliment, or a slightly exaggerated problem she herself had overcome.

"Well, I'm not giving my key back. It's an insurance card of sorts, for me," said Alice.

"Just remember that I have a doorbell."

"Yes, ma'am."

Kaisa reached for a recipe card box in the cupboard. "I decided to make a lemon pound cake. My neighbor is back, and I think she would like it. A couple of weeks ago, I made a cardamom braid and left it behind her door. I know she was around, as the loaf disappeared."

Oh, my God, that again! Kaisa hadn't mentioned the mystery woman since the day she had discovered the supposedly blood-stained mink coats on the neighbor's balcony. Alice had hoped that, with the medication, the hallucinations had stopped. She decided to ignore Kaisa's statement about the neighbor. She realized that someone living in the building had enjoyed a wonderful Finnish *pulla*, her mom's special coffee bread. Tom had done some investigative work and talked to Kaisa's neighbors. No one was aware of a woman living next door to Kaisa.

"If I remember right, isn't the lemon pound cake your favorite?"

"Yes. It's a White House recipe. I can't remember for sure which president's wife's specialty it was, but I think it was Lady Bird Johnson's."

Kaisa gathered ingredients from the cupboard and the refrigerator. She missed the large pantry in her old house as well as the large professional-style multi-burner gas range. Alice and Tom had insisted that she exchange the condominium's gas stove for an induction one. Kaisa's loud objections had been of no use.

"It's for your safety," they'd said. "You don't want a fire, or the gas left on by accident," they had said. Kaisa admitted to herself that the smaller living quarters and safety features in it were exactly what she needed. Her pride did not allow her to admit it to her daughter.

"Looks like I am low on flour," she mumbled to herself.

"You want me to go get some?" asked Alice.

"No. Thank you, though. You know, once I decided that I can still drive confidently, I've been doing some shopping myself. I do appreciate your picking up things for me, though, so don't get me wrong."

Alice felt warm both emotionally and physically. She realized she still had her coat on and hung it on the back of a kitchen chair.

"Mom, you'd be proud of me. I talked to Mrs. Smith about Stephanie."

Kaisa looked up from her recipe. "It's about time. Did you talk sense into that awful female?"

"Turns out there may be another side to the story. Mrs. Smith—Melinda—says Stephanie is the one who decided to leave home. She was not thrown out. Melinda seems quite reasonable, not at all the Dragon Lady the kids call her. Stephanie wants nothing to do with her mother, so Melinda and I are working behind the scenes to get some help and also to involve the Albrights."

"Well, what a tangled web we weave."

Alice smiled. "Thank you, Sir Walter Scott."

"Just be careful. I'm proud of you for wanting to help the girl, but take care that you all, and I mean all, come out of this with some sort of clarity for the future."

"It depends a lot on how the issue is received by the Albright boy and his parents. We've seen no sign of him, and it's a mystery whether Stephanie has even told him about the baby. I'm assuming she has and he's made himself scarce. Of course, I don't know what Stephanie does on her phone. Mr. Smith has left a message on Dr. Albright's answering machine with no results."

"Pam hasn't said anything?"

"No. But my thorough, old-school daughter is gobbling up all information available about pregnancy and childbirth. I wish Stephanie did the same."

"Pam is a treasure," said Kaisa, "but I'm prejudiced. And your husband? Where's Tom in all of this?"

"You know Tom. He's steady and calm. He's taking all this in stride, but I sometimes go overboard and end up in a dither."

"You think?"

"I know, I know. I need to work on that."

"Good idea," said Kaisa. Her fingers suddenly slipped and she dropped a large glass canister of sugar on the tile floor, shattering the canister into small, sharp slivers.

"Move away, Mom. I'll take care of this. The glass pieces are all the way over by the living room door. Your slippers are no match for the broken glass."

"I can…" insisted Kaisa, reaching for the broom.

"No, have a seat." Since Kaisa had been taking the new medication, Alice hadn't seen Kaisa's fingers work less than perfectly until this incident. "This is no big deal. I have a Tupperware canister you can have."

"I'm not having any ugly plastic canister on my countertop, thank you very much. Where were we? Oh, yes. You need to be careful of how much you abuse that sweet man of yours."

"What are you saying?"

"I'm just saying that even a saint has his limits."

Chapter 17

Crystal had been an obstetrics nurse for twenty-some years. She had always wanted to be a nurse, but specialized in childbirth due to the positive environment in the labor and delivery rooms. Where most nursing dealt with illnesses, witnessing and being an integral part of bringing a new life into the world on a daily basis was invigorating and affirming.

Although the hopeful and forward-looking atmosphere ruled most days, there were still times of trouble, pain, and despair to the point of making a woman weigh her decision about having children. Today had been one of those times.

Crystal had worked the 11:00 p.m. to 7:00 a.m. shift. For some otherworldly reason, most babies chose to be born in the deepest, darkest hours of the day. At the beginning of her shift, there was one patient to care for: Natalie, who was well on her way to delivery. This baby was Natalie's third and the process was familiar to her. Having her husband fully engaged as her coach added to her comfort. Crystal made periodic checks on Natalie but was able to concentrate on necessary paperwork. Looking through the patient's history, Crystal noted that Lisa Hughes, her high school quartet sister and colleague at the hospital had been the attending obstetrician in Natalie's previous deliveries.

Lisa, Crystal's idol, was a well-liked doctor whose

services were sought by women even in surrounding communities. She was a brilliant, Ivy League-educated woman, who had received countless offers to practice in famous hospitals in large cities. But Lisa had wanted to establish her practice in Haudenosaunee Hills, to provide services to people she knew, people her parents and grandparents had known. Lisa loved history and maintaining traditions. She had even kept her childhood home, an enormous, ornate Victorian, which she renovated little by little. Her quartet sisters had fondly made fun of her roaming around alone in her immense space.

I wonder how she's doing, thought Crystal. After years of success in her profession and various positions of responsibility in organizations in her community, Lisa had started to yearn for a change and had joined Doctors Without Borders. She had accepted an assignment in Afghanistan. Since then, Crystal had not heard from her. Alice's daughter Pam was taking care of Niles, Lisa's Siamese cat, a forlorn feline who had lost his mistress and, right before that, his angora buddy, Frasier. To add to his misery, he had had to move to brand-new surroundings at the Fitzpatricks' home, and they didn't let him go outside. A great deal of stress for a little creature.

Crystal was counting months in her head. *Lisa's year should be up by now...* She was deep in her thoughts when the automatic double doors opened and an orderly wheeled a wheelchair through the doors. In the chair, a young girl was groaning and writhing in pain. The girl announced that she wasn't supposed to be there, that she wasn't due for another few weeks but her water had broken.

Crystal got up and notified the other nurse on duty of the new patient. Crystal was relieved she already had a patient assigned to her. She immediately felt guilty about her thoughts. After all, she was an equal opportunity nurse, caring about all patients equally and fairly. Secretly, she had to admit to herself that she very much appreciated future mothers who were prepared, asked questions, and understood that some pain was to be expected in the birthing process, and that medications were not always the answer.

As the night progressed, Natalie gave birth to a baby boy. The sex of the baby was welcome news to the father, who, after two girls, couldn't wait to have a football and fishing buddy and expressed his thoughts for all to hear. Crystal sympathized with Natalie. *What if the baby had been a girl? How can men still think that way, especially since they themselves are the sex determinants in the process of fertilization?*

The young girl was having trouble. Her parents had been called, but she continued to labor alone. Crystal anticipated a less-than-stellar outcome in her case. The girl's teeth bore obvious signs of meth use, and in such cases the baby's future was less than ideal.

After a horrendous night of screaming and thrashing, the teenager gave birth to a premature baby, an underweight boy whose first cry was weak and hesitant. He was immediately taken to the Neonatal Intensive Care Unit. The girl was not ready to be a mother, and Crystal's heart sank. She caressed her own belly, thinking how lucky her baby was.

****

"What a night!" Crystal proclaimed to Gavin, who was having breakfast at the kitchen table. She shared some details, with Gavin grimacing at appropriate spots.

"I made some oatmeal. Want some? And there's blueberries I took out of the freezer."

"Thanks, honey. I'm living backwards, having breakfast first and then going to bed!"

"In that case, consider this dinner."

Crystal enjoyed her bowlful of warm, healthy food. She looked up.

"Hey, have you, by chance, heard any news of Lisa or heard from Lisa herself? Her year in Afghanistan should be over by now."

"No, I thought maybe you had. I get paid for the lawn mowing and snow removal, but that's an automatic bank transaction with no contact with Lisa. I just assumed she was still on her assignment. I thought Tom told me she was still on assignment in Afghanistan."

"Remember, we thought after the terrorist attack that Lisa would come home immediately. I wonder if the Doctors Without Borders kept the personnel there or moved them somewhere else. I know it was a long time ago. I don't think there's anyone we could ask. She has no relatives that I know of."

"Any particular reason you need to know about her now? Not that you shouldn't. You are good friends, after all."

"No specific reason. Just wondered if she was back. Of course, that's silly of me. If she had returned, she would've been in touch, I'm sure." Crystal did not want to let Gavin know, and she almost didn't want to admit it to herself, but she hoped beyond hope that Lisa would be around to deliver her baby when the time came.

After her sleep, Crystal called Alice.

"Hi, I just thought I'd check on how the meeting

went with the social worker."

"It went fine, much better than I expected. And, there are new developments. Denise, that's the social worker, urged me to talk to Mrs. Smith. Funny, but she's not what I thought her to be—Mrs. Smith, I mean, not Denise—you know, the nose-in-the-air type who doesn't even acknowledge us regular folk. She's actually quite nice. She says that people misunderstand her shy and quiet demeanor for being uppity."

"Interesting," said Crystal. "I don't know the woman."

"She says the situation is a bit different from what Stephanie has let us believe. Stephanie left home on her own accord. She was not thrown out."

"Really? Well, that changes things. If it's true, of course."

"At this point, I'm apt to believe the mother. She also said they have tried to get in touch with the Albrights. They believe the father of the baby couldn't be anyone but Michael. So far, the Albrights have not responded. We'll have to wait and see.'

"I had time at work to look through some stuff. We had a teenage mother last night. Terrible case, but that's beside the point. Anyway, there is a support group in town for teenaged mothers. I don't know what the format is for the meetings, but I'm assuming it's a group where teen moms can exchange ideas and feelings and maybe learn something new."

"I'll definitely look into that for Stephanie. Thanks."

"By the way, have you heard from Lisa? I know you have Niles, and she was so attached to him. Has she checked in with you at all?"

"She did, but that was way back in the fall. She was

doing well and had decided to sign up for another year. Remember the horrific experience she had in Kabul a year ago?"

"The attack on the maternity ward of the hospital where she worked. Mothers, pregnant moms, and babies killed by explosions and gunfire…"

"Yes, how could I forget that! Lisa must have lived through it without being scathed or she wouldn't have decided to stay an extra year. Of course, she has nobody in her life to tell her to come home, to stay out of harm's way."

"True. So she'll be back next year. Didn't she leave in January a year ago?"

"Yes, she did. I did hear that she's been in touch with Abdul Naziri about the Afghani culture. She was worried about not acting appropriately or according to local customs. She did get training by the organization before she left, but questions come up when you are living within the culture. Could be he's also helping her sort out the unthinkable attack, I guess, with her using Dr. Naziri as a sounding board. But you know what I really think? I think she has a crush on him. They were introduced right after he moved into your house—I mean Kaisa's house—with his kids."

"Hmm. Very possible. What's not to crush on? A handsome university professor with an impressive resume, after all."

"And five small children?"

"There's that," Crystal reflected.

"Come to think of it," said Alice, "what about Christine? Any news from her?"

"How on earth did five children remind you of Christine?"

"I don't know. You know how my brain works: Trying to go a hundred miles an hour in first gear. I guess I conjured up an impossible scenario in my head—Christine with five children? Impossible! Christine no, Lisa yes."

"I haven't heard a thing. The last I knew she was working with your husband to buy her old house, and somehow her brother bought it instead. She came to town when her mother was going downhill, and visited her, if you can call it that. Carol was pretty much comatose during the last few weeks of her life. Christine sat by her mother's bedside for hours on end, which must have been a discouraging experience with no response from Carol. She was cremated, but there's been no memorial service. It's been a year already. I wonder if Christine and Magnus are planning something sometime."

"Tom sees Magnus quite often. We'll have to check with him."

"Let me know, and keep me posted on Stephanie's situation. And, like I said, if there's anything I can do to help, don't hesitate to call me."

People always say that, but very few really mean it, thought Alice. Crystal was genuine and real. She could count on her.

Chapter 18

Lisa Hughes stood by the small two-burner stove in her apartment in Kabul preparing vegetables to go with naan bread and eggs. She had easily adapted to a diet that was mostly organic and healthy. With almost a year and a half spent in Afghanistan, her view of the world had widened considerably. It was one thing to see various countries as a tourist, eating fast food and staying in American hotels. It was another thing entirely to live in a different culture for several months or years. Lisa realized she was born as one of the most fortunate people in the world. Even the loss of her parents in a boating accident didn't dampen the thought that she was lucky beyond belief and that, to feel worthy, it was her duty to help others who couldn't even dream of her charmed life. Her thoughts turned to Crystal's mother, Lola, who was known to disappear occasionally into some near-wilderness in an exotic country and return with invaluable memories and stories.

Although the conditions in the hospital in Kabul were acceptable, they were a far cry from the sterile world in which Lisa maneuvered in the States. The people were lovely, and she was growing closer to them as she learned more of the local language. There was a dispute among the native speakers whether that language was called Dari or Farsi. Some people also spoke Pashtu. To complicate things, there were dialects for each. Lisa was sure she would easily be in her eighties before she could master any of the languages receptively, let alone speak them. She relied a great deal on the people around her who could interpret what was said.

Childbirth itself had not changed from the beginning of time, only people's attitudes toward it had shifted from thinking of it matter-of-factly to considering it a process requiring professional help. Lisa remembered hearing that her mother had been born at home, with her grandmother assisted only by her grandfather when the midwife's car had broken down on the desolate road to their farmhouse. There were young people today back home who preferred to give birth at home. Lisa had never made house calls, but the time in Afghanistan was slowly changing her mind. A large percentage of Afghani women had their babies at home, and the hospital admitted only the more complicated cases.

Lisa ate her meal looking out into the garden. It was obvious it had once been a lush spread of flowers, bushes, trees, and water fountains. Some flowers were still successful in painfully bringing forth tortured-looking blooms. With her busy schedule and no ability to travel, Lisa had not ventured out into the countryside of giant, red poppy fields. Abdul Naziri had been more than charitable in giving her small but important details on how to deal with her environment and its dangers. A jaunt into the hinterlands of Afghanistan was not recommended, especially not for a woman alone. In fact, it would have been considered insane.

While in her job, Lisa had experienced firsthand how precarious life was. A terrorist group had opened fire and used explosives after storming into the maternity ward. Lisa was attending to a mother who had just had her baby. They were able to hide in a closet amongst sterilizing equipment and blood pressure cuffs. Twenty-four people, including pregnant women and newborns, were killed in the massacre. The event was too horrific to comprehend. Yet despite sleepless nights and seriously considering a request to end her commitment half way through, she'd valiantly reported to the new job site. Toward the end of the year, she felt increasingly more comfortable, although she continued to be easily alarmed at the sound of a motorcycle or a car backfiring.

For Christmas, Lisa hung shiny red and green ribbons on a painted-leaf begonia growing in a pot on the table of her one-room apartment, the extent of her decorating for Christmas. She thought of her friends back home...

Alice would have her whole family involved in finding and cutting a spruce in the woods, decorating it together with family and friends, admiring every shiny ball and every Santa's elf and red bow ornament while singing Christmas carols and drinking eggnog and glögg.

Crystal would have a small tree brought in, dug up from their own Pure Earth farm and its roots wrapped in burlap to allow for replanting after Christmas. She would hang handmade decorations on it, preferably made of recycled materials.

Christine would have a decorator come in and do a fabulous job preparing her condominium on the seventeenth floor of a Seattle luxury high-rise for her annual extravaganza of a "money-is-no-object" Christmas party. Or, on the other hand, Christine might just as well travel home to Haudenosaunee Hills and spend a quiet Christmas with Magnus in the childhood home both were attached to. Christine was a woman of substance and means. She was also kind and considerate, which kept her approachable.

Lisa missed hard winters and high snowbanks. She missed her friends. She missed her cat. And—she surprised herself—she missed Abdul Nazari. Abdul, the brilliant, widowed professor with Middle Eastern good looks, who now lived in the Weston house, where Christine, Crystal, and she had spent so much time with Alice twenty-five years ago, in the bedroom now a fairyland for one of Abdul's daughters. His house was the opposite of Lisa's stately, quiet, Victorian residence. The old Weston house had been turned into a lively home for growing children. The noise generated by the Nazari crew was, at times, overwhelming, and while everything was in its place at Lisa's house, Dr. Nazari's place looked very much lived in. Lisa enjoyed the interruptions when she was discussing her upcoming trip with the Political Science professor, and she was flattered when one of the little girls asked her to braid her hair or wanted to polish Lisa's fingernails. She had allowed herself to think she could get used to family life, the type she had never had herself. Yet, just a month ago, she had committed herself to staying another year in Kabul.

Lisa cleared her throat. It was scratchy and she felt slightly feverish. She felt run down and weak against any viruses or bacteria attacking her. She hoped for a good night's sleep.

Chapter 19

The freight train that always stopped below Denise DuBois' apartment window on Tuesday and Thursday afternoons was in its customary location. Denise, or Deedee, as her family and friends called her, could count on setting the clocks of her kitchen appliances by it. The scheduled train seemed to be always on time, and only the train cars were different from day to day. She had never bothered to find out why there was a stop on this stretch of the rail. There was no railway station, no industrial complex nearby necessitating a loading or unloading. As often was the case with a less than sufficient rail system, one train had to stop and wait until another train had passed a junction, allowing the second train to use the same rail down the track.

The outside walls of many train cars had colorful graffiti in the form of cleverly arranged alphabet letters overlapping one another, painted in bright purples and reds, yellows and blues. On others, there were haphazardly spray-painted obnoxious words or messages—either political opinions or exclamations of a sexual nature.

Deedee was curious to see what the theme of the day was today. The train car two stories below her sported clearly legible capital letters in white paint edged with black, CLARK LOVES NATASHA, the message contrasted on a bright red heart with an arrow through it.

How sweet! Enough to lift your spirits! thought Deedee. Other cars had clear maroon sides, left alone by lovers and hoodlums alike.

She gathered her coat, scarf, and purse, stepped out into the hallway of the building, and closed the heavy door to her loft apartment. She had chosen it on a momentary impulse and, more to the point, for the lack of another choice when she moved into town for a job in a nearby small city that had no acceptable apartments to offer. She'd needed to find something quickly and now considered finding a place in Haudenosaunee Hills a lucky break. Her true taste in styles ran from country cottage to Colonial to Victorian, old and antiquey, all a far cry from the cold, industrial warehouse space in a newly renovated factory building. Her apartment was a source of envy for many of her friends, with its exposed red brick walls, galvanized metal heating and air ducts shining in the ceiling, and large water pipes embellishing the walls. All one vast space, areas for various functions and activities exposed to each other. Deedee was thankful for the bathroom door, at least.

Her furniture, gathered through the years from flea markets, inherited from aunts and uncles who downsized or passed away, or pieces she bought on a whim because it pleased the eye—all were styles from various decades and centuries. Some of the old, beloved pieces would have fit together, not as a furniture store kind of unit but as furnishings and accessories that could live together in harmony. However, to make them live in a factory warehouse was a travesty.

One of these days, I will find a place more suitable for me and my eclectic possessions.

Deedee had always known she was adopted, yet her

adoptive parents had not told her anything about her birth parents, only that they, Brigitte and Jean DuBois, were not her biological mother and father. Deedee loved her parents of French descent. She was pleased that they even pronounced their last name authentically. She had not insisted on more information. Perhaps they didn't have any more facts or knowledge beyond what she already knew, and she was satisfied with that. However, her complexion was darker than what would be typical of a Caucasian child, and, as a ten-year-old, she had often fallen asleep at night making up scenarios in her mind about circumstances of her birth.

She imagined having been born to a wealthy Middle Eastern couple who gave her up for adoption due to her being a girl.

She conjured up a story of an American white high school girl getting pregnant by an exchange student from Kenya. This had actually happened in Binghamton, where Deedee had gone to school. That story had a good ending with the boy going to college in the States and then gaining citizenship. He married the girl a couple of years later.

She made up a scenario of a rape and nuns taking the baby in until adoption. Was this why she had no trouble memorizing words to hymns and could easily memorize the catechism or prayers her grandmother introduced her to?

When she told the various tales of her birth to her mother, her mom laughed and encouraged her to be happy with her life, content with reality.

Deedee's lack of knowledge about her origins had led her to choose social work as a career. She first got a job in Canandaigua and later received a promotion that led her to Haudenosaunee Hills. The new job specialized in child protective issues, an area where Deedee's strengths lay and which gave her the most satisfaction. Her parents supported her in her decisions, her mother boisterously bragging about her big-hearted, socially responsible daughter and her father humming a soundless murmur of satisfaction.

DeeDee decided to walk to the restaurant by the lake—a good hike, but she needed it after sitting all day in her job. The weather was warm. Spring had arrived with force. Her mother used to say the wind was soft and gentle like a cow's breath. There were leaves in the trees again, and there was a special aroma in the air, a smell of new growth and wet soil, the opposite of the odor in the fall when, without excuse, dying matter emitted a heavy, rotting scent.

As Deedee was not a shopper, she hardly ever went downtown. Outside of an occasional concert at the old renovated opera house, nothing beckoned her. She noticed a new proprietor had taken over the high-end men's clothing store, and she passed a man she had often run into in her job site at the social services building. As in any weather, he had on a worn-out down coat and flailed about a large cardboard sign with the message: *The end is coming. Are you saved?*

Deedee had not built a large friendship group in Haudenosaunee Hills. She had left behind a couple of good friends from school days, who were in frequent touch with her through social media. She had also extricated herself from negative romantic entanglements. *Come to think of it,* she thought, *they shouldn't even be called romantic.* The men in her life had been either chauvinistic control freaks or people pleasers who offered to give her the moon from the sky and turned their own lives inside out trying to please her. She was well aware that a major factor in her process of choosing had been her thought and hope of changing these men. After all, she had a master's degree in social work, the same field that clearly points out the futility in trying to change someone.

The Italian restaurant had opened a couple of years ago with an Italian couple cooking true old-world dishes. It had quickly become the locals' favorite. It was open again now, having closed its doors for a few months while the décor was changed from the usual to the authentic with Tuscan murals on the walls and dark beams in the ceiling. There were fewer customers today, which was not a negative to Deedee. She wasn't fond of crowds and noisy places. Walking in, she looked around and quickly waved to a tall man by the window and walked over.

"How are you?" asked Magnus, pulling out a chair for her.

"Doing fine. Same old problems and sad stories at work. Otherwise, I can't complain." She took off her jacket and sat down. "And you?"

"Keeping busy. I've got the master bath almost done and started on the other bathroom on the upper floor. It was a task getting the clawfoot tub to the second floor from the garage. It took six guys to maneuver it through the doors and the stairway."

"You're lucky you still have it. Your parents were still of the generation who saved everything: 'You never know, you might find a use for it someday.' "

"Exactly. I spent a long time restoring that tub in the garage. I must say it was a brilliant idea to keep it. It'll come in handy bathing the baby. How much longer do you think we should wait?"

When Magnus had met Deedee through the partner parenting group, he had found her to be good-looking, ambitious, kind, and a sweet person with a bright intellect and a great sense of humor. Through their meetings, first in person and later via FaceTime, he felt that he had gotten to know her quite well and found her to have all the qualities his future child should inherit. She even had characteristics he found to be an extra plus—Deedee could sing and she was athletic, both talents he did not have.

It had bothered Magnus that Deedee was young and appeared to be soured on men in general. She openly announced that she had no intention to tie herself to a man. She simply explained that roles between men and women were still greatly undeveloped and there was no equality to be found. She'd once said, "Why would I want to be someone's unpaid maid?" Tongue in cheek? Maybe, maybe not.

Deedee had told him she was adopted and assured Magnus that his being gay was only a positive. She was looking for an intelligent, self-assured man to father her child. She didn't need a man in her everyday life.

"I know you're getting anxious," Deedee said, "but I'd like to wait till the busy summer is over at least. When we decide to do it, I want to give the effort a hundred percent of my attention. Don't forget, I'm still in my twenties, so we have time."

"Right, for another two days."

Deedee smiled.

As Magnus reached for the early birthday present he'd brought, an old, antique opal ring, Alice and Tom walked in. Alice was baffled for a minute. *What is Denise doing with our friend Magnus? Is Magnus proposing? To a woman?*

When his friends came over to the table, Magnus made the introductions, and Deedee burst out laughing.

"This must look a bit strange to you. I can just see what you two are thinking! Good to see you again, Alice. Nice to meet you, Tom."

Magnus asked the two to join them for dinner.

"We won't disturb you." Tom twirled around as if to leave, turned back around and stared at Magnus. "Were you proposing?"

Magnus and Deedee laughed louder. "Not even close. This is just a birthday present," said Magnus. To prove there was no diamond, at least, Deedee opened the box and took out a beautiful opal ring.

To give a girl a ring of any kind must mean something, thought Alice, but she said: "Happy birthday!"

Tom was thinking with a furrowed brow. "So how long have you—what's the word in a case like this? How long have you known each other? Been together? Kept company?"

"We've known each other for a couple of years, when we met at the Partner Parenting meetings. We've gotten to know each other and feel that a child would benefit from having us as parents."

"That's wonderful!" gushed Alice.

"That's good," said Tom with a lower, less audible voice. It was questionable whether "good" referred to the relationship or the proposed waiting period.

Alice and Tom declined the invitation to join the two for dinner and found their own table for two. They looked back at the table by the window and watched Deedee and Magnus lean close to each other and speak animatedly as if they were concocting a major conspiracy.

Chapter 20

Alice insisted that she accompany her mother to doctors' appointments. Her reasons for being present were several: She needed to know firsthand the status of Kaisa's illness. She knew her mother didn't always listen fully, and if she did, she didn't remember what was said. Alice wanted to have all information available from all sources, when it came to her mother and Parkinson's in particular.

What a worrywart! thought Kaisa. Her Parkinson's showed surprising signs of halting. She knew, of course, that Parkinson's was a progressive disease, and that getting back to her pre-illness days was an impossibility. She was still driving herself, and small lapses in her memory were no more noteworthy than what her completely healthy contemporaries reported. Most of them looked for their car keys or cell phones on a regular basis or missed an appointment or two due to misplaced appointment cards and the resultant failure to write the date and time on a monthly calendar.

Young people had their calendars on their phones along with the rest of their lives. Kaisa was appalled at the dependence on cell phones. *How did we ever manage without them? Today, people walk around, their eyes riveted to the small screen, oblivious to their surroundings. I suppose it's easy to check on your grocery list on the phone or to flash your phone at the machine reading your pass as you check in to board a plane. Maybe it's more convenient to read a book on your phone than to hold an actual paper copy in your hands. And maybe it's necessary to be reachable by everyone every second of the day. How unpleasant! I need my time, my peace and quiet when I want it. I do know I am an old fuddy-duddy. I also know that being against technological advancements is downright antiquated.* Kaisa slipped her cell phone into her pocket.

Flowers brought on by April showers were coloring the landscape. Daffodils, jonquils, and tulips in a variety of colors filled the flowerbeds between the building and the lake shore. *What a beautiful spot I live in! It's not a match to the lakes surrounded by birch trees in Finland, but close!*

Kaisa's Finnishness was like a barnacle. It stuck to her with cement-like hardness, able to resist all efforts to budge it. Not that she had even tried. In the early years as a new immigrant to the Finger Lakes, she had tried to be more American—to engage in small talk, to dress more casually, and to participate in various social groups—only to realize that her natural steadfastness and a more formal style suited her better as a Finn and as a judge's wife.

The wind picked up, rattling the slightly open sliding glass door to the balcony. Kaisa reached out to close it. Outside, on top of the tulips and daffodils, were sheets on paper, carried by the wind from one spot to another. More sheets were flying down from above. Following their path, she gazed up and saw the papers were fluttering down from a low stack on her neighbor's balcony.

There! That's definite proof there's someone living

in the condo!

Alice and Tom still made fun of her for insisting on the existence of a woman next door. Kaisa was panicking. Somehow, she had to go down to the yard level to investigate if there was a name on the papers. She put on her sturdy rubber-soled shoes and started down the steps on the side of the building. She almost slipped, so she decided to use another method for her descent. She sat down on the step and scooted down on her buttocks carefully, one step at a time. She knew she was a sight, but nothing stood in the way of her determination.

She made it to the bottom of the stairs. It was May, and balconies were decked out with summer accessories: small tables and chairs, wind chimes, and indoor plants brought outside after freezing was no longer a danger. The neighboring balcony was empty except for a rusty, lightweight metal TV tray the wind had obviously knocked over. On the floor was a smooth rock, painted to look like a striped cat, an unmistakable paperweight that had failed in its job and let loose of the pile of papers.

Kaisa started to gather the papers and fought with the wind to catch them. With her hip still healing, she moved slowly, and the effort was frustrating. She had a great urge to read what was written on the documents but didn't want to appear suspicious or nosey. She picked up all the papers she could see and headed back to the steps. With her hands full of witness material, she had difficulty negotiating the steps, and she fell on the unoperated hip.

"God damn it!" She was not one to use swear words as a habit. She sat still, sideways on a low step. She carefully moved one limb after another, testing them for damage. Except for a slight soreness on her good hip, she determined she had escaped disaster. She folded up the stack of papers, stuck them in the waistband of her jeans, and climbed the stairs on all fours. She made it to the top, wiped her hands on the back of her pants, and walked inside.

Kaisa shook with excitement. She would finally find out her neighbor's name. She would be able to prove she wasn't hallucinating. After sitting in her favorite reading chair, she smoothed the papers in her lap.

A business letter-sized sheet had examples of various exotic languages in the world, each one in an alphabet more unrecognizable than the next—various Native American ones and unfamiliar languages of tropical islands. Kaisa remembered seeing something like this before, but couldn't place it. A yellowish ten-by-six narrow paper was a receipt of items purchased at a hardware store in Dennis, Cape Cod in 2014—a canvas, rope, and a small boat anchor. She was perplexed. "What the hell?" she said out loud. This made no sense. She looked at the next sheet—a page from a manual for a cell phone, and more sheets of extra pages from the same manual. A large bottle of bleach bought at a Dennis grocery store was the only item listed on the next sheet. None of the sheets had an identifying name on it.

Kaisa's imagination ran wild. *Who would buy a canvas, rope, an anchor, and bleach all on the same day?* She admitted she had watched entirely too much television—and especially true cold cases of murder—after the death of her husband two years ago. The receipt was for items needed if you wanted to get rid of a body by dumping it into the ocean. And bleach? An agent used to deep-clean signs of blood...

She got up quickly—and immediately grabbed her hips. She was now feeling her escapade.

The mink coat with blood on the lapels—there has to be a connection! Kaisa's heart was pounding. What had she stepped into?

The remaining sheets of paper had information that appeared pertinent or maybe not, lyrics to an old Bob Dylan song, and a multi-sheet European train schedule. Kaisa struggled to find a thread connecting the documents. The only thing that made sense was a murder that apparently took place in 2014 somewhere in Dennis, Massachusetts or near it. It also made sense in light of all this evidence that the woman living next to her was the murderer, or at least an accessory. *No wonder the woman has been so secretive!*

Kaisa smoothed the papers and laid them in a neat pile on the kitchen table. She pulled a plastic clip from the potato chip bag and clipped the papers together. She gingerly walked into the hallway and placed the clipped stack outside the neighbor's door. She hesitated, but rang the doorbell. No answer. Again.

Kaisa's hip had started to ache, and when touched, the area was tender.

Alice will kill me, but I think I probably should see a doctor. What the heck, she'll kill me if I don't see one! Kaisa got the last appointment of the day with her GP in town. She decided Alice didn't need to know about this visit to the doctor. She showered, had a snack, and drove across town. An X-ray showed no sign of a broken bone. Returning to her condominium, Kaisa noticed that the papers at her neighbor's door were now gone. She rang the doorbell again. Again, no answer.

Kaisa spent a sleepless night with her sliding glass door locked and macabre scenarios swirling through her head. She knew she needed to do something about this, but what?

Chapter 21

Alice invited Kaisa for dinner on Saturday. "Why don't you come a bit earlier and you can spend some time at the piano? We could take a sauna before dinner, too..." She hesitated. "Or after dinner, if you'd like that better."

"Thank you. Sounds great. What can I bring?"

"You know you don't need to bring anything, but if you insist, we always love your *pulla*, and I happen to know you enjoy making it."

"That's a deal."

What is this? Did Alice find out I snuck to the doctor's office the other day? Why the call right now? Kaisa conceded she was getting paranoid.

At Alice's, she rang the doorbell and walked in without being acknowledged. *Payback!*

"Hi, Mom!" Alice looked out the window and pointed with her index finger. "Look at how you parked."

"What now?" Kaisa showed signs of being slightly alarmed.

"You're way off the driveway, onto the lawn."

"Okay, I can go back out and make sure the car is well within the confines of the paved area and parked in a fashion acceptable to you. I just didn't want to step into a puddle and get my feet wet."

"I'm sorry, Mom. I'm just a little tense. Believe me,

I really don't care about the car or the lawn."

What did I predict? This Smith girl is making my daughter crazy. "Why don't you come and listen to me play for a few minutes. You always used to like that. Of course, my fingers aren't as nimble as they used to be, but I can still produce a recognizable tune. But first, here." Kaisa handed Alice a braid of *pulla*, a shining light-brown loaf adorned by pearl sugar. Alice had a mind to object to her part as an audience but thought better of it, and they settled in the living room, Kaisa at her grand piano, now "stored" at the Fitzpatricks', and Alice in one of the wing chairs facing each other by the fireplace.

Kaisa played the first movement of Beethoven's *Moonlight Sonata*, the only one of the three movements she felt confident enough to attempt. A slow tempo these days was better. *Curious, that in this piece, the slow movement is the first one. Highly unusual.* Her fingers moved left and right on the keyboard with only an occasional glitch that made her cringe and inconspicuously tilt her head toward her right shoulder and squint her eyes.

"Brava!" Alice clapped her hands toward the last notes of the sonata. "You still have it!"

"I don't know. I believe I'm more like the old man on TV years ago, a black junkyard owner. What was his name? Do you remember?"

Alice wrinkled her forehead. "I do remember the program, I think. His name 'and Son' wasn't it?"

"Yes. That's him."

Alice waited. "And?"

"And what?"

"You said you believed the same as he did. What is

it?"

"Oh, right. He said he used to have wild oats, but as an old man, he only had shredded wheat. I feel like that, too, about a lot of things. By the way, where is everybody?" Kaisa looked around.

"Tom went fishing with Bobby, and the girls are kayaking. They'll be back by dinner."

"How are things going?" Kaisa decided she would be satisfied with superficial answers, although she knew the issue at hand was a cornucopia of troublesome, messy details.

"There's actually been a lot of progress. I talked to Mrs. Smith. She's not at all what you and I have thought. Turns out neither she nor her husband asked Stephanie to leave home. The girl decided first to move to her aunt's house, and then said yes to Tom and me and our offer for her to stay with us."

"Hmph," said Kaisa. "What do you know."

"And, get this." Alice became animated. "Mr. Smith has called Dr. Albright twice. He finally got an answer. The doctor, his wife, and—here's the kicker—their son Michael had no idea what Mr. Smith was talking about."

"No kidding!" Kaisa was genuinely surprised. "Stephanie never told Michael? That's something! So what happens now?"

"I'm working on getting some communication going. Stephanie still won't talk to her parents."

"Does Stephanie know that you are aware of her deception as far as the so-called evictions?"

"Yes. It was a pretty sad scene. Lots of crying, lots of apprehension, lots of fear and trepidation, but she agreed to start seeing a counselor who specializes in youth services."

"Well, that's something. What was the attitude of the Albrights?"

"Right now, I think they are sorting it out with the Smiths. It's Michael I'm worried about. According to Stephanie, both of them knew what they were doing. She told me that one time during sex the condom had broken, but they hadn't thought anything of it."

"The optimism of youth." Kaisa sighed.

"Well, but for the grace of God, there go Tom and I," said Alice, without much thought to who her audience was.

"You mean to tell me you and Tom weren't virgins when you got married?" Kaisa feigned disbelief.

Alice saw a faint grin on her mother's face. "Okay, Mom."

"Moms know a lot more than the kids think, right? Pam doesn't have a whole lot over on you, does she?"

The house all of a sudden became noisy with the whole family back from their activities. Bobby proudly produced two large, shiny lake trout.

"Beautiful!" exclaimed Kaisa while hugging her grandchildren.

"Who's going to clean these?' said Alice, knowing from past experience that Tom was an expert at fileting a fish and would not want her to use his dangerously sharp filet knife.

Pam and Stephanie settled on the couch to check on their social media.

After dinner, Alice warmed up the sauna. They urged the rest of the family to take their turns first, as Kaisa was a serious sauna enthusiast and spent more time on the highest bench in hotter temperatures than most and didn't want to rush for the sake of people waiting for their turn.

"I'm so pleased with your progress after surgery," said Alice while the women were placing their folded clothes on the chairs in the dressing room.

"Me, too," said Kaisa. As Kaisa removed her pants, Alice was alarmed.

"Turn around." Alice had Kaisa stop with her right side facing her. "What on earth is that?" Alice cried out.

"What?"

"Can you see this? You have a huge black-and-blue mark on your upper thigh in the back."

"I do?" Kaisa could not turn her head enough to see it.

"Geez, Mom, what happened?

Kaisa contemplated her answer for a moment. You don't get a bruise and not feel it. She decided to play it safe.

"I was moving fast and hit my thigh on the corner of the dresser in the bedroom. It smarted a little, but I didn't think it would leave a mark."

"You're lucky, Mom. You could've broken something."

Not that again, thought Kaisa, relieved that she didn't have to come clean about going to the doctor without Alice.

They settled on the highest bench in the sauna and threw water on the rocks on the stove. The heat hit them instantaneously and almost violently. Both of them enjoyed the attack and alternated between sweating and a refreshing, cool shower. Quiet and relaxed on the bench, Kaisa unsuccessfully tried to hide her self-satisfaction as she stated, "Well, I finally have proof that I'm not nuts."

"What do you mean?"

"There really is a woman living next door to me."

"You saw her?"

"No, but I found old papers that flew down from her balcony. There were all sorts of receipts for purchases of suspicious items you would use to get rid of a body—you know, rope and canvas, for instance. And remember the mink coat on the balcony with blood on it? This is disturbing, but I think the woman killed somebody, dumped the body, and is keeping a low profile."

"Where are the papers now?"

"I should've kept them, but I put them by her door in the hallway."

Alice rolled her eyes.

"I didn't want to have her think that somebody had them and maybe took them to the police or something."

Alice threw more water on the rocks. She breathed through her mouth to avoid burning her nostrils. "Where did you say you found the papers?"

"They were flying off her balcony."

"And they conveniently flew onto your balcony?"

"No, I got them by the lake." Oops. Kaisa knew she'd just gotten caught.

"Mom, didn't I tell you, you can't go down those stairs?"

And didn't I tell you to mind your own business? Kaisa said, "Nothing happened. You really need to stop playing mom with me. The time will come sooner or later for you to get your chance at that. Don't rush it."

"Okay, okay. So what are you going to do about those papers?"

"Like I said, I don't have them. I'll do some more investigating before doing anything official."

"Was there a name on these papers?"

"No, not a one."

"Figures," mumbled Alice under her breath.

Chapter 22

The Fitzpatricks and the Smiths got out of their respective cars, having arrived almost simultaneously. Both couples had accepted an unexpected invitation by the Albrights to get together and discuss the dilemma they found themselves in. The first meeting was to take place without Stephanie and Michael, although their lives were the topic of conversation.

Probably a good idea, thought Alice. *We don't know the possible reactions to things. The discussion might get heated, and the kids don't need to witness temper tantrums thrown by adults.*

The Albrights lived in a large, well-kept, Tudor mansion in an established area of town. The wide street had a median with decorative blooming trees. The manicured lawns and the bushes shaped into smooth spheres and triangles advertised the skill of the gardeners. Doctor Albright opened the thick, heavy door to his guests, and the two couples stepped into a marbled entryway with a gigantic chandelier hanging from the beamed ceiling. The ornateness and sparkle didn't match the almost rustic beams, in Alice's estimation. *Well, money can't buy taste.*

They were led into a library where all the walls were covered with countless books, new and old, some of which appeared to be entire sets of an author's collected works. They sat on black leather sofas which faced each other.

"May I offer you a glass of sherry?" asked Dr. Albright. Everyone accepted the offer except Melinda, who shook her head without uttering a word. Alice wondered if Melinda didn't drink due to her parents' alcoholism.

With a delicate sherry glass in her hand, Mrs. Albright sat in an armchair. Dr. Albright remained standing. Alice understood that stance to mean he was in charge of the situation, the leader of this discussion group.

Instead of tackling the reason for the gathering, Dr. Albright had everyone introduce themselves and suggested they use first names. "I am Robert."

"Clare," said his wife. The rest took their turn— Melinda, Craig, Alice, Tom.

"Melinda and Craig, Alice and Tom," repeated Clare, as if to reinforce her memory. "You are the history teacher, right?" she asked, nodding to Alice.

"Yes. I've taught in the high school for over twenty years now, but not always the same courses."

"And you?" Clare inquired of Melinda.

Melinda crossed and recrossed her legs. "I'm just a housewife."

Both Clare and Alice looked at her in surprise.

"Oh, stop!" said Alice.

"There's no such a thing as 'just' anything," said Clare.

"I do keep busy with the house. I'm old-fashioned and cook everything from scratch, and I sew a bit. It all takes time."

"My wife is way too modest. She doesn't just 'sew a bit.' She designs and makes the garments from start to end. No store-bought patterns or anything. She made the outfit she has on." Craig, obviously proud of his wife's talent, was impervious to Melinda's embarrassment as he made her the center of attention. Everyone was looking at the clothes she wore—a lightweight short-sleeved summer suit with a perfect fit.

"My hat's off to you," gushed Clare. "That outfit is beautiful. The workmanship is superb! And to cook from scratch, that's amazing. I've had to resort to ready-made meals now and then, but Robert's schedule is unpredictable, and my job is all-consuming."

"I didn't know you work. What is it that you do?" Alice asked.

"I'm a translator. I work for a publishing company and translate works from French and German into English. I work from home and always have. Sometimes I wish for different scenery."

Robert Albright cleared his throat.

"Well, here we are. The four of us are about to become grandparents, and the future mom and dad are still in high school. Let me get one thing clear— Stephanie definitely wants to keep the baby, correct?"

"Yes," said Alice immediately, and equally immediately regretted opening her mouth. This question was directed to Stephanie's parents, but there she was, jumping right in, as usual.

"Yes." Melinda backed Alice almost inaudibly.

"Why on earth didn't she tell Michael right away?" asked Clare. Alice opened her mouth, but felt Tom's hand on her arm and got the message.

"Stephanie is a quiet girl, rather introverted, and has never wanted to cause trouble for anyone," Craig said, "She was afraid of what the response would be and thought somehow that ignoring the issue would make it disappear."

"They are so young," said Clare.

"They are young, and their potential for their future is amazing," chimed in Robert. "Michael has been accepted to Rochester Institute of Technology for the fall. I had wanted him to be a doctor and continue in my practice as an orthopedic surgeon when I retire, but he wants to be an engineer. I do hope he can still do that. What are Stephanie's plans?"

"She has wanted to be a teacher and has been accepted to Syracuse University, but she changed her mind. When Stephanie found out that Pam was not going to a four-year college, she declined Syracuse's offer. I have to admit I was a little ticked off at that point." Craig's face reflected his statement.

Tom spoke up. "Our daughter is an amazingly practical young woman. She has not made up her mind about a career and decided to go to the local community college for her first two years. She can get the core courses taken care of and, after deciding on a major, transfer to a university. And, as Pam says, I'll save a slew of money. She's right."

"That's actually not a bad idea for Stephanie, either." Craig looked at Melinda.

"You're right," Melinda agreed.

"But," said Alice, "what about the baby? We have now placed our kids in college, but where's the baby?" She was getting impatient.

Everyone was quiet. Clare spoke first.

"Let's face it. The baby is the most important issue. We don't want our children to have to sacrifice all they've worked for, but if you make an adult decision to have sex, then you act in an adult fashion and take care of the consequence."

"Right," Alice agreed, "there is no schedule that says, 'You graduate high school in year X, from college in year Y, and get married and have your first child by year Z."

Craig sat up straighter. "What about marriage? In my day, when you got a girl in trouble, you married her. What do you think, Bob?"

"Robert."

"Oh, sorry. Robert."

Alice was irritated. "In trouble? That's such an unfortunate word when speaking about a child. Besides, in today's world, nobody has to get married. To think that you must do it is antiquated."

"That is entirely up to Stephanie and Michael." Robert looked serious. "They are so young and hardly know what they want of life. They'll be eighteen soon, and at that point they have a right to decide what they want. Not that these few months till they hit their birthdays will all of a sudden make them mature and wise. We will support Michael in his decisions through college and, if needed, beyond."

"We'll do the same for Stephanie, won't we, honey?" said Craig, taking Melinda's hand. Melinda nodded.

"And until Stephanie figures out what she may want, she is welcome to stay with us," Tom said, with Alice smiling up at him.

On the way to their cars, Alice suggested, "Hey, want to get a bite to eat at the café and talk some more?"

The café had removed the heavy glass panels in their windows, and screens let in the breeze from the lake.

"I'm not hungry," said Melinda, and ordered a cup of coffee. With simple hamburgers and French fries on everyone else's plates, Alice said, with ketchup dripping from her chin, "What about that house, huh? All the antiques and the books must have been in the family for decades. Clearly old money."

"What's old money, really?" said Tom. "When does money turn from new into old? I'm sure, although I don't know the history, that the first Vanderbilt's possessions were not considered old money. I wonder what the cut off for change is? Fifty years? A hundred years? What if a representative of a generation goes bankrupt? What do you call money that's old but there's a lot less of it?"

Craig remembered a friend who "didn't have a pot to piss in," although on the outside he looked like someone with money. "In reality, he hated all the old stuff he had inherited but didn't have the means to get rid of it and buy new. You never can judge a book by its covers," Craig decided.

"Well," said Tom, "I'm sure the Albrights have a pot or two to do with whatever they want, and as far as books, they just might have read them all. Books like that have some value, even if they smelled like a library basement."

"So…" Craig crumbled up his paper napkin into a ball. "What now? Am I right in thinking you will talk with Stephanie and try to get her to talk with Michael? She probably still won't talk to us."

"We'll be happy to do that," said Tom. "And from what I gathered, although they didn't say it so many words, Bob and Clare will have a good long talk with Michael."

"Robert," said Craig.

"Yes, that was very clear. Robert, not Bob. From now on, should I have him call me Thomas?"

Chapter 23

Lola and Mauno had now been married over a year. Married! Who would have thought? Lola, the feminist extraordinaire, free spirit, who didn't need a man in her life. Lola realized that with age she had bent her requirements for many things and flexed her ideas for the sake of others. She expected the same in return from people in her life, not to speak of the fact that her marriage was, on the surface, a matter of expediency, a legal matter rendering her life uncomplicated. She felt rather Machiavellian. This feeling was eased by the fact that, as Mauno had been in love from the beginning, Lola had slowly developed deep feelings toward Mauno beyond the obvious attraction she had felt from the beginning.

Not only was she married, she was about to become a grandmother. Grandmothers were old people, women with their gray hair in a tight bun at the back of the neck, skirt and blouse covered by an apron, feet in orthopedic shoes, and obvious difficulty getting up from a couch. Or they were women with bright red lipstick, glasses on a chain around the neck, poorly fitting bras, and obviously dyed hair showing the form of the curlers even when combed out. Lola ran around barefoot in the summertime and wore secondhand, colorful outfits she discovered in flea markets, especially long, flowing skirts. She paid very little attention to the line of her eyebrows. She felt young, no different from the days of the Vietnam War protests. The only change was the color of her hair and the fine wrinkles covering her body. She also struggled with the idea that being a grandmother all of a sudden obligated her to love the idea of grandmotherhood, to be eager to hold that baby in her arms. Lola loved Crystal with all her heart. She always had. However, she was not like other women, who couldn't wait to hold a baby, any baby.

Lola had grown up in a large family where babies were always present, either her own siblings or her cousins, all gathering for Sunday dinners at her house after mass. There was noise and chaos, yelling and hugs. After dinner, Lola sneaked off to her room or a secret spot in the attic with her paper and pencils. The lonely activity of drawing comforted her, while other children in the extended family were entertained by games involving running around and yelling.

Lola was different from her brothers, and, as years went by, the connection to her siblings grew looser and looser. Today, she barely knew where each of her four brothers was. Their interests had been vastly different from hers. She loved art, while they preferred car racing, guns, and beer parties. The growing gap between them resulted in a lack of communication. She assumed that her brothers had taken care of the Giordano family name's continued existence on this earth. There had been notices of birth of babies. With Lola traveling the world, she often saw the notes when they and the babies were several months old, and she chose not to acknowledge them.

Now that she was older, she felt a slight regret for shutting out the rest of her family. Looking at Mauno and his children, grandchildren, and countless cousins, she realized the richness of it all. Lola now looked at them as her family as well, and couldn't wait to bring Crystal and Mauno's daughters together.

Even today, her mind was occupied by a granddaughter. Kaarina was graduating from the Finnish upper-level school, with university studies as her next step. However, before that, she was taking a year off, and, come August, she was heading to Japan for an exchange year. Lola felt so very happy for her and, she had to admit, a little bit jealous. Kaarina had all the adventures ahead of her, all the excitement the world could offer. Lola remembered her skydiving friends in Thailand, the close group of climbers on Mt. Kilimanjaro in South Africa, the farm workers in Slovenia she had joined for a summer, the man in France who had hired her with under-the-table pay to work as a guide in his chateau in the countryside. Part of the pay had been all the wine she could drink from his vineyard—rich red burgundy that had gotten her in trouble with the following day's obligations a couple of times.

As she brought back memories, she realized she hadn't sent Crystal a letter from the magical winter journey to Ylläs Fell, well above the Arctic Circle. She didn't want to stop her custom of sending Crystal handwritten letters from all destinations on her trips. How did she forget? The man in her life had disturbed her routine. Funny that Crystal hadn't mentioned the absence of a letter. Of course, she too now had a man mixing up and reorganizing her daily life. Lola wondered where she had stashed her stationery in the move from Kaisa's cottage to Mauno's house.

Lola ordered six red roses from the most reputable

florist in Naantali, the closest city to the island. Six seemed to be low in number, but she knew the price of roses was conveniently and shamefully raised for the graduation. Per custom, the graduates would receive congratulatory roses from relatives and friends. The group picture of the students each year looked like a sea of roses, with people's faces almost secondary. *Seems like a waste to me,* thought Lola. *All those beautiful flowers, fated to wilt and die in a week's time.* Six was a good number for that reason also.

She looked forward to the enormous bash the graduation party was going to be. She had learned that Finns were reserved and quiet, even at big parties, unless, of course, alcohol was served, in which case they tended to become rather talkative. They discovered their courage to speak English, and although, in a typically modest fashion, they maintained that their English wasn't very good, they could carry on a perfectly fluent conversation.

Chapter 24

Crystal lifted her tired legs onto the ottoman, a round leather stool she had had to air out for two years before bringing it into the house and using it. Lola had sent it to her years ago from Morocco, informing her of a possible smell caused by the tanning products of camel urine and pigeon excrement. Not only was the stench possible, it was overwhelming! Now that it had been thoroughly cleansed by the pure air of the Finger Lakes, the footrest was comfortable and a favorite of Crystal's for its shape, size and decorative stitching.

The weight gain caused by Crystal's pregnancy, as well as the hormones, made her tired and sleepy. She admitted that part of the exhaustion was her age. A pregnant woman in her forties was considered high risk, especially if she was carrying her first baby.

She wondered how Stephanie was faring. Of course, women were physically able to have children from a very early age. Unfortunately, their emotional maturity could not match the body's capabilities. Stephanie should be having a wonderful experience. However, the internal turmoil Crystal had observed in her affected the girl's mind and spirit.

Crystal reached for the letter she had received from her mother. The last one had been written in Kaisa's cottage in Finland in August of 2019. With Mauno in Lola's life, Crystal had felt that her mother's travels had possibly ended. Perhaps she could consider the letter from the cottage the final chapter, and she could now bind the letters into an autobiography for Lola. Yet here it was, another chapter...

As Alice was always interested in all things Finnish, Crystal wanted to share her mother's letter with her.

"This letter came as a total surprise," she said to Alice on the phone. "I'd like to read it to you, okay?"

"Of course, you know I'd love to hear it."

"Here goes:

"My dear Crystal,

"It's a beautiful mid-May morning here! I have said this before, but there is no earthly way I can thank Kaisa enough for allowing me to tag along with her to this wonderful place. I have now experienced all of Finland's four seasons. I am equally amazed at and thankful for each of them. I was convinced I would never travel anywhere again, but little did I know that the most incredible trip of my life was ahead of me.

"When Mauno found out that the Ylläs ski resort in Lapland was going to close the season earlier than usual, he arranged a ski vacation for us in the beginning of March, right after we got married. I looked at it as a honeymoon trip, really. Mauno rented a private cottage, and I expected to find a place like Kaisa's.

"After a fourteen-hour drive, we arrived in a quaint village covered by three feet of snow. The roads were plowed but not sanded or salted, keeping the scenery pure white and virginal. The cottage was a log cabin with every possible convenience, including a sauna, of course, which we took advantage of nightly. Mauno talked me into jumping into the snowbank after the hottest heat we could stand. What an experience! Did

you know that rolling in the snow is actually a colder experience than jumping into a lake through a hole in the ice? Why, you might ask. I found out that when you climb out of the lake, the water flows down your body and disappears. When you roll in the drifts, the snow will stick to you for a long time, freezing you inside and out.

"We skied and walked, had a ride in a sled pulled by a reindeer, and another by a team of huskies. There were some people around who had rented snowmobiles. We found them disturbing in this pristine world. The loud noise of the motor and the smell of gasoline ruined the natural peace. All in all, there were very few people, which made us feel rather safe. Instead of eating in restaurants, we cooked reindeer sausages and salmon on the open fire outside. For a couple of days, it snowed, and we watched huge snowflakes flow down as if in a slow-motion film.

"We made an overnight visit to an ice castle. I froze my behind sleeping on a gigantic block of ice covered with layers of hides. Although not the most comfortable experience of my life, it was one of the most memorable. The restaurant with ice tables and chairs eased the discomfort by its mere uniqueness.

"The greatest treat was watching the northern lights—a dance of green red, purple, and white formations across the clear sky, a sight you didn't want to leave. A couple of times, we spent a long time admiring the miracle, with our necks bent in an awkward position until we gave up and lay down on the snow.

"This was a trip I want to make again. Hopefully, you and your family will be able to join us. 'Your family.' It sounds so strange as, for so many years, it was just the two of us. Now we both have new people in our lives. I

am grateful for that, as well. I promise I won't be traveling alone anymore and, you'll be pleased with this: Mauno has made me understand that carrying a cell phone is actually a good thing. I promise to keep in touch more and hope that you'll stay well and happy for the months before the big moment.

"Wishing you all the best. Say hello to Gavin for us.

"I love you. Mom

"Just think of how many times I told my mom that she needed to have a way to get in touch with me quickly or for me to touch base with her, but no! Now, a man comes along and, presto, there's a phone!"

Alice laughed. "Both of us have stubborn moms. Yours is far away again after you thought she might actually settle down near you. My mom's here, but in la-la-land some of the time. I just need to look after her, like I seem to look after a lot of people. Hey, I've gotta go. The social worker is calling. Talk to you later."

"Bye," said Crystal thinking of Kaisa, and Stephanie, and Alice.

Chapter 25

Stephanie tried on various outfits. Her pregnant belly bulged out prominently. Her mother was trying her best to reestablish a mother-daughter relationship with her by buying her maternity clothes and books about childbirth.

Why waste your money on clothes you wear for two to three months? So what, if your belly stretches out your regular clothes or if your waistline is under the belly? You see loads of old men walking around with their pants under their beer bellies. Stephanie felt that so much was made of fashions unnecessarily.

Stephanie also felt that her recent actions had done a lot toward making the whole situation more tolerable. Alice had forced her to get in touch with Michael, who had sounded strange on the phone. He seemed baffled that she hadn't returned his calls or answered his texts. He had been under the impression that she had dumped him without a reason, severed all ties inexplicably. Michael was hurt that he had heard of her pregnancy from his parents. Stephanie had tried to explain how overwhelmed she was and how she'd thought he would definitely dump her if she didn't dump him first. She agreed they had a lot to talk about.

At Deedee's suggestion, Alice had also talked Stephanie into joining a teen mothers' support group she was now getting ready to attend. *What on earth could these girls give me? They're all in the same miserable situation I'm in,* thought Stephanie. Yet she wanted to talk to someone who was going through the same experience as she was.

Stephanie had tried on most of the clothes in her closet and dresser, with piles of them now on the floor. She had picked a pair of shorts and a T-shirt advertising a local pet grooming establishment. A cute Pomeranian with a bone in his mouth stared out from Stephanie's midriff. She started to leave the room but turned at the door and went back to dutifully pick up all the clothes and hang them in the closet or fold them neatly in the dresser drawer.

Pam dropped Stephanie off at an old school building, now used for various events, meetings, and trainings.

"Text me when you're ready to be picked up," said Pam. "Good luck!"

Stephanie looked at all the young girls in the room, two of them familiar faces from her school. Others were most likely girls from out of town. A couple of teens knew each other and carried out a muffled conversation. Others were checking each other out.

The leader of the group, a young woman herself, entered the room through a back door. She introduced herself as Jackie. She informed everyone that she was in her first job as a social worker and that just a few years ago, she had been in the same situation as all the girls in the room. She immediately earned a great deal of trust by the statement.

After introductions, Jackie inquired about what had motivated everyone to attend the group. The answers ranged from a straightforward, "My mother made me come," to an almost belligerent, "It ain't nobody's business." Stephanie related to both statements. However, when her turn came, she demurely stated, "I want to talk to people who are experiencing what I am experiencing and maybe get answers to some questions I have." She wanted to add, *I want to know how many of you are happy about what happened. How many of you have no clue what this means for your future? How many of you love the baby's father? Do all of you realize that your life as you thought it would be is now history?*

The farther the group got into the discussion the more astonished Stephanie became. It became increasingly clear to her that she had lived a very sheltered life.

A girl with colorful tattoos covering her arms and neck announced that she had gotten pregnant deliberately. Another, shy, very young-looking girl said that by getting pregnant, she had hoped to make her much older boyfriend marry her and take her away from her home situation where her father was emotionally abusive to all her family members, yet the boyfriend had moved to a different state, never contacting her again.

Most of the others said they had been caught by surprise when they found themselves pregnant. It became obvious that all of them had trouble dealing with reality. A rather thin and pale mother-to-be said she wanted some hints to make sure she ate healthy for the baby's sake. She admitted that she was living on ramen noodles, rice and beans, and other inexpensive foods along with snack foods like potato chips, cookies and candy. Other girls looked at each other with an obvious glance of familiarity with what was being said. Stephanie thought of the diverse meals made with natural, healthful ingredients that Pam's mother made, with fresh fruit available any time she wanted a snack.

Some expressed they were afraid of touching a baby and had never even changed a diaper. While most girls responded by expressions of disbelief, Stephanie could easily relate to the lack of experience. As an only child, she had never worked nor had she ever been asked to babysit for anyone.

Jackie led the group with the confidence of a professional. She deflected nasty comments, kept the conversation going, and gently brought into the discussion those who were hesitant or bashful.

It became clear to Stephanie that, although she hadn't delved into the topic of pregnancy, she already had a great deal more knowledge about it than most in the group.

At the end of the meeting, Jackie disclosed that, in upcoming meetings, there would be guest speakers on many topics, including birth and care of the newborn. The tattooed girl was heard to say, "Well, duh! Isn't that why we're here?" Some participants were quick to inform Jackie that they would not be able to come next time as their work schedule prevented it.

On the drive home, Stephanie reflected on her experience. "You wouldn't believe how weird some of the kids are," she said to Pam. "Some had a million tattoos and piercing and wild hair—you know, like yellow and blue, with long hair on one side and the other side shaved."

"Really?" said Pam. "You know some famous people who look like that, and they are perfectly okay people."

"I know. I just can't imagine them as a little baby's

mother. And, that's just on the outside. Not that I know a lot about these people, but geez! Then there were some who aren't eating! Can you imagine? Or they're eating crap. What are they doing to their baby? On the way out, one of them even lit a cigarette! What a loser!"

"What did you expect? A Sunday School class?" asked Pam, and immediately added, 'Sorry."

"I don't know. Some of them were there, because their mothers dragged them there. They just didn't seem interested."

You weren't exactly the epitome of inquisitiveness before this meeting. "Well, maybe their curiosity will grow as time goes by," Pam said out loud.

"I don't know." Stephanie shook her head. "I don't think some of them will ever come back. They had all sorts of excuses for not showing up next time."

"That's sad," said Pam.

"Yeah, I know."

Chapter 26

Dear Charlotte,

On your big day, allow me to congratulate you for your great accomplishment! The whole world is now open to you. Congratulations also on your scholarship. You will make a wonderful teacher and the children in your classroom will be very lucky to have you as a person to admire. I wish you all the success in the world!

With warm thoughts,

Mrs. Fitzpatrick

Fifty-three done. Twenty-four more to go. As had been her custom for years, Alice was writing her personalized cards to all the graduates—Pam, Stephanie, and Michael among them this year. Notes to these three would be the easiest and the most difficult to compose. The graduation ceremony was scheduled to take place outside, a brave decision every year, as the weather can never be trusted completely.

Each year, there were fewer and fewer seniors, the number going down by five to ten per year. There was talk about a merger with the neighboring school district, but it remained as talk only.

The smaller number of students means fewer notes to write, thought Alice.

"How are you doing?" asked Tom, standing in the doorway to the office/craft/classroom.

"Fine. After the first ten, it becomes drudgery, an

effort to find ways to say 'Congratulations' without sounding repetitive or ideas to keep the notes personal. I know and remember most kids well, but there are those who moved to town later, and, as I didn't have them in my class, it's tough to find something interesting to say about them. Yet I can't leave them out, either."

"Well, you put yourself in this predicament years ago when you started this."

"I know. You're right. When do you stop, though? They tell me the kids look forward to a message from me. Some have even saved them for twenty years! They say it shows I care, in some cases that someone, anyone cares."

"Let me help by cooking dinner," offered Tom. "By the way, is it me or has Stephanie all of a sudden taken an interest in food? I don't mean that she eats more or eats less than before. She seems to study labels and ask a lot of questions. Is she thinking of a career that's somehow food-related, not that a career of any kind is utmost in her mind these days?"

"I don't think so, but I have definitely noticed it, too. This started right after she went to the pregnant teenagers' meeting. I'll tell you more later. Thanks for doing dinner. This gives me a chance to make some headway on the notes."

Later in the evening, Alice and Tom sat in the living room with their bedtime herbal tea.

"You know, I had to talk Stephanie into attending the meeting with the pregnant girls, but it seems that she really enjoyed it. I don't know how much they cover factual information and helpful material, but just that she was among girls who all share something unique was good for her."

"Like an exclusive club of sorts." Tom smirked.

"Tom, that's not fair. You don't need to be sarcastic! Those girls are having a hard time, some more than others. You wouldn't believe some of the life situations Stephanie has been telling me and Pam about. There are girls in the group who don't have a family of their own, or if there's a family it's totally dysfunctional. Some of them have even lived in the street at some point. I really feel for them. There's this one girl…"

"No, she's not moving in with us," said Tom sternly.

"I know." Alice was annoyed. "I'm just saying. You mentioned Stephanie's interest in food. It's not just food. It appears that she was shocked by what the girls eat or don't eat, and wants to do something about it. She asked me if I would be willing to teach classes for them on healthy foods and easy cooking. They have no clue about nutrition and some of them live on garbage. No, I don't mean literally, but might as well. They eat non-nutritional stuff. It's worse that this so-called food goes right into their babies. So, anyway, I said yes, that now with school soon over, I would do it."

Tom was quiet for a while. Alice looked around the room moving only her eyes.

"You would do it? Is it part of the curriculum? Is there a curriculum?"

"No, I don't know, but it would be extra, like a bonus class."

"Is there a budget for it?"

"Oh, I wouldn't ask for any pay. Totally voluntary."

"And who would pay for the food used for the cooking demonstrations?"

"I don't know yet, but we can work it out."

"We can work it out," Tom repeated. "And, which

'we' is this? You and I? You and the girls? You and Social Services? And, I suppose it would all happen in the industrial kitchen of the old school?"

"I think so. If that's not possible, I could do it here in our kitchen."

Tom got up quickly, spilling his tea.

"I have to put my foot down," said Tom wiping the tea spills on the knee of his trousers. "I know you mean well, and you are a wonderful person trying to help anyone having a need of some sort. Alice, there has to be a limit. Having Stephanie here with all her problems and quirks is taxing for all of us. She's seventeen and can't fathom her actions could be troublesome to anyone. She'll change as she matures and will become more altruistic, but right now, she's a taker and you, my dear, are the biggest giver I've ever known. For years I've watched you sacrifice yourself, your time, and your personal hopes and wishes to make someone else's life better. You don't need another commitment, another job to prepare for, especially one that has no resources attached to it, no support system, no administrative structure behind it."

"Well, if I'm such a giver, you certainly have benefitted from my generosity for years!"

"Alice, I've said this to you before—You can't be all things to all people. Can we look at this calmly and reasonably? It's obvious there's a great need and I'm happy although a little surprised that Stephanie has spotted it. Let's investigate and see if it's possible through Social Services to somehow fund classes like this."

"Things like that take time." Alice was frustrated. "You know how slowly the wheels of bureaucracy move.

The young mothers and their babies need help now!" Alice was in tears. She stormed out of the room. She regretted there was no door between the living room and the kitchen—she would have slammed it!

Later, in bed, Tom grabbed his CPAP mask. *My life of masks. One type to help Magnus drill or weld in his restoration project, yet another to keep me from snoring when I sleep. And then there's the mask of hiding my true feelings in an effort to please others.*

"I thought of something," he said, turning toward Alice.

"Mmm," said Alice inaudibly.

"What do you think of this? We can present the idea of the nutrition classes to the Smiths and the Albrights. After all, they have all sorts of money and could easily foot the bill for the cost of the food. I don't know if it's feasible, but it would be even better if Stephanie could bring herself to present the issue to the future grandparents. And here's something else: Kaisa could teach the classes. She has a Master's degree in Home Economics and knows a thing or two about nutrition and cooking. She is also a grandmotherly type the girls might relate to."

Alice couldn't help but chuckle. Her mother might be grandmotherly at times, but she was just as apt to shell out judgment when she thought it was due. Alice imagined Kaisa's expressions when dealing with the tattooed and pierced young ladies.

Tom continued, "Teaching would give Kaisa something to think about, something that would steer her away from all the imaginary nonsense."

Alice sat up. "You're right. Why is it that you're always right?"

"It's because I'm a man."
Alice threw her pillow at Tom.

Chapter 27

Although it was early in the season, tourists had already started to crowd parks and other attractions in the Finger Lakes. Boats of all sorts were visible on the lakes after a long winter. On the roads, there were long, sleek limousines on their way from one winetasting to the next.

Magnus and Deedee decided to devote a Saturday to responsible winery hopping and climbed into a luxurious stretch limo, large enough to accommodate a dozen or more passengers.

The lush greenery of the hillside vineyards, with blue skies above and the blue lake below, created the scenery that lured people back to the area year after year. Magnus felt at home in his childhood landscape, and Deedee loved the beauty of it all, although scenery or surroundings had not been criteria for choosing a job or a place to live.

Sitting on an enormous deck with a view of one of the myriad vineyards and the lake beyond it, Magnus and Deedee took in the summer day's charm and allure with all their senses.

"I was just thinking," said Deedee, "I know this is your old stomping grounds, and you bought the house and are doing a fabulous job restoring it, but what happens when the project is done? I mean, you don't have a job, and it's terrific that it's not crucial that you have one, but do you have hobbies that would keep you here? Your parents are gone and your sister is way out in Seattle, and you don't have other local relatives, either, right? You have good friends, but friends don't necessarily make you stay put."

Magnus got up. "Want another Riesling?"

"Please," said Deedee and wondered if she had hit a nerve. How deeply rooted was Magnus in Haudenosaunee Hills and how willing was she herself to set down roots being barely out of her twenties? If there were a child involved, these questions needed to be answered.

"Try this slightly sweeter version," said Magnus returning with two glasses of clear, golden liquid.

Deedee took a sip.

"Hmm," she pondered out loud, "exquisite bouquet, rather fruity." She lifted her glass delicately.

"Oh, yes, light-bodied, with quite a mellow finish," Magnus said. They burst out laughing. "Before you make me sound even more gay than I am, we'd better stop."

"True," said Deedee.

"This really is pretty good," said Magnus, looking at the scenery through his Riesling. We should probably leave the rest of the critique to the wine snobs. I know that wine is the answer. I just can't remember the question." He pretended to think hard.

"Who said that? You did not come up with that yourself. Besides, I've heard it before."

"I don't know." Magnus lifted his glass to an unknown person. "Here's to Mr. Anonymous!"

"To get back to what we were talking about," Deedee reminded Magnus, "do you think you'll live here the rest of your life?"

"I really don't know. You asked about what I would

do after my house is finished. I could see buying another old house and restoring it, maybe several of them. The job's kind of grown on me. I like to work with my hands and I like seeing the big changes. When we have a child, we should both be nearby, at least for the first few years. Of course, in life, nothing is guaranteed, and whatever you do involves risk. You don't know if I may want to move away, I don't know if you might fall in love and get married, and so might I. We can't stop living our lives because we want a child."

"If I wanted to get married, why wouldn't I want to give myself a chance instead of involving a gay guy?"

"I don't know. Because you feel sorry for me? You know I want a biological child and can't very well produce one by myself?"

"That's not true. It's also not true that I'm thinking of having a husband. In my job, I see enough trouble and turmoil in regular marriages."

"All caused by men?" Magnus was perplexed.

"I can't say that, but this I am sure of—people today are too selfish to engage in truly devoted, dedicated relationships. It was different before."

"Before? When?" Magnus was not convinced.

"Well, like at the time our parents were our age."

"Could be," Magnus agreed. "I know my parents were married for decades and I never saw any lack of dedication. There certainly were no fights. Of course, their parents and the entire extended family had cooler temperaments than other nationalities. My dad's family was from Sweden, pretty much all the way to the original Mr. Lindqvist, a cobbler who came here in the 1700s. My mom, I'm not sure. I think she had English, Irish, and Scottish ancestry with some German thrown in."

"Like most Americans," noted Dedee. "My family, well, you tell me. I have no clue. Just looking in the mirror I know I'm not Swedish or English. I get my dark complexion from at least one parent if not both. My adopted parents don't know, either."

"I was thinking…" Magnus lifted his glass and raised his brow in question. "Want another?"

"Since we have the limo, why not? I like the first Riesling better."

DeeDee thought about her origins. She had decided a long time ago that race didn't matter, that skin color didn't mean anything except to indicate how much sunshine your earliest ancestor was exposed to thousands of years ago.

Sipping on the next glassful, DeeDee said," You were about to say something earlier. You said you were thinking about something."

"I was thinking that we should get DNA tests done. That would give us some answers, and for the sake of our future child, it would be useful to know what genetic features are in the offing for them or what illnesses they have a genetic disposition for, and for us as well. My mom had dementia. I would like to know if, perhaps, I will develop it, too. My mom certainly kept her mind busy, and didn't slow down physically, either, until the dementia was diagnosed. My dad died of pancreatic cancer. Not much anyone can do to fend that off."

"That's actually a good idea," agreed DeeDee. "Do you want to order the tests or should I?"

"I saw an ad where they had a special, two for one. I'll have to see where that was."

"Magnus, you are a millionaire. What do you care?"

"If I didn't care, I wouldn't be a millionaire long."

Magnus nodded emphatically, as if to say, "So, there."

"I suppose," said DeeDee, wondering to herself how it was important to Magnus to save on an item under a hundred dollars, and yet he was willing to shell out a pretty penny for the private limousine for the day. She decided there were certainly strong frugal Scottish genes in Magnus's system, but those genes were confused by some obviously spendthrift ones from other cultures.

Chapter 28

Alice had decided, as she had countless times in her life, that it was time for her to pay attention to her own wellbeing. Now was a good time to proceed, as school was almost over and she would soon have more time for herself. The school year of no contact with the students outside of the screen had made her feel deprived, and the effects had continued into following years. Sitting during so much of the time, instead of being on her feet, walking about, had stiffened her body, and she had put on a few pounds on her already plump figure. She was convinced that holding onto unwanted pounds was the result of stress, for the most part. In addition, Stephanie's move into the household had added a great deal of tension.

"This is it!" said Alice and climbed onto her bicycle. She felt unsure of her capability, and the saying, "It comes back to you, like riding a bicycle," didn't ring true to her. The seat felt oddly hard and the handlebar was in an uncomfortable position.

This is probably fine for competitive riders, but I'm not doing a Tour de France! Alice thought. She had trouble working the numerous gears determined to be necessary by Tom. With every shift of the gears, Alice felt less than competent and feared the chain would jump off its predetermined path and get tangled beneath her feet.

"You'll get the hang of it," Tom had said when he

presented the bike to her. "Here's the manual, if you need help."

Alice rode up the hill to Crystal's farm. *Of course, I had to choose the most difficult incline around here for my first time out.* She pushed up the hill, using a gear much too high for the effort needed. She sweated through her shirt and finally arrived at the Pure Earth Farm. She removed her helmet, sweat pouring down her face in rivulets. Her hair was matted down on her head.

I really am not suitable to be seen in public, thought Alice and scratched the neck of Rufus, the border collie, who had come to greet her.

Crystal was having a glass of juice on the patio.

"Hi," she called out to Alice. "Is that a new bike? Snazzy!"

"Yeah, a little too snazzy for somebody like me. I really don't know what I'm doing. Tom thought this bike would be good for me. I'm not so sure. It has all sorts of bells and whistles I'm not used to. When I was a kid, I had a bike with one single gear and a foot brake on the pedal. If the chain came off, I could easily put it back on. This one..." Alice shook her head. "This one needs a mechanic with a master's degree!"

"You're funny." Crystal chuckled. "You're just not used to it. Maybe we can go for a ride together and I can teach you. By the way, do you want some juice?"

"No, thanks. I have water. Look at this, the water bottle attaches to the top tube, and if I want to, I can attach a long flexible straw to it and drink as I go without using my hands!"

"The top tube? Listen to her!"

"Hah! Don't I sound like a professional already?"

"You may need no lessons at all, but I too should do

some exercise. I was just diagnosed with geriatric gestational hypertension."

Alice was alarmed. "Oh, no, that's really dangerous, isn't it? Wait, did you say 'geriatric'?"

"I did say 'geriatric.' It's just another more official word for old, when you talk about people. The medical community has to have their own vocabulary. Just like hypertension instead of high blood pressure or adiposity for fatness."

"Well, I am the poster child for adiposity," said Alice, "but what about the hypertension?"

"It's not to be ignored. It's quite common with older women in the second half of their pregnancy. It'll be good for me to ride again."

"Great! Today, I think I'll be happy if I can make it home. My thigh muscles are feeling that hill."

"Just let me know when you want to ride. I do get tired quite easily these days. I'm not seventeen."

"Yeah, I know," Alice smiled with compassion.

"Speaking of seventeen-year-olds, how is Stephanie doing?"

"Stephanie seems to be taking her pregnancy more seriously these days, although she's hard to read. Joining the support group seems to have opened her eyes. There are girls in that group living a life Stephanie knew nothing about. You and I see them in our jobs, but kids are so self-absorbed they walk through life without noticing life around them. It's really interesting. Stephanie doesn't look down on these girls. She has a lot of empathy and is looking for ways to help them somehow. It's actually great to see the depressed girl is disappearing. She has even agreed to meet with Michael and face reality together with him, whatever that may mean. Her mother is trying to reach out to her but is playing it safe. She doesn't want to jeopardize the recent progress."

"That's great to hear."

"I don't know where it'll lead, but things are looking up." Alice lifted her right leg half way over the tube of the bike. "Hey, don't look at me. I'm always so graceful getting on this thing." Alice succeeded in getting on her bike after two tries.

****

The next morning, Crystal's phone rang at work.

"Hi," said Alice in a rather subdued tone. "If you can't talk, let me know, but you won't believe this: I'm a victim of my own bicycle! I was riding down your hill last night, got my controls mixed up, and plummeted full force into the ditch at the bottom of the hill."

"Geez," said Crystal. "Are you all right?"

"Considering that my foot is broken, I'm doing fine."

"I'm so sorry! That hill of ours!" Crystal felt, however unreasonably, guilty about owning the hill of bad luck.

"It's not your fault!" said Alice. "I was wondering, though, and I hate to even bring this up, but would you mind hosting Stephanie for a few days? I know she's supposed to be a family member at our house, but I realize I've failed on that score. I feel like we have a houseguest, and with a broken foot, things look a bit overwhelming. Silly, I know. Like I said, I hate to do this, especially since you have the blood pressure problem, but maybe Stephanie can be of some help to you. You have a way with younger people. Of course, if by some miracle Stephanie says she'd rather go home to her parents, all the better."

"Not silly at all. I'll be happy to have her for a while. Let me just talk with Gavin. Don't worry. Everything will work out. Gotta go. Talk to you soon."

Alice leaned back on her pillow and lifted her leg up on the bed.

Why me? Why now? Tears came into her eyes first making her vision foggy, then obliterating the view of the entire room until Alice's eyes were fully closed and she cried loudly and vehemently, letting out all her frustrations and guilt, her resentments and feelings of insufficiency.

Chapter 29

A low-to the-ground red sportscar swerved into the Fitzpatricks' driveway, and a young man in tennis shorts and shoes of the latest fashion stepped out.

Michael rang the doorbell and waited, and waited. He was about to turn around and leave when Alice opened the door.

"Hello," she chirped, surprised at the glee in her voice. *Must be the painkillers,* she thought. "Sorry it took so long. I don't know where everyone else is. They're all so used to having me rush to the door, that even with this..." She pointed to her crutches. "I'm still the doorman."

"Hello. What happened to you, Cougar—I mean, Mrs. Fitzpatrick?" Michael was genuinely surprised and concerned. The nickname had slipped out so very naturally, Alice had to smile. She was thankful her nickname was rather innocuous compared to those for other teachers.

"Well, when you don't practice riding a complicated bicycle on flat land first, you know..."

"You crashed, huh? Did my dad do your foot?"

"No, it was another orthopedic doctor. I know your dad is super, but I didn't happen to get him. Well, come on in."

"Stephanie!" Alice called out. A rude gesture, but forgivable due to her difficulty moving.

Michael stepped into the foyer and removed his shoes, a habit he had learned at the Smiths' house.

"Stephanie, you have company," said Alice, as if Stephanie couldn't see Michael herself, as she now stood next to him.

Alice had an inkling as to why Michael had appeared at the door. She juggled several possible scenarios. It could be the Albrights had convinced Michael that Stephanie was not going to have a virgin birth and he should step up and assume his role as a father, or perhaps Michael had come to break up with Stephanie, or maybe they actually had agreed to meet and have a date of sorts.

"Hi," said Stephanie.

"Hi," said Michael.

They stood staring at each other. Alice stood staring at them, then swung her crutch to take the first step. "I…I have to…I should…do things."

How very elegant of me, just the kind elocution you expect from a respected educator, thought Alice, and chuckled to herself. She was the adult in the room, and probably more uncomfortable in the situation than the kids.

"Can we sit on the back deck and have a drink? I mean a soda?" Stephanie called after Alice, who was making herself invisible.

"Absolutely. Help yourselves."

"So," said Stephanie.

"So," said Michael. He leaned on the railing of the deck and popped open a cola can. "Well, where do we go from here? What are your parents saying?"

"I haven't talked to them. I can't."

"Why not? Is there something more you haven't told

me?"

"No. I just feel that I am such a disappointment to them. You know, my parents aren't like yours, born with a silver spoon in their mouths, people who have met with nothing but success in their lives, able to deal with anything. My mom and dad clawed their way out of very pathetic situations in their childhood and made something of themselves with no formal education beyond high school. Then I come along and ruin it all for them. It would have been better if I had had an abortion." Stephanie started to cry.

'You don't mean that." Michael took Stephanie by the shoulders and pulled her to him "This baby has two parents, don't forget. I have some rights, too."

"What rights do we have? We are seventeen, for God's sake!"

"We are, but not for long, and when we turn eighteen, we can make our own decisions."

"Where do you get that Pollyanna attitude from?"

"What does that mean?" Michael was baffled.

"It means that you're not looking at things realistically. What decisions can we possibly make? You can decide to give up your dream to go to RIT and, instead, get a job at a fast-food joint. You can decide to live on pasta and canned meat. You can decide to do nothing with your life except go to your minimum wage job, maybe even two of them, and try to come up with money to support a family. I can decide the same thing, but the baby needs its mother. It probably won't even make sense for me to work, with the price of day care these days. We can't afford to live."

"If I am a polly...something,"

"Pollyanna."

"If I am a Pollyanna, you're the most negative person I know. What happened to you? Do you love me?" asked Michael.

Stephanie bent back her neck in frustration, as if to get an answer from the ceiling. She sighed.

"Yes, I love you. I've been miserable without you."

They stood hugging for a long time.

"We can work it out. I think our parents have talked to each other, and they probably have a plan." Michael wasn't sure what discussions had taken place, but he sensed that Stephanie's talk with her parents would go a long way toward solving some issues.

"I thought you said we need to make all our decisions and don't need anybody else."

Michael paced the deck. "I didn't say that. I just mean that our parents would probably listen to us, and we could all come up with a plan together. Let's face it—we won't make it alone."

"I know it." She sighed. "Will you help me?"

"Of course. Help you how, exactly?"

"Come talk to my parents with me. I'm too afraid to go back after storming out. They are so disappointed with me."

"They love you, I'm sure of that."

Stephanie hugged and kissed Michael.

"Why did you wait to tell me, Stephanie? I had all kinds of terrible thoughts when you didn't answer my texts or calls."

"I was scared. I didn't want to ruin your life any more than I had already done."

"No way! So it's not going in the order we thought. You know—high school, college, job, then marriage, house, kids. We just mixed up the order a little."

"Oh, and don't forget the two-car garage and a dog somewhere in there, too. You really think our parents will all support us?"

"I actually do. It's not like we've given them trouble all our lives. We're good kids."

"Good kids who couldn't control ourselves and had sex!" Stephanie sounded flustered.

"Are you beating yourself up for that? For God's sake, Steph, sex is normal. We just had bad luck."

"I guess so. I've also been thinking of all the other people. What are they saying? I don't even want to know."

"Who cares? It's none of their business. Put that out of your mind. Promise me that you or both of us will talk to your mom or both parents, like soon, okay?"

"I will," said Stephanie and felt a nervous stomach developing at the thought of facing her mom. Not only did she feel guilty for getting pregnant, she couldn't bear the thought of discussing the lie about being thrown out of the house.

"Oh, hi!" Tom had appeared at the door. "How goes it?" He made a conscious effort to sound and appear as casual as possible, having sensed the less than comfortable air around the two.

"Fine," said Stephanie and Michael as a duet.

"Uh, I was just leaving," said Michael, and he hugged Stephanie and headed out into the foyer to put on his shoes. Without bothering to open the car door, he jumped into the driver's seat, revved the engine, and motored away with Stephanie's admiring glance following him.

"Everything okay?" asked Tom.

"Everything's okay. I think things are going to work

out. We're going to talk to our parents after I talk to my mom first."

"Good for you," said Tom. *It's amazing how little understanding and finesse seventeen-year-olds have,* he thought to himself. *They'll have to face some serious truths and adjust to reality. Michael may even have to give up his sportscar...*

Chapter 30

Already a year had passed since the Taliban charged into the maternity ward. Lisa had been shocked and horrified at first, spending a great deal of time pondering the cruelty of man, the blatant inhumanity exhibited all over the world. She studied the history of the area, and looked forward to the time she would be able to engage in deep discussions with Abdul again. As a political science professor, not only did he have knowledge of the recent developments, he knew the root causes of problems, the role of religions, and the interaction of various civilizations reaching back eons.

Lisa's immediate horror had turned to a strong desire to devote even more time to improving the status of women. Dealing with females in burkas felt both rewarding and hopeless. She spent long days at the hospital, went home exhausted, and fell into bed, sometimes without dinner. Yet she couldn't sleep. She tossed and turned, or took short catnaps. Many times she wished she had a bottle of wine or some whiskey around, which would have meant breaking the law in a dry country. She considered sleeping pills, but turned down the idea as an option that only masked symptoms.

In the hours she was off duty, Lisa would attack a task or a project with vigor, only to drop it, having lost interest.

She couldn't think. She would make notations on a

difficult case at the hospital and, halfway through, lose her train of thought.

On a June morning, a young woman had been in hard labor for over twenty-four hours. When obvious fetal stress developed, Lisa made a decision to perform a Caesarean section.

After the patient was prepared for surgery, and the healthcare team was ready, Lisa was handed a scalpel. She proceeded to make the incision. As the scalpel approached the incision site, Lisa's hand started to shake. She stopped. Alarmed, she took a deep breath and waited. The personnel assisting her looked at each other alarmed.

"Are you all right, Dr. Hughes?"

"Yes, I'm fine," said Lisa and made a second, this time successful, attempt at incising the skin layers.

After the operation, Lisa ran out of the operating room and out of the building. She sat on a stone bench next to an aromatic low-growing plant. The smell of the flowers reminded her of the attack a year ago. She got up and walked around the ancient courtyard, kicking small rocks ahead of her.

What is wrong with me? I can't sleep. I can't concentrate. I'm nervous and jerky, and I only have two speeds: full force ahead or full stop.

Lisa went back into the building and could not help but sense the secretive talk that had taken place after she left the operating room. Lisa requested to have the rest of the day off. Once in her apartment, she made a cup of tea, Afghanistan's national drink, choosing from her diverse assortment, and reviewed her symptoms again. It was now clear to her that she needed to admit what she had suspected for a long time—she was suffering from post-traumatic stress disorder. She could tolerate some symptoms to a degree, but she absolutely could not function in her job and perform surgery with shaky hands.

After another sleepless night, Lisa called the administrative office of Doctors Without Borders to discuss her dilemma.

"What is it that you want to do?" asked the official with a heavy French accent. "We can refer you for an examination. We can also agree to an early release from your commitment, if that's on your mind."

"Let me think about the early release option. It hadn't occurred me that I could opt for that. I would definitely want to have an examination, regardless."

It didn't take Lisa long to come to a clear understanding of what she wanted to do. The answer had been handed to her on a silver platter: Go home. Once in the States, she could address her problems in familiar surroundings, choose the psychiatrist and therapist she wanted to see, and get well...or at least better. She missed her friends, her home, her hobby of gardening. She wondered if her beloved feline companion would still remember her and whether he would readjust to living with her in a big, quiet house without the busy goings-on of an active family he now enjoyed. And, she missed Abdul and his children. Nothing quiet about them.

Lisa made arrangements to return home on July fourth. Although it was a complete coincidence, what better date, she thought, to arrive at home and reclaim her independence once again.

July fourth was a Sunday. When Lisa landed at JFK, she heard the pilot announce the temperature in New

York: 75 degrees with slight rain. A cool, cleaning rain she hadn't felt for a year and a half! She was almost disappointed that she couldn't run right out into it and feel it on her face, but she had to stay within the Transportation Security Administration's corral of those cleared at the checkpoint.

The small plane's route from JFK to Rochester flew directly over Haudenosaunee Hills, now under a thick cloud cover. When Lisa exited the airport in Rochester, she deliberately stepped out from the covered walkway into the rain and lifted her face to it. After a while, she wasn't sure what was rain, what were tears flowing down her cheeks. Lisa shivered. Her body had registered the temperature, much lower than what she was used to. She put on a light coat, located her rental car, and headed out to the lake country. It felt strange to drive again. She was tired from delayed and cancelled flights, yet excited to be in familiar surroundings which, at the same time, felt strangely foreign.

Lisa turned the key in the lock and opened the heavy Victorian door to her house. No one knew of her arrival, as she'd wanted to return on her own terms.

I'm home! Lisa walked through her house. The old floor boards creaked more than usual. No one had been in the house except for Tom, who had stopped in periodically to perform a safety check.

Lisa lifted dust covers off the antique furniture, opened windows, and propped up the lid of the grand piano. She sat down and played parts of her favorite classical pieces, cringing at every wrong note. She walked into the kitchen and wondered if there would be water, but of course there was. Gavin needed it for the summer to water her perennials. She took a glass of

147

water and went back out. Looking around on the porch, she realized all the window boxes were filled with red and white geraniums and blue scaevola: red, white and blue for the Fourth of July. Who had done this? Gavin? Crystal? Why grow flowers at an empty house for nobody to see? Of course, they were visible from the street, and, Lisa had to admit, they added a great deal to the look of the house, making it appear as if someone lived in it. Smart! She would call Crystal and Gavin as well as Alice and Tom, but not until the next day. Tonight was for her—for her to leave behind the anxious doctor fretting about the lack of materials, lack of knowledge about childbirth, superstitious beliefs, and lack of willingness to dedicate money for women and their care and, ultimately, their babies. She looked forward to her morphing back to the woman she used to be, concerned but not consumed by worry.

She was deep in her thoughts when she heard the horrendous sounds again—numerous gunshots in a series and individually, whistles of ammunition flying through the air... She covered her ears and closed her eyes. In a few seconds, she realized it was fireworks, in honor of the Fourth of July. She knew the origin, but the reaction was raw. She talked herself into a calm state, and was feeling normal by the time she walked up the stairs to sleep in her own bed for the first time in a year and a half.

Yet she spent another restless night in fragmented sleep, waking up every time a train passed through town and signaled its approach to the railway crossing, a sound she had been accustomed to in the past, to the point where it was nonexistent to her ears. This was the exact sound that had given her the impetus to travel, to experience something different in her life. She almost felt gratitude toward the whistle.

Through the night, Lisa twirled around in her mind all things past, present, and future. She had had her adventure, even more than she had asked for. Now was the time to concentrate on the present. She pulled up the familiar covers and slept till midmorning.

Chapter 31

Kaisa walked into Alice's house carrying a reusable shopping bag.

"Where are the kids?" she asked.

"Hello, Mother," said Alice. "I thought the rule was that we use doorbells. Privacy, as you said." Kaisa ignored her daughter.

Bobby appeared in the foyer, aware a task awaited him. Kaisa dangled a chain of keys in front of her grandson. "I have some more stuff in the back of the car."

"Looks like you're handling the crutches a lot better now," Kaisa nodded toward Alice.

"They're not bad, but I can't wait to get rid of them. I've really taken my freedom for granted all my life. I had no idea of how confining this is."

"Tell me about it! And imagine those who are too old or too heavy to use crutches and end up in a wheelchair." Alice hadn't thought of that.

"I really have to lose some of these pounds, walking, maybe, to start with, or swimming. Definitely not bicycling for a while."

"No kidding, but that's a good idea. You really should do something about your weight. I know, I know, I harp about it too much, but it's only for your own good."

"Yes, Mom, but to remind me of something I feel awful about just makes me mad and resentful."

"Okay, no more said. You're an adult."

No more said until the next time. Alice could understand her mother's so-called caring about her weight, if she were mortally obese. She only needed to lose twenty pounds or so to feel and look better. Kaisa had no idea what it was like to have extra weight. She still weighed the same as she did on her wedding day almost fifty years ago. Kaisa didn't wear her worries and her stress on her body like Alice did.

"Mom, I really have to hand it to you. You recuperated superfast from your hip surgery and are now getting around like nothing ever happened."

"Thanks, you know how stubborn I am. I did all my exercises religiously as directed. I also think it was all for the better that I forgot to take some of my prescribed medications. They were for pain, after all. What's a little pain? I'd suffer some pain instead of poisoning my body with chemicals." Alice shook her head, wondering what other self-diagnoses and therapies Kaisa was using.

"Take those into the kitchen, please," Kaisa said to Bobby.

"What did you do?" asked Alice, staring at the assortment of casseroles, salads, and baked goods. "I'm not totally helpless. I appreciate this, but it's been a couple of weeks. The first few days, it was helpful, but now I'm okay, really."

"Well, I had some free time and, when I cooked for myself, instead of freezing the overage I decided to give some to my neighbor and bring some to you. Besides, you know how much I actually enjoy baking, so this is no big deal."

"Thank you, Mom. Don't get me wrong. Like I said, I do appreciate it. Want some coffee?" It did not go unnoticed by Alice that Kaisa had mentioned the neighbor again.

"You know me, I never say no to coffee. It's total addiction. I once tried to wean myself off caffeine, remember that? I slept for three days straight even though I had an excruciating withdrawal headache. I succeeded, but slowly went back to it. I figure that's about the only vice left in my life. I should be able to enjoy it."

"Far be it from me to deny you coffee," said Alice. "Mom, you said that you have some free time. How would you like to do something with that time and help some people?"

"I'm not joining any charity group of uppity women who get together and donate money to art galleries and opera houses."

"No, Mom, the need here is a bit closer to the ground. You know the support group for teenaged pregnant girls, the one Stephanie is attending?"

Kaisa nodded.

"Well, they have different topics they cover in their meetings and healthy food isn't one of them. Stephanie has noticed that some of the girls live on sugary, fatty snack foods and soft drinks and could use some down-to-earth advice and direction on what to eat to keep themselves healthy and to have a healthy baby."

"And you think I am the person to set them straight?"

"Mom, you have a master's degree in home economics, you love cooking, and you like to help people. Why not you?"

"Are the girls really interested? You think they'd listen to what an old grandma has to say? And where would the food come from? You know, I can lecture to people till I am blue in the face, but chances are they won't listen. Lectures are boring. You need a kitchen where they themselves can actually do some cooking. They need to feel the textures—the smoothness of a watermelon, the fuzzy skin of a kiwi, the roughness of the scales of a pineapple. They need to smell a raw onion, and garlic, fresh fish, and the pungent aroma of boiling cabbage. They need to be hands-on like you were from the time you were tall enough to reach the countertop using a stool."

"See how excited you get about your favorite topic, Mom? I doubt these girls would have the means to cook with fresh fruit and vegetables or fresh fish all the time, but that's exactly the idea. There is a kitchen and there are utensils. All they need is someone like you."

"Hmm…and how often would this be?"

"That is negotiable. It can be a one-time event just to try out and see how it's received by the girls. If it goes well, a bigger plan can be worked on. Some of the girls have jobs, and their work schedules are rather unpredictable."

"How old are they?"

"This group has girls between sixteen and twenty."

"Is this like a court-ordered obligation for them?"

"No, I guess support and talking to people in the same situation as you yourself isn't a court issue. It's supposed to be relaxing and a place where they can exchange ideas and feelings. It is completely voluntary."

"It's certainly a worthwhile issue to address," said Kaisa. "I just don't know if I'm the right person to do this. Let me think about it."

"Sounds good," said Alice. *She'll do it.*

"So, speaking of Stephanie, how's she doing, now that she's at Crystal's?"

"She's doing very well. I was afraid she would take the request for her to go to the farm as an afront, but that didn't happen. Crystal says she told Stephanie from the beginning that although she wasn't officially an adult, she needed to act like one. Crystal has had her actually cook meals, clean house, do laundry, et cetera, and Stephanie has been fine with every task. She hasn't objected and she's done a good job."

"Are you surprised? That's what you have done with Pam. Why didn't you do it with Stephanie? She was here like a guest at a full-service hotel."

"I know. I should have asked more of her. I guess I felt sorry for her with that horrible Dragon Lady mother of hers, or so I thought."

"Asking a child to pull their weight is not mean. It's acknowledging their abilities, it's building their self-esteem, it's preparing them for the life ahead of them."

"Mom, I don't need a sermon. I tried my best. In addition to Stephanie, the whole co-ordination between her parents and the Albrights and getting Stephanie help form the Social Services all fell on me. It was tough, and it still is."

"From where I sit, it looks like you offered to take that responsibility. You are a wonderful person, Alice, but you need to learn to let go of some things. When is Stephanie coming back, or is she?"

"I know I should let go, but when I see something that needs to be done, I just do it. I don't know when she'll come back. Secretly, and this is horrible to admit, I'm hoping she doesn't. The issue of the kids' future is being discussed by the Smiths and the Albrights. I hope they can work out a solution that is good for everybody involved and…" Alice hesitated for a second, "one that doesn't involve me or my family. Of course, Stephanie is Pam's friend, and I hope that will always be the case."

"You've done a lot. I hope the grandparents-to-be realize that. Stephanie may understand the depth of your involvement with introspection and a great deal more maturity. Sounds like what Crystal is doing is completely on the right track."

How can it be that my mother is capable of stroking me and striking me in the same breath?

"I'm going to work! See you later!" called Bobby from the foyer, dressed in his fast-food restaurant uniform.

"You know, Mom, boys are so much easier than girls," said Alice and waved to her son.

Chapter 32

Lisa got out of bed, taking her time with every aspect of it. She opened her eyes and instead of looking at a ceiling of nondescript beigey color, she saw an expanse of white brightness and an ornate chandelier her mother had found in an antique store decades ago. She sat up and looked around. She saw period wallpaper and furniture to go with it. Everything looked unreal to her—the brass pulls on the chest of drawers, the fixtures that had once been gas lights on the wall, the fainting couch in the corner. All reminders of a time long ago, all still part of her house, all of it dictated by Lisa's innate need to connect to her past. Lisa got out of bed and walked to the window. A beautiful summer day, a perfect day for a homecoming.

Lisa deliberately put on shorts and a tank top, the least amount of clothing acceptable in the street in decent society—a far cry from what was required in Kabul. She looked forward to her first cup of coffee on the porch. Her bare cupboards brought her back to reality. She had no coffee. She had no tea. She also had no car, as the one in the garage didn't even promise to start. Dead battery.

The walk to the coffee shop was long, but just what she needed after a long plane ride the day before.

Haudenosaunee Hills provided a welcome contrast to Kabul in its smallness and lack of cacophony. There were no cars honking, no people yelling, no dogs barking. Only a few cars, some of them soundless electric vehicles. There was also music wafting from the music store, where instruments were sold and repaired, a lovely sound for passersby.

The coffee shop smelled of a rich roast. Lisa ordered scrambled eggs, a fruit cup, and coffee. People went in and out of the shop. So far, she hadn't run into anyone she knew. She decided to call Alice.

"Hi, it's Lisa," she said.

"Lisa! Wow! Are you calling from Afghanistan?"

"No, I'm back right here in good old Hills. Got back yesterday. Would it be okay if I came over? We can talk and I can get Niles. How is he?"

"Niles is fine. You know what they say… Dogs have people, cats have staff. Here he's had a whole complement of very eager staff, not just his mistress. Lots of attention, some of which he didn't even want. Yeah, of course you can come over. I'm just surprised. I thought your second year wouldn't be up until January."

"It's a long and maybe even a disturbing story, so can we leave it to a later date, when we have nothing else to talk about?"

"Sure," agreed Alice, dying of curiosity. "Come on over. My foot's in a cast, so I'm not going anywhere. There's lots to talk about. Any time is fine with me."

"Great, I'll just have to get my car going. See you later. Wait! What did you say? Your foot's in a cast?"

"Yes, for another few weeks. I'll tell you when you get here. Welcome back to Haudenosaunee Hills!"

Lisa called the vehicle assistance company and started to walk back toward home. *Hopefully all the old car needs is a jump start.* Luckily, she was right.

The small city felt familiar and homey. Lisa drove

around for a bit to see if anything had changed. She noticed a few boarded-up businesses on Main Street, among them a Chinese restaurant and a dry cleaner, both brand new at the time of the beginning of Lisa's assignment to Kabul. It's hard to be a small business owner in a small town.

Alice's house was just as it had always been, a large yet cozy ranch in a grove of poplars.

Standing on one foot, Alice opened her arms wide for Lisa. Their hug was long and warm, expressing Lisa's gratitude for being back home again and Alice's relief for having her friend safe at home, away from a dangerous corner of the world.

"How are you?" asked Alice, hobbling into the kitchen.

"Very tired." Lisa sighed. "Tired from the trip back, tired from the entire time away, tired from the experiences and the stress. Glad to be at home. Tell me, what's new?"

"Well, I'll start with this stupid foot. I decided to start bicycling again, and, of course, on my virgin voyage, I crashed coming down the Pure Earth Farm hill. You know how steep it is. I'll be all right. No biggie. Tom's real estate business is doing very well. Pam and her friend Stephanie both graduated high school and will be going to college in the fall, at least Pam is. Stephanie is pregnant and has been living with us, but she's now at Crystal's."

"Wait, I can't quite keep up. Why was this girl living with your family, and why is she now at Crystal's?"

"That's a long story. I'll have to tell you the details at another time. Anyway, the biggest news is that Crystal and Gavin are having a baby in a couple of months. Let's see... Lola is living in Finland now permanently. She married a Finnish friend of my mom's."

"Lola? Lola got married? I'll be darned!"

"My mom has been doing okay lately. With a new medication, she's shaking a lot less, but she's having hallucinations. She thinks there's woman living in the condo next to hers who killed someone and disposed of the body. Can you imagine?"

"Oh, dear," empathized Lisa. "That's not very common, but it can happen with Parkinson's patients."

As Lisa spoke, Niles sauntered into the room, stopped on a sunny spot on the rug, sat down and yawned deliciously. He proceeded to give his front legs a bath, paying no attention to Lisa or Alice.

"There, you see? The king has arrived," said Alice.

"The King of Siam, he thinks." Lisa got up and scooped Niles into her arms. "I think this king has put on weight while I was away." Lisa hugged her cat.

"I'm so sorry. I have a feeling that with all the people in this household, he may have been fed a little more often than was necessary."

"Don't apologize. Cats usually eat until they are no longer hungry, dogs eat till they burst."

Lisa sat back down, rubbing Niles's neck.

"What about Christine?"

"Haven't heard too much about Christine. She hasn't been around, that I know of, since her mother died. There hasn't been a funeral or a memorial service, either. It could be that Carol didn't want one. Magnus, by the way, is still restoring his house. I haven't been in it for a while, but Tom tells me it's coming along great. Oh!" Alice got animated as if she realized something important. "Get this! Magnus has a found a woman to partner with to have a baby. Her name is Deedee—Denise, actually—and as it happens, she is the social worker I dealt with getting some answers to Stephanie's situation. Deedee is absolutely gorgeous. With her dark beauty and Magnus's handsome Viking looks, the child they produce will be an amazingly beautiful human being."

"That's wonderful! Tell me more about Stephanie. How did you get involved in her life?"

"You really want to hear? I don't want to bore you with all the messy relationship stuff," said Alice, but continued the whole story in minute detail.

Lisa was thoughtful. "Interesting how all cultures are capable of making pregnancy and childbirth an enormous issue. In cases where there really isn't an issue, they make one up."

"I've been babbling again. I would love to hear more about your experiences, but I'll let you go and rest." Alice had noticed Lisa's heavy eyelids.

"I need to get some groceries and reorient myself to living in the States again."

Alice got up. "Give me a call if you need anything. Oh, here." Alice picked up the cat carrier she had retrieved from the closet. "With my foot, I'm not going to be much help here, but I can hold the carrier. You can do the fighting."

Niles demonstrated his ability to spread and lock his legs much wider than the width of the opening of the cat carrier. After a struggle and numerous scratches to Lisa's bare arms, Niles was trapped, and on his way home.

Chapter 33

Pam walked home from her fast-food restaurant job. She usually rode her bicycle, but recent developments made her want to think, to straighten out the knots in her mind, which required a long, leisurely stroll.

Summer was going to go by fast, and a new chapter in Pam's life was on the horizon. She looked forward to college. She had always enjoyed school and learning, which was easy for her. Where her classmates were apprehensive about tests, Pam loved being tested and looked at exams as a way to challenge herself. Her test results were always first rate, and she was thinking of ways to make the challenges even greater. She loved essay questions that allowed her to expand her ideas and concepts, to write as much as she wanted. She had always found multiple choice questions to be an insult to the students' intelligence. College would be different. It would be harder. She would love it.

As most of her friends prepared to leave town to attend a university, Pam felt as if she might be left behind. She herself had made the decision to attend the local community college for the first two years, but now she felt a few misgivings about her decision. Her friends were moving on to a new school, new friends, new place to live. She, most likely, would live at home, and there was nothing new about the community college just a mile away.

Pam stopped at the bank to deposit her paycheck. If she kept her job while going to college, maybe she could afford to move away from home after she turned eighteen in the fall. She already had quite a bit of money saved, and she had received several surprisingly large scholarships. She knew her parents were committed to paying for her tuition. She wondered whether that commitment would expand to room and board outside a college dormitory situation.

Some of her teachers had questioned her decision to attend a local two-year college when she could have been accepted by any Ivy League university. Pam felt strongly about issues of money and status and trappings as indicators of having "made it." She felt sorry for Stephanie's parents, who seemed to be trapped in a rat race of "more is better," and she had no respect for people who flaunted their pedigree that somehow enabled them to buy a spot at the big-name universities.

Pam was undecided regarding her future career. Stephanie's situation had shaken her, and more and more, she found herself observing human behavior as a fascinating phenomenon. She knew that whatever her career choice, it would somehow involve seeking answers to what made people tick.

Pam walked faster, and by the time she reached her front door, she was warm, perspiration running down her temples. She walked into the kitchen and had a tall glass of water. Something was missing.

"Mom?" she called.

"Hi, honey," Alice answered from the back deck. "How was your day?"

"Not bad. It's nice now that I can work days. Hey, what happened to Niles's food and water dishes?"

Alice came through the sliding glass doors, knocking over a flowerpot with her crutch.

"These damned things! I can't wait to get rid of them."

"Where are Niles's dishes?" Pam repeated. Niles himself was usually hiding in one of his favorite places. Pam was used to his antisocial behavior and had paid no attention to the absence of the cat himself.

"Oh, Lisa came and got him. Isn't it great she's home? Something happened to make her return earlier than planned."

Pam was quiet. She sat at the kitchen table and slowly rolled and unrolled a placemat depicting Finnish flora: bluebells, bachelor buttons, twinflowers, and heather.

"Why didn't you tell me she was coming to get him? I couldn't even say goodbye. I was the one Lisa asked to take care of Niles, not you. And I did, all of it—the food and water, the litterbox, the veterinarian's appointments, and so on."

"I'm sorry," said Alice. "I didn't even know myself. She just called this morning and said she'd be over in the afternoon to get him."

"You know, this sucks. First you manipulate it so that Stephanie moves out with nobody talking to me about it, and now you think it's okay to whisk Niles away with no warning. Am I really part of this household? Do I matter at all?"

Alice's heart sank. Pam was right. She hadn't given her daughter's feelings any space in her thinking. How could she be so insensitive? Another sign she was running on overdrive again.

"Pam. I apologize. I could've handled this better."

"Yeah, you could've. What's next? You're gonna tell me that you're sending Bobby to a boarding school some place, God knows where? That Dad's taking a big job in a city far away? That Grandma is moving back to Finland? You are moving people around in my life like chess pieces on the board until there's no one left standing but you and I. Checkmate!"

"Honey, I've given you plenty of freedom to live your own life."

"Yeah, by not paying attention to me and my feelings. You're always busy with this project or that, involving new people in your circle. You don't have time to care for the relationships you have. How you have time to create new ones, I'll never know!"

"Pam, if I remember correctly, it was you who asked if Stephanie could live with us, for example."

"Well, you remember wrong. I came to you to talk about Stephanie's situation. I didn't ask you to take her in. It just tickled you to be the answer to yet another problem, as if your schedule wasn't full enough."

"You didn't seem to object, and I thought you rather enjoyed having Stephanie here."

"Of course, she's my friend, and what was I going to do after the fact?"

Alice had been standing on one foot. She felt the burn and sat down at the table.

"I know I have this 'savior complex.' I feel that if you're not part of the solution, you are part of the problem."

"This time, you've created a problem for your family. I wish I could have more of a mother for myself. I guess I'm selfish, but I don't like sharing you with the rest of the world to this extent."

"I've tried to raise you to be an independent, self-assured young woman, and I thought I had succeeded."

"I am independent. I have self-esteem, maybe too much. I have times when I think I don't need anybody, but, deep down, I know I do. Look at you and Grandma. You are both independent, but you still need each other. I don't feel needed."

Alice got up and hugged Pam. "My dear, dear Pam..." Alice choked. "I need you so much. I'm just no good at expressing it. How can I make this up to you?"

"Can we do something together, just you and me? I mean, you and I?" Pam rolled her eyes.

"Of course, and it's okay to say 'you and me.' It's just the two of us. You're not writing a college essay. You don't have to be perfect."

"Somehow, I feel that I do. After all, Grandma is perfect, and you are perfect, so why shouldn't I be perfect as well?"

"Oh, my, we do have a lot to talk about." Alice sighed and took out her phone. "Now, let's schedule this spontaneous women's outing for us."

"Mom, do you hear yourself? Spontaneous things aren't scheduled. That's an oxymoron."

"Okay. I'll let you orchestrate this. I already feel guilty for not doing a big party for your graduation. When I'm well again, and Stephanie's situation has settled a bit, we'll celebrate properly. If what you'll plan for the two of us is to happen any time soon, remember that I still have these sticks of death, so no bungy jumping." Alice lifted a crutch.

"That's a deal." Pam smiled. "I love you, Mom."

"I love you, too."

Chapter 34

Kaisa looked at the time. It was eleven a.m. That meant it was seven hours later in Finland, or six p.m.—or was it a six-hour time difference? She couldn't remember if Finland had voted to do away with daylight savings time or not. There had been a great deal of discussion about it as a useless custom, now that farmers don't necessarily have to follow the sun's schedule in order to get their work completed in the fields. They can climb into their gigantic farm machines with either heat or air conditioning in the cab, plus music of their choosing. Besides, for most of the peak days in the summer months, the sun never sets long enough to call a night truly dark.

Kaisa called Lola. They hadn't spoken for weeks. Lola answered immediately, "Lola Kuusinen." Kaisa knew people answered their phone by stating their name, but she wasn't aware that Lola had taken Mauno's last name.

"Hi, Mrs. Kuusinen. What made you become a Kuusinen? That's not a very feminist act."

"Well, you know, when in Rome, and all that. Here, it's much easier to be a Kuusinen than a Giordano."

"I get it," said Kaisa. "How are things?"

"We're enjoying the summer and the sun that never sets. It's beautiful when you get used to it."

"I know it. We didn't celebrate Midsummer Solstice

this year. Wouldn't be the same without you."

"And I had saved all those branches and twigs for the bonfire. I'm thinking that one of these summers I'll come back and we can create a solstice celebration again. I still have my house on the lake. I've been talking to Crystal about it. She and Gavin are using it now as a handy spot to go swimming and to launch their kayaks. I considered selling it, but you know how the market is right now. Mauno says I should keep it, and when we travel again we'll have a place to stay. Of course, that's extra work for Crystal and Gavin."

"Are you kidding? They'll be happy to have the lake house when it gets beastly hot here."

"I suppose you're right. How are you doing? How is your health?" Lola was always hesitant to ask, anticipating less than positive news.

"You know, I'm on a new medication and my shaking has diminished quite a bit. It's not gone, mind you, but there's considerably less of it. And my hip, well, it's almost completely healed. I've been religious about doing my exercises."

"That's fantastic! With your..." exclaimed Lola with the last part of the sentence disappearing into a loud murmur.

"What's that noise?" asked Kaisa.

"Oh, we are in our boat, sailing back home from a small island that has interesting birds nesting on it every summer. The sound you heard was a Coast Guard boat speeding by."

"Sailing in the Baltic! How wonderful," gushed Kaisa. "So are you planning on coming home—I mean, here—when the baby is born?"

"I'm seriously thinking about it. Right now, Crystal

has a slight medical problem with hypertension, but she has this girl Stephanie—well, why am I telling you? You know she has Stephanie living at the farm, and I hear she is a great help. Who knows how long she'll stay. As you know, she's having a baby of her own around the same time as Crystal. I think they're due like five days apart."

"I've heard Stephanie absolutely loves living on the farm. I also hear there may be some positive developments in Stephanie's relationship with her parents. The Smiths and the Albrights—you know, Michael's parents—have agreed to give a sizable donation to a support group for teenaged pregnant girls and, specifically, to fund a nutrition program for them. And guess who's going to be the hands-on instructor… Yours truly!"

"You're kidding! What made you decide to do this?"

"I have my home economics degree, which I never used in a job."

"Maybe you didn't," Lola interrupted, "but your knowledge in the area certainly was known to everybody in town. You were too busy to actually teach, hobnobbing with Richard's lawyer friends and cooking amazing party food for every possible soiree."

"Of course," continued Kaisa, "there's the danger that I'll be teaching outdated information, but I figure that as long as I can give practical advice, how can I go wrong. Protein still comes from the same sources as it did fifty years ago and then some, and vegetables and fruit have never gone out of fashion. The main idea is to get these young girls to eat healthy foods for their own good and for the sake of their babies. If I can expand the curriculum to include hints on cooking economically, all the better. Cooking from scratch, basically, shows them how to make several different types of meals out of one big chicken or how to make creamed soup out of vegetables that have seen better days."

"You're great at that! It'll be such a difference from what kids eat these days."

"You've got that right."

"I miss your cooking, especially the great spreads you prepared for one thing or another. The Finnish dishes you prepare are rare even here. You seem to be much more Finnish than the Finns in Finland these days. Often, people eat pizza, hamburgers, kebabs, and even sushi. No difference from what you get in any American city. When Mauno's granddaughter graduated at the beginning of June, they had a huge party for her. The food was mostly regular American fare with some Finnish touches like pineapple and ham on a pizza. By the way, it's funny, but most people here eat their hamburgers and pizza with a fork and a knife."

"That's true. I had forgotten that. So, they are still having big graduation parties?"

"Lots of people, lot of food, lots of alcohol in some circles."

"I see. Pam also graduated, as well as Stephanie. With Alice's broken foot…"

"Alice broke her foot?" Lola was alarmed.

"Yes, she started bicycling and crashed. She's on crutches for a while still. That's why Stephanie moved to Crystal's. Anyway, Pam insisted that any party would be too much, so it was postponed until fall and they'll have a "college entrance party."

"That's a good idea."

"Well, I just thought I'd check with you. Let's talk

again soon."

"I'm glad you called. I have to get off the phone anyway. Mauno needs my help in getting the boat tied to the dock."

"Happy mooring!"

Chapter 35

Stephanie's stomach was making somersaults from early morning on. She had slept fitfully, thinking of what might happen in a few hours when she and Michael faced the dreaded meeting with her parents. Stephanie had severe cramps. The discomfort made her wonder about labor and delivery, the severity of that pain compared to what was already unbearable, and this wasn't even pregnancy-related. Stephanie got up at six a.m.—an ungodly hour for a teenager—made herself a cup of tea, and put a heated bean bag on her belly. She was sure the warmth was pleasant also for the baby.

Crystal had woken up and spoke to Stephanie calmly, assuring her that her intestinal problem was most likely caused by the stress she experienced anticipating the discussion ahead. Stephanie sat in a recliner and after a couple of more bathroom trips, fell asleep until Crystal reminded her that Michael would soon arrive to pick her up.

Stephanie dressed in a loose sleeveless shift, comfortable on a hot summer day. She couldn't get her mind off potential disasters as a result of the upcoming meeting. She regretted having involved Michael in a problem she alone had caused by lying. However, she knew she needed his emotional support in this difficult situation. She had heard from Pam that her parents and Michael's had committed to donating a large amount of

171

money to the nutrition program. Stephanie hung onto the hope that this gesture of good will was a sign of a positive outcome for today's dialogue. Yet she entertained bizarre scenarios in her mind:

Would her parents, especially her mother, tell them that as Stephanie had lied about having been thrown out of the house and as she could never be trusted again, they wanted nothing to do with them?

Would they tell them that they would support them emotionally, but that Stephanie needed to move back home, allow Michael to live in the dorm at RIT, as was originally planned, and that they were not old enough to take care of themselves, let alone a baby?

Would they say that since their children had acted like stupid kids, they would need to grow up in a hurry and act like responsible adults and parents and get jobs to support their family?

Would they offer to take the baby and bring him or her up as a sibling to Stephanie, and send her and Michael off to college?

Would they tell them they had found a couple who was anxious to adopt?

Would they offer to give them all the money they needed as long as they never had to see them again?

Stephanie had to rush to the bathroom again. She sat on the toilet and decided that none of the scenarios was acceptable. None was likely. None had potential to be even vaguely true.

Stephanie met Michael on the patio where he was talking with Gavin.

"You ready?" she asked.

"Sure. Are you?"

"I have to be, I guess."

They sat in the sporty two-seater and drove down the hill.

"This is so much more difficult for me than it was for you with your parents. You hadn't lied to them." Stephanie sighed, trying to hold together her long hair blowing in the wind.

"I couldn't lie. I knew nothing. My parents told me about the baby, remember?"

"I know, I know. I should've told you. It's my mom. I'm so apprehensive about her. I don't ever want to hurt her. She's had such a hard life, and now she's doing so well, and I had to ruin it all for her."

They drove through town in silence.

"Stop at the gas station there." Stephanie pointed. "I have to go again."

A few minutes later, they pulled into the driveway of a large McMansion with a three-car garage.

"Do your parents have three cars?" asked Michael. "I never noticed that before."

"One has an antique jalopy of my grandpa's in it, or that's what Dad calls it. My dad's restoring it. It's an old barge with fins in the back. You know the type. I can't imagine how a really poor guy could have big car like that in the day."

"Aah," said Michael. "Maybe he bought it second or third hand."

Both Stephanie and Michael stood at the front door straightening their clothes and hair as if in preparation for a job interview. Stephanie felt she had made herself an outsider by leaving her parents and the house, and she felt uncomfortable walking in without ringing the doorbell.

"You're ringing the doorbell to your own house?"

Michael's eyebrows were raised. Stephanie shrugged her shoulders.

Melinda opened the door and gave Stephanie and Michael each a hesitant, awkward hug.

"Come in. I fixed us some snacks. I thought it was too early for lunch."

They walked into an almost-all-white living room with some carefully thought-out touches of yellow and gray popping up in the abstract paintings and the pillows on the large sofas. Melinda followed interior design trends meticulously. Stephany remembered various style changes during her childhood.

On the coffee table in front of them was a large, round serving platter of fresh vegetables: cherry tomatoes, broccoli, pepper wedges of all colors, cauliflower and carrots with a bowl of dip in the middle. On the side were a small bowl of cashews and an assortment of cheeses and grapes.

"This is nice, Mom," said Stephanie. "So colorful and healthy."

"Thank you," said Melinda. "I thought I should have something healthy for you, you know, with the baby and all." Her eyes moved to Stephanie's belly. "How are you feeling?" Melinda rubbed the fleshy parts of her palms together, obviously agonizing about the situation.

"I'm fine," said Stephanie, "except right now, my stomach's upset. In fact, excuse me for a minute." Stephanie left the room.

Melinda looked at Michael. Michael was ill at ease.

"She's just a little nervous, that's all," said Michael. "No biggie."

They sat in awkward silence.

"Hello, Michael," said Craig Smith, walking into the

room, obviously fresh from the shower.

"Mr. Smith," said Michael and got up, watching carefully to see whether Craig would reach out to shake hands. He did, and they shook.

"Nice wheels you've got there."

"Yeah, when my brother graduated college and got married, his wife didn't think his car from the college days was sending a suitable message for a family man, so he gave the car to me."

"Well, lucky you. It's a beauty. Take care of it."

"Yes, sir," said Michael and grabbed a carrot.

Stephanie came back into the room and Craig went to hug her. Melinda's eyes were watering.

"So," said Craig, "if you two get married, is that the end of the car?"

Michael quickly swallowed the cashews in his mouth so as not to choke. "Sir?" he asked.

"I'm sorry, said Craig. "I didn't mean to jolt you like that, but let's talk about what we need to address—your future."

Stephanie was surprised at how the talk that was supposed to be mainly between her and her mother had turned to her father grilling Michael.

She toughened herself and said, "First of all, I need to apologize. I was caught by surprise when I found out I was pregnant, and I just wanted to hide. I acted like an idiot. I apologize to you, Michael, for not telling you, and I apologize to you," Stephanie nodded toward her parents, who were sitting close together as a unit, "for being totally unreasonable. Mom, I am so sorry I lied when I left. I wasn't willing to accept responsibility for my actions and I had to find someone to blame. To say that you threw me out was a way to get empathy from

Aunt Sharon and from my friends." Stephanie's voice broke.

"I have big shoulders," said Melinda. "We all make mistakes. It's all forgiven. You are so young and have big things to think about. My reactions should not be among them."

"Mom, it's never okay to do or say something that hurts another human being." Stephanie got up and hugged her mother. Both cried.

"The question is," said Craig, "where do we go from here? As you probably know, we and the Albrights have spoken. We will all help the two of you and our grandchild, but we'd like to know from you what it is you would like to do. Do you want to get married? Live together? Live with us? The Albrights? Maybe you don't want any of that?"

Stephanie and Michael looked at each other.

"We definitely want to be with each other," said Stephanie, with Michael nodding fiercely, "but, well, how? We have no money, so I guess we have to ask you for help. And you just said that you will help, so we are really grateful for that."

"We can talk about details later, but you need to think about Michael's plans for college and about a place to live. Both the Albrights and we will contribute toward what is needed. This is not to say that anything goes. You need to live within your means and start to pay attention to where your money is going. And, Stephanie, you need to think of your education as well. Your plans will probably be shelved at least for a little while, but, please, don't trash your dreams! Loads of people go to college while married with children."

"But they have incomes," said Stephanie. She

reached for a piece of broccoli, thought better of it, and withdrew her hand.

"Incomes or student loans. You don't need to worry about that. Like I said, your mother and I will help. You don't know how lucky you are. You both have parents who are in a position to help. Nothing like our parents." Craig glanced at Melinda, who gave him a warning look. He missed it and continued, "We had to scrape and fight for everything we have. And it wasn't easy, let me tell you. We were lucky to get through high school before we were smack in the middle of the working world, nobody giving us anything."

Melinda touched Craig on the arm with an obvious *That's enough* message.

"We understand," said Stephanie. "I feel terrible that you had to work so hard, and I'm thankful that I'm not in the same position. You deserve every happiness in your life together now. I feel so guilty for ruining it all for you."

"Stop," said Melinda. Her look at Craig spelled clearly, *And you had to bring all that up again!* "It's all okay," continued Melinda. "Dad gets a little carried away sometimes."

"I'm sorry," said Craig, holding back on his desire to explain himself more clearly.

Stephanie changed the subject. "By the way, the money for the nutrition program. Thank you so much! It means a lot to me. You should see the need there is in that group of girls. Knowledge about nutrition is only a small part of it."

As Stephanie and Melinda discussed the various pregnancy-related issues, Craig invited Michael to take a look at the old car in the garage.

"Wow! That's amazing! What year is this?"

"It's a 1965 Cadillac. It still needs a lot of work, but it'll be great, don't you think?"

"You bet!"

"You know how today's cars are actually computers. In Melinda's father's day, if something broke, he could easily fix it himself. You can appreciate this as an RIT student—engineering, was it?"

"Yes, sir," said Michael.

"As they say, the world is your oyster. Keep that in mind."

"Yes, sir," said Michael again. He thought he was starting to sound more like ROTC than RIT.

On the way back to the farm, Stephanie and Michael reviewed what had just happened.

"That wasn't so bad," said Michael.

"I'm exhausted," said Stephanie.

"Aren't pregnant women supposed to be exhausted?"

Stephanie laughed. "Pull to the parking lot!" she said. They were passing a chiropractor's office.

"Okay." Michael stopped the car precisely within the designated yellow lines.

"Give me your hand," Stephanie reached over. She placed Michael's hand on her abdomen, to the right of the belly button. "Feel that?"

"Do you still have the grumbling stomach?"

"No, silly, that's the baby kicking."

Michael looked at Stephanie with his mouth open. "No way!"

Stephanie nodded. "Way."

"How cool is that!'' said Michael in awe.

Chapter 36

Lisa spent the first week at home counting her blessings. She walked from room to room studying pieces of furniture or accessories one at a time. She looked at each piece carefully from all points of view: beauty, functionality, history, her emotional attachment to it, and monetary value. Of particular interest to her were pieces handed down by her grandparents. In their day, some of the furniture had already been antique when they acquired it. Lisa had heard rumors that the dining room set with tapestry-covered chairs had originally belonged to the Roosevelt family, but there was no way to prove it. The drawers of the matching sideboard were full of intriguing items from a time long ago.

Who uses a special spoon to serve nuts, or an oyster fork, or asparagus or sugar tongs? She wondered about those and other items. Her favorites as a child had always been the ice tea spoons with a leaf for the bowl and a thin silver straw as a handle. Most guests didn't realize the long-handled spoons were straws, and Lisa loved to surprise them by putting her lips around the spoon handle. Her mother's friends mostly laughed at her childish shenanigans, but some rather uptight types showed their obvious disapproval.

She picked up a silver bowl: a first prize won by her father in a Haudenosaunee Hills Garden Club annual contest.

This is lovely, but so thoroughly unnecessary. She thought back to her small apartment in Kabul and felt warm and ashamed at the same time. *You don't need "stuff" to be happy.* She thought of the measures people go to in order to protect their belongings—cameras sending a warning to your phone when a stranger approaches your front door, alarm systems to keep away potential burglars, or, at the very least, house sitters while you are traveling. *Do I really care if someone runs away with my tomato server or the Victorian tea set?* Yet she handled each piece with care, caressing each cocktail stick and its handblown glass rooster at the end.

Lisa remembered her patients back in Afghanistan, their daily struggle to keep their families warm and their children fed. She was immensely fortunate, yet the abundance left her feeling empty. Of all her friends, Crystal seemed to have the correct look on life. She didn't have the burden of previous decades and past generations weighing on her shoulders. She didn't have "stuff." Crystal's mother Lola's family hadn't been poor, but they had nothing extra, nor did they aspire to more. Lola had always been an adventurer, only periodically returning from her world travels to her little house by the lake to rest, it seemed, till the next destination beckoned her. She, and consequently Crystal, were not saddled with extraneous possessions.

Lisa was torn. *This "stuff" really is more of a nuisance than a blessing. The time it takes to polish the silver, to dust all the tiny nooks and crannies on the Victorian furniture, and to keep all the rarely used crystal sparkling is time wasted!* Lisa decided to do something about it, yet felt a twinge of despair at the idea of getting rid of things her mother had taken pride in.

History and the connections from one decade to another had always been important to Lisa. Her belongings were a physical manifestation of that connectedness.

Outside, Lisa walked around the house. It was too late for this season, but she started to plan a vegetable garden for the following year. A garden had always been her father's pride and joy. With Lisa in medical school when her parents died suddenly, the garden had lost its importance and been plowed under. But Lisa knew both Crystal and Abdul had perennial berry bushes and strawberries, so she could get replacements for her garden from them. Crystal and Gavin were professional gardeners and would have whatever advice she needed, too. *Abdul doesn't know a blueberry bush from a juniper.* She thought of him with affection. When he bought Kaisa's house, he inherited Kaisa's vegetables, fruits trees, and perennials.

Abdul. Lisa tasted his name in her mouth, a name she had heard countless times in Kabul. Each time, she had felt a small jolt in her chest. *The man is so brilliant, so kind, so handsome!* Lisa had to admit she was, in her mother's word, "smitten." All the information she had gotten from Abdul prior to her trip to Kabul had been invaluable. He obviously loved his old country and knew a great deal about it. He was extremely busy in his professorship, and, as required, with publishing pieces about his expertise, the Middle East. He was also both father and mother to his children. Lisa would see them later. She had been invited to dinner at Abdul's house.

Although she knew the concept of time had some fluidity in the Afghani world, she stuck to her old habit of arriving on time and drove to the house through the lane bordered by birch trees Kaisa and her husband had planted in the early years of their marriage about fifty years ago. All Abdul's children ran outside to greet her, from the toddler to the teenager. The littlest one handed her a bouquet of flowers, making Lisa feel like a celebrity being met by a welcoming committee, though Abdul was a far cry from a pompous or overbearing dignitary. His children respected him without fear and showed their affection freely.

After the dinner of lamb, rice and carrots, once the smallest children were tucked into bed, Lisa and Abdul walked into the garden and sat in the gazebo with their tea. As they settled down, Lisa noticed a large car driving by at a crawling speed on the road bordering the garden. The car appeared to slow down deliberately, then speed up again after a moment. Lisa had an uncomfortable feeling.

"Did you see that?" she asked.

"You mean the car? Oh, yes, sometimes people still drive by, curious as to who has bought the old Weston place. At first, I thought maybe even Haudenosaunee Hills has a racist component. I've heard people call me 'that black man.' And, of course, there probably is racism, like everywhere else, but these cars are innocuous. I wouldn't worry about it."

"I'm just a little jittery."

Lisa looked at a garden she, Alice, Crystal, and Christine had played in as children, and where later they had exchanged secrets about boys and dates. Even later, as the Chrysalis quartet, they had practiced their vocal quartet pieces in the gazebo, surrounded by the smell of apple blossoms and the beauty of early summer flowers, all within the surrounding high, white fence that kept the deer and the rabbits away with variable success.

Now, she saw obvious signs of neglect and deterioration: dying bushes, overgrown areas by the fence, empty spots where Kaisa had had her annual flowers. There were several flower beds where spring and early summer plants had finished their blooming and not been dead-headed. Lisa felt sad, and hoped Kaisa would not have to see this. She would be distraught, or maybe even angry, as only Kaisa could be.

There was no end to the topic of Afghanistan in the discussion between the couple. Lisa was attracted to this fascinating man, but she had started to wonder if their mutual interest would be too limited, and told Abdul so.

"I am sorry," said Abdul. "I have been pondering the same, but I thought that Afghanistan is what you would want to talk about, especially with me. I am your encyclopedia when it comes to my country."

"You think your knowledge is the only reason I like you? No, I like you because you are you. I want to learn more about you beyond the common interest in Afghanistan. What are your interests, your hobbies, your dreams?"

"I am actually quite boring," he replied. "My children are my life, and whatever free time I have, I like to read and watch movies. Very mundane."

"What kinds of books? What type of movies?"

"I like mysteries, something that keeps me guessing. The same with movies. And you? What are your hobbies?"

"I, too, am pretty boring, if that's what you call it. I read, too, mostly about people's relationships of one type or another. I like books about women's issues. I read, and play the piano, walk and kayak, not seriously, but enough to keep limber."

Abdul patted the slight bulge at his midriff. "I should move more, too, but it is hard. After a busy day, I just don't feel like taxing my muscles. I did have a twelve-pack, when I was younger, you know."

"A twelve-pack? You mean a six-pack? Cans of drinks come in twelve-packs, like soda and beer." Lisa smiled.

"Oh, that's right. You should know your anatomy as a doctor, after all!"

Lisa felt good. It was a relief to laugh again. Maybe more of that would help her get rid of her nervousness, her jumpiness at loud sounds, and her reactions to people who spoke at a volume close to yelling.

"By the way, did you go back to your practice?" inquired Abdul.

"No, not yet. I decided to take a few weeks off before getting back into the grind again." Lisa was afraid to think how she would be able to cope with the pressure. A break would give her a chance to reevaluate her life, to put things in correct perspective, whatever that might mean.

After making a date with Abdul to go kayaking, Lisa drove home feeling more and more contented.

Chapter 37

Kaisa emptied a heavy canvas bag on Alice's kitchen table. The contents resembled materials owned by a serious scrapbooker.

"Okay, girls, I need your help in figuring out what materials I can use in the first class, the meal planning segment." Alice, Pam, and Stephanie viewed the papers, scissors, and culinary magazines with curiosity.

"This is what I thought," said Kaisa. "I'll have all the students tell everybody what their favorite food is. I'll write their choice down in my notebook and use the list later on. Hopefully, the choice isn't potato chips. I'd like to show how you can modify something to make it healthier. I'll then have them create a whole meal using pictures from these magazines, paying attention to what they think is healthy."

"Why can't they just tell you and the class?" asked Pam.

"There's a method to my madness. There are only a few magazines. That makes the girls interact with each other, share materials, et cetera. I can only watch and see who is taking this seriously, and who would rather just sit on the periphery. So you are my guinea pigs. I'm only giving you two magazines and two pairs of scissors."

"Nothing like aggravating us right from the beginning," said Alice. "What is the purpose here? To learn to cook healthy foods or to share and be nice like you learn in kindergarten?"

"Yes," said Kaisa and winked at her daughter. "So, tell me your favorite foods."

"Mine's Polish sausage and mashed potatoes. They have to be served together," said Pam. "The sausage cooked so that it bursts open."

"Mine, I think, is Alice's chicken with garlic and sundried tomatoes in a Parmesan sauce over rice. Oh, and a vegetable to go with it, like broccoli," offered Stephanie.

Alice hesitated. "I have so many. I have a theory that some people are born with better functioning taste buds than others, and, let me tell you, I have the most efficient ones. I eat everything. I love all kinds of food, and it shows. Just look at me. Well, maybe I won't eat raw oysters or squid. My favorite? I have to say salmon with yogurt dill sauce, new potatoes, and sweet peas."

"Grandma, what about you? What's your favorite? And be truthful," said Pam.

"I'll tell you today, but I probably won't tell the class. It's blood pancakes with lingonberries."

"Eew!" said everyone simultaneously.

"Are they really made of blood?" asked Stephanie, horrified at the thought.

"They are. They look like a chocolatey dessert, but they are a rich main meal packed with protein and iron. Okay, get to work on your meal planning."

Alice, Pam, and Stephanie looked at each other. Fast as lightning, Pam grabbed one of the two magazines. Stephanie looked surprised and hesitated to touch the remaining copy. She picked up a pair of scissors. Alice took the magazine and, using all the arm muscle power she had, ripped it in two and handed half of it to

Stephanie. Pam cut colorful pictures of fresh fruit and vegetables. Stephanie studied recipes carefully and only after determining the ingredients to be healthy did she cut out a picture. Alice had a good time ripping pictures off the pages.

"Ten more minutes," announced Kaisa and turned to look at Alice. "You have coffee made?"

"In the thermos," said Alice. She thought of coffee as a poison definitely deserving a spot on the healthy list. Other than fresh fruit juices and water, liquids are most likely forbidden. *Thank God for those doctors who say that red wine is good for you!*

The ten minutes were up.

"What do you think of this exercise? Do you think the girls would find it useful and fun?"

"I think most of them will. Those who are negative about everything probably will do the exercise and secretly like it, but won't say so," Stephanie offered.

"Let's see what you came up with and, by the way, I'm impressed with how you solved the dilemma caused by lack of scissors and magazines." Stephanie and Alice smiled.

"Sorry," said Pam.

All the pictures they'd ripped and cut out depicted healthy, balanced meals.

"Well," said Kaisa. "The results are great with this group of students. You obviously know what healthy food consists of, whether you practice it or not. It'll be interesting to see what happens in the group."

"Stephanie will report back to us on the opinion of her peers," said Alice. "I'll be curious to see about cooperation between the girls. It'll show a lot about their life skills in general."

"Indeed," said Kaisa.

"I hate to ask you, Pam, but would you mind giving me a ride back up the hill?" asked Stephanie. "I could call Crystal or Michael…"

"No problem," Pam interrupted. "Maybe we can stop for ice cream on the way at the lakeside stand," and added, turning so that Kaisa was sure to hear, "you know, the healthy kind."

Kaisa gathered her supplies into the bag and went to the piano. She played, this time using Alice's sheet music from her high school and Chrysalis days, light accompaniment for the quartet. Alice hummed along, breaking into words now and then, lyrics she hadn't forgotten for over twenty years.

"Mom, you're still doing great!"

"What do you mean 'still'? It sounds like you anticipate my demise."

"No, no, I just mean that you've always been good at the piano. Maybe not as good as Lisa, though. By the way, Lisa is back in town."

"Yes, I know."

"What do you mean you know? Why didn't you tell me you knew?"

"Why should I tell you? I figure you had her cat and Lisa probably came to get him first thing. I drove by my old house to look at the garden. What a mess, by the way! There was Lisa, sitting in the gazebo with the professor. They looked quite cozy. I know they've been in touch throughout the time Lisa was in Afghanistan and even before, but do you think there's something romantic going on?"

"I'm not sure, but if there were, I'd be thrilled for Lisa. She's so alone in the world with no family," said

Alice.

"If she hooked up with him, she'd go from no family to a very lively household. Whew!" Kaisa wiped her forehead for effect.

"Well, Lisa is used to big changes in her life, and can adjust better than most of us," Alice assured her mother. "Mom, do you think it's healthy for you to go back to the old house? Isn't it better to save yourself from bringing back all the memories? I wouldn't think it's good for you to see that the garden has been neglected, that all your hard work for years was for naught. Why would you do that, torture yourself like that? I know how attached you were to the place."

"Nonsense," said Kaisa. "I want to bring some irises and other perennials to the beds by the lake and just wanted to check that they were still there. So if I want to ask Dr. Naziri for some rhizomes toward the fall, I know they are still available."

"Right," said Alice. *Likely story!*

"Besides," Kaisa continued, "I was afraid that if I had told you I saw Lisa, you would have accused me of hallucinating again."

Alice rolled her eyes.

Kaisa lifted up her index finger as if for an important notice. "I'm keeping an eye on the drapes of the condo next door. I think they are closed tighter on some days than others."

"Whatever," said Alice and wondered when Kaisa's next doctor's appointment was. She definitely needed to join her mother and explore whether a medication adjustment could help the problem.

Kaisa returned to the topic. "What did Lisa say about her plans? You talked to her for a while, didn't you?"

"It was her first full day back. She was super tired and just pretty much came to get Niles and left. She said she had a lot to tell. I'm sure we'll get together soon. What an experience she's had! Tom and I have been wondering whether the Taliban attack at the maternity ward influenced her to stay an extra year and then caused her to cut that year short."

"Horrendous! It would definitely have left a mark on me."

Alice didn't answer. *Thank God Mom doesn't have to experience anything traumatic. It would send her over the edge, no matter how strong she says she is.*

Chapter 38

Summer was rushing by as if in deliberate haste. August brought with it an abundance of ripening produce, a sea of color in flowerbeds, and department stores full of back-to-school items from serious electronics to children's backpacks with pictures of the most recent kids' movie characters. So many people seemed to live several weeks ahead. It wouldn't be long before Halloween decorations appeared on the shelves.

Michael felt strange. He squinted his eyes, even with his aviator sunglasses, as he looked toward the sun from his seat on the lifeguard's perch by the pool in the park and then called his peer to take over during his break. Listening to his fellow graduates, Michael wasn't sure if he should be out there looking at dormitory accessories, things like bedspreads, lamps, et cetera. Way back in March, his mother had seemed to have a plan regarding the décor of his dormitory room and had forced him to get in touch with Frank, another freshman, assigned to him as roommate at RIT. A nice enough guy, who had his own definite idea on how their room should look. Michael truly was not interested in dorm room décor, especially when he knew that he wanted to be with Stephanie. When he'd felt the kick in Stephanie's belly, the baby had become real to him. Before, it was all about the drama of Stephanie's being pregnant. Now, he felt the existence of the brand-new person growing inside the girl he loved.

After the talk he and Stephanie had with her parents, he felt more adult. The parents had actually said they would go along with what he and Stephanie wanted to do. The Smiths trusted their decisions and would support them. Michael felt honored to the extreme. Now it would be up to him and Stephanie to prove to everybody that they deserved the trust and confidence in their ability to decide the direction their lives took.

To bounce off some ideas, they had talked with Crystal and Gavin. The couple was always ready to listen and treated them more as their equals than as immature kids. Stephanie had reported a big difference between Alice and Crystal. Alice seemed to be more of an authority figure. She acted as a mother, directing your every move. Maybe the fact that Stephanie also knew her as a teacher added to Alice's air of authority. Michael had felt it, too. Crystal and Gavin were, however, encouraging without parental overtones.

Michael called Stephanie, who had just decided to give Rufus a bath.

"I think I know what we should do," he said.

"Oh?" asked Stephanie trying to keep Rufus from shaking while still covered in suds.

"You still want to live together?" he asked.

"Yes. You do, too, right?"

"Yes. That's why I think we should talk to Mr. Fitzpatrick about an apartment to rent. I think we should live close to our parents within a commuting distance to RIT for me. It's only a half an hour. Nothing new here, I know, except for the Mr. Fitzpatrick part. We have already talked about it all. I think it's more adult to talk to a realtor than to rely on our parents to find a place."

"For sure. When do you want to go see places?"

"I can get an appointment, or do you want to make it?"

"Okay, I will. You have a job, and I'm free as a bird."

****

Tom greeted Stephanie and Michael in his real estate office. They sat down to discuss options.

"So, a new chapter starting in your lives, huh?"

"Yes, sir," said Michael.

"Well, the rental situation is not too optimistic, like I told you on the phone." Tom looked at Stephanie. "Still, I've got a couple of choices here. There's a cute two-bedroom rental in the middle of town, within walking distance to just about everywhere. There's another one a bit farther away, but still in town. For that one, you'd have to buy all appliances. And this is a real beauty." Tom showed them a sheet with pictures and a list of features. "It's in the next town, but the entire downstairs of the house. And then there's this condominium with no yard at all. None of these places has a garage. So, as you can see, all of them have some sort of less-than-perfect feature attached to them."

"We figured that would be the case," said Michael. Stephanie thought he sounded so very mature. "Let's just go and see what they look like 'live,' so to speak."

"Okay. I'll get all the keys. Follow me."

The first place was perfect, except for the fact that it was a second-floor apartment. Stephanie had trouble picturing herself with grocery bags, a baby, and a stroller, trying to navigate the narrow stairway.

The second one had a bare kitchen and its location was in the wrong direction from town, leading them even farther away from everything while increasing Michael's commuting time and distance.

In the same direction was the house with the downstairs apartment, even farther away than the second one, although otherwise suitable.

The condominium, although new and sparkling clean, had only one bedroom, and the absence of a yard was a definite deterrent to Stephanie.

When they finished the tour, Stephanie and Michael looked discouraged.

"If it was just the two of us, we could consider the places in town, but we can't do the upstairs with a baby, and a yard would be super nice," said Stephanie.

"Hmm." Tom pinched his chin together from the sides. "There is this other place. It's out of town, but it's worth looking at, I think."

"Okay," said Stephanie, defeated. Michael was quiet.

They sat in the car and followed Tom.

"This is interesting. We don't even have the baby yet, and already he is dictating where we live."

"Or she," said Stephanie.

"Oh, right."

Tom headed north in front of them, driving along the lake.

"This is out of town, too," said Stephanie in disappointment.

"But at least it's in the right direction if we think of my commute."

Seven or eight miles out of town, Tom turned onto a secondary road.

"This is the same road that leads to Crystal's cottage," said Stephanie.

As they pulled into the yard of Lola's house, a small clapboard cottage with a picket fence, Tom got out of his car and asked, "So, what do you think?"

Stephanie stayed in the car. "What do you mean? This is Lola's place and Crystal and Gavin's summer cottage now."

"I do know that," said Tom.

"What's going on here?" Michael had not followed the conversation carefully. "This is a rental?"

"It appears that way. Crystal told me that after talking with her mother in Finland, the decision was to rent the place, but not just to anybody. They seemed to have a special young couple in mind."

"What the fu..." Michael caught himself. "You're kidding me," he corrected. He didn't usually swear, but this occasion was so momentous, a swear word had almost managed to slip out.

"Let's go in. You may hate it," said Tom, smiling.

"Fat chance of that," said Michael.

"I've been here with Crystal many times. I love this place," said Stephanie.

They opened the gate to the fenced-in yard and walked through a garden in great need of tender loving care. Tom unlocked the door and showed the young couple in, thinking that these kids were the youngest people he'd ever showed a place to in all his years in real estate.

They stepped into a spacious room with a kitchen on one wall, the ever-so-popular "open concept." There was a gigantic map of the world on one wall, full of push pins with heads of various colors. Stephanie knew these to be markers for the places Lola had traveled to in her search of adventures and excitement—red for Spain, purple for

Slovenia, green for Austria, yellow for South Africa. She wondered whether the colors signified something. She looked for a pin for Finland. White. Maybe for snow. In the corner, there was a fireplace that spelled "cozy" to Stephanie. She walked around, admired the lake view from the large window, and saw a lean-to shed with a kayak and a large pile of brush in it.

Michael appeared. "Yeah, those twigs and branches have to go. Looks pretty trashy, doesn't it?"

"No," asserted Stephanie. "Crystal told me that's material for a June Midsummer Solstice bonfire that was supposed to happen for the last two years but didn't. It's a huge undertaking and people just don't have time for that, especially when the people involved are getting older and older. Younger people don't seem to be interested. We can do that, though! We can have a Solstice celebration next summer and keep a tradition going."

"We can, can we?" Mchael was hesitant. "So you've already decided on this place?"

Stephanie smiled widely.

Michael had followed his father's advice for things to keep in mind when visiting potential apartments. He could almost quote it verbatim...

"Pay attention to the type of heating. There's a big difference in your heating bill depending on the type of fuel used. Check on the tightness of the windows. Ask about insulation. Find out if there's a municipal water and sewer. See if there's a need for radon mitigation, or if there are signs of damage by humidity: mildew or mold. And make sure you know who and where the landlord is. You don't want an absentee landlord."

Michael had been overwhelmed. He had no idea

there were so many important things to pay attention to.

After checking his list with Mr. Fitzpatrick, Michael declared, "I looked at the important things with Mr. Fitzpatrick." Tom smiled to himself. *A little information sometimes brings out the experts.*

"Everything looks solid," Michael continued. "If there's a faint mildew smell, it's because the house is mostly closed up and needs a thorough airing. There's a fireplace for a secondary heat source, and the house is connected to the town's water and sewer systems. And," he added, "this is a few miles closer to Rochester and RIT."

"Wow!" Stephanie stared at Michael with a look of admiration. Michael stood a little straighter.

"You haven't asked about the rent amount," said Tom.

Stephanie and Michael felt defeated. It wasn't fair that they were shown this fantastic possibility and then have the rug pulled out from under them. Both sets of parents had made a promise to help, but it was shameless to have them pay high rent while the real renters were unable to contribute to what was needed.

"Well," said Tom, "I don't think you could get a better deal. Lola has decided that she'll let you have the house rent-free for four years, as long as you take care of the lawn, the garden, and the snow removal. Of course, you'll pay for your own utilities, TV, wi-fi, and so on. This way Crystal won't have the responsibility for two houses, Lola gets to keep her place without selling it, and you'll have a great place to live with some responsibilities."

"Yes, sir." Michael was responding to the "with some responsibilities" part of Tom's statement.

"I'm not going to sermonize to you," continued Tom, "but living in a house, your own or someone else's, is a big responsibility. A house needs attention like a baby. Even if you're young, you're up to it, I'm sure, plus you have a slew of people who support you and love you. Do you want to take a couple of days to think about it? The house isn't going anywhere and it won't be offered to anyone else. I can keep my eyes open for possible apartments that come on the market."

Stephanie and Michael looked at each other, leaned into each other's shoulder, as if expecting support to flow in both directions through the physical contact, and said in unison, 'We'll take it."

Tom smiled. "Okay then. It will probably be a good idea for you now to talk to your parents. A rental agreement is also in order, even if there's no rent money changing hands."

"Oh, yeah," said Stephanie.

"Absolutely," added Michael.

On the way to Crystal's, Stephanie sat as close to Michael as a two-seater would allow, disturbing Michael's ability to shift gears manually.

"Can you imagine this?" she enthused. "How lucky can you get? Do you realize how many wonderful, caring people we have in our lives? It's almost unbelievable. You know, we'll owe a debt of gratitude to so many people, especially when we get on our feet and can pay them all back somehow."

"I know it. I get it that our parents support us, but just think—Crystal, her mother, and Mr. Fitzpatrick are all pulling for us. And Crystal and Mr. Fitzpatrick concocted this devious plan, 'a tangled web' to deceive us."

"Yeah. Shakespeare said it right."

"That wasn't Shakespeare. He's gotten a lot of credit for it, but it was really Sir Walter Scott."

"Are you sure?"

"Is your belly like a basketball?"

Stephanie put her head on Michael's shoulder. "You're so smart," she said and closed her eyes.

Chapter 39

Kaisa recalled her first teaching assignment a month ago. She had pondered long and hard about her choices for clothing and accessories as well as making her demeanor suitable for an educator. Would she want to come across as a grandmotherly type full of empathy, understanding, and assurances, or as a hardliner who made sure her suggestions were listened to and her advice adhered to? She could wear jeans and a T-shirt but thought of them as too casual, trying to convey a message of "I'm just like you, I'm your buddy, your new best friend."

She put on a dress, looked at herself in the mirror, and saw a woman on her way to her Tuesday morning bridge club.

She tried on a lightweight suit. Maybe good for a funeral.

In the end, Kaisa had compromised and gone back to her first choice of jeans. She added a short-sleeved blouse with red and white poppies. Not too casual, not too formal. She grabbed a long apron to give herself the air of a chef and headed out to the old schoolhouse.

Kaisa looked at the group of girls sitting around a long table, a dozen big-eyed young faces, a dozen young bodies in shorts and T-shirts, all visibly pregnant.

They are so incredibly young. I'll have to remember that "a long time ago" to them was 2010.

Kaisa directed the girls through the sharing of their favorite foods exercise, which revealed a great deal. Some of the girls had very little knowledge about basic food groups, let alone what constitutes a balanced meal. Some appeared to be disinterested until Kaisa told them some odd bits and pieces about different foods, among them that tomatoes were actually berries but had been declared to be vegetables by the Supreme Court in 1893, or that some people's dislike of Brussels sprouts and cilantro is genetic, or that the rhyme *Beans, beans, they're good for the heart. The more you eat them, the more you fart* is only true for the fact that they cause flatulence. By the time Kaisa got to the end of the rhyme, she had the approval of her audience, who were barely out of the stage of body function humor in their development.

The meals created out of magazine pictures had a range of carbo loads to fairly well-balanced platefuls.

****

During their meetings, Kaisa would lecture lightly about a topic, after which the class moved into the kitchen. This was the most popular part of the sessions, mainly because it involved action and movement. Kaisa was sure all her students had trouble sitting still, which was understandable with their sugar-loaded diets.

There had only been a couple of mishaps involving food. While making a fruit-and-vegetable smoothie in a blender, an important lesson was learned—It is crucial that the lid of the blender is in place before the blender is turned on. The secondary lesson following the mishap was the importance of keeping your working surfaces clean. A sharp knife was a great tool for teaching the girls how to hold and use a cutting utensil correctly. Only three bandages were needed for the whole class. Kaisa realized it hadn't even crossed her mind to worry about accidents. She would give extra strong warnings and pray for no lawsuits.

Now, in the fourth meeting, Kaisa had the girls cook an egg two ways. Boiled and fried were familiar choices. Someone mentioned hearing of "poached" but had no idea what it meant. It was new to most that to make a perfect boiled egg, either soft or hard boiled, you needed to use a timer. Some wanted to fry their egg "over easy" as it was their father's or cousin's favorite. Kaisa explained that "over hard" was easier than "over easy" which is harder, more difficult. The girls were confused until some of them realized the word play.

An addition to the meal was spinach, either cooked to go with the fried eggs or raw with the boiled.

One student stood on the side looking bored. She told Kaisa she was a short order cook at a local diner and sick of seeing eggs.

"I get it," said Kaisa. "Have you made scrambled eggs, regular and soft?"

"Yes," said the girl. Kaisa had her demonstrate how they are made. The girl was thrilled to be in the position of an instructor.

After the class, Kaisa drove to Alice's house.

"I'm surprised at the lack of knowledge of the girls," Kaisa said to Alice, "and I'm even more surprised at how eager they are to learn. If you give them a job or some responsibility, they seem to bloom! Don't parents teach their kids anything anymore? Most of them look like they haven't lifted a finger all their lives." Kaisa paused. "Well, from what I can gather, some of them may have lifted the middle finger a bit! You only have to look at their fingernails—long, painted talons. I can only imagine what grows under them. You certainly can't do anything with claws like that. I bet most of them even have fake nails, and with what money? Those things aren't cheap. Same with the expensive tattoos and piercings."

"Mom, you didn't say anything to the girls about that, did you?"

"No, of course not. With those nails, though, I'll have to watch that they make sure to wear gloves at all times in the teaching kitchen. I bet they don't even need a knife for peeling an orange, if they ever eat an orange."

"Of course, the bigger the holes in their knowledge base, the bigger the difference you'll make. Good going, Mom! I talked to Stephanie after the first class. She said the consensus of the class was that you are 'awesome for your age.' Of course, she said this from the point of view of an observation, not a scientific examination, but you have reason to be proud!"

Kaisa laughed heartily. "There's an endless potential there. I just hope they can keep it together. Their lives seem rather helter-skelter." Kaisa looked out into the meadow of wildflowers. "At their age, I was probably equally bewildered about life, but at least I wasn't pregnant."

"You never know, Mom. I've learned this from all the years of teaching: In any given class, there may be a Pulitzer Prize-winning playwright and an Olympic gymnast right next to a future homeless person or a prisoner convicted of murder. And what's even more amazing, you can't tell at that point who will be who."

Chapter 40

Stephanie wrapped a white silk ribbon around the stems of the flowers she had picked in the garden with Crystal's permission—purple cone flowers, Russian sage, butterfly bush, and white dahlias, a lovely combination of varying hues of violet and white. She was taking the bouquet to Clare Albright later in the day. Michael and Stephanie were having dinner with his parents. The invitation had come immediately after Michael returned home from their apartment-hunting excursion. Stephanie wondered what the dinner gathering would be like... More or less a discussion about how to handle the finances of their future? Or a more personal getting-to-know-you-better event? Stephanie hoped for the latter.

When Michael picked her up, she saw he was wearing dress slacks and a crisp, ironed shirt with a sweater hanging on his shoulders. It was held in place by the sleeves tied together loosely in the front. *How preppy can you get?* She was secretly happy with her own wardrobe choice, too—a pair of white slacks and a navy top with white polka dots. She wore sandals with low heels. *All in all, not a bad looking couple!*

Michael looked at Stephanie admiringly and gave her a long kiss. There was great temptation in the air, and they were alone, but both agreed that it was important to be on time for the dinner.

Michael never used the front door but entered the house through the garage and the kitchen. Today, that seemed inappropriate somehow and they walked to the front of the house and stepped into the foyer.

Stephanie had been in the house before, but usually in the TV room with many other teens or in the kitchen grabbing a bite to eat with Michael before a football game.

"Hello," called Michael.

"Hello," answered Clare, her arm stretched out toward Stephanie for a handshake, but she then withdrew her hand. Stephanie felt alarmed and dismissed, but Clare immediately came toward her and gave her a big, warm hug.

"You know, hugs are better than handshakes. All the bacteria in your hands. This is a lot better," she looked at Stephanie in the eyes and confirmed, "in so many ways."

"Oh, these are for you," said Stephanie, handing the bouquet to Clare, while trying to see how much damage the flowers had suffered in the surprise hug.

"How lovely!" said Clare. "Come right in. Robert will be with us momentarily. He had an emergency phone consultation."

Michael directed Stephanie to the large living room where the furniture was arranged in well-designed groupings perfect for comfortable conversation. On the coffee table were large books in carefully placed stacks of three or four. A charcuterie board with cheeses, pâtés, and grapes looked tempting beside the books. Everything was calculated, everything was organized to a T. Although Stephanie felt awkward in the midst of so much class, so much sophistication, she somehow felt relaxed. She knew deep down that the Albrights had already accepted her, at least Mrs. Albright had, as proven by the fact that they had agreed to the deal on the house Crystal had offered. Stephanie also remembered the donation to the support group's nutrition classes.

Robert appeared in the doorway. "Hello, good to see you," he said. Let me get us some drinks. What would you like?"

"Water is fine..." started Stephanie. Robert raised his eyebrows. "Or," Stephanie continued, "if you have some fruit juice..."

"Looks like the food course, what is it again? Cooking class? Nutrition course? has done its job," said Robert and winked. "Son, you'll have a cola, I take it? You two don't mind if we have something stronger?"

"Not at all," said Michael.

"I'll help you," said Clare to Robert. They disappeared into the butler's pantry.

Stephanie had kept her gaze at eye level with Michael's parents in the room, but in their absence she looked around the room in awe.

"Who are these people on the walls?" She nodded toward the large portraits in ornate, gilded frames around the room, the women dressed in shiny fabrics and lace, their hair in dos from various time periods. Stephanie recognized the Victorian opulence and the Empire style, especially the high waistline just under the bust, a style suitable for a pregnant woman. There was a man who looked like George Washington in a white wig and what appeared to be a military uniform. Next to his portrait was one of a pale woman, whose curly hair peeked from under a large, decorated bonnet. A man dressed in simple black clerical garb was pictured in a smaller painting.

Michael was thoughtful. "You know, I think they

are all my ancestors, but I'm not sure who they are."

"Here we go." Clare brought in glasses of apple juice and a cola to the young couple. Robert followed with martinis, walking gingerly to avoid a spill.

He raised his glass after handing one to his wife.

"Here's to all that's good from now on, and here's also to the next generation of Albrights!"

"Stephanie was just asking who the people are in the portraits. I'm ashamed, but I really don't know," said Michael to his father.

"Well, this couple..." Robert stood near the wall and pointed to the pair who seemed to be from the 1700s, "is Reinhardt Albrecht and his wife Louisa. They were German. The name Albrecht goes back to the 1300s and was changed to Albright somewhere along the way since these two." Robert raised his glass next toward the Victorian beauty and the man with bushy sideburns. "This woman is Theresa Albright from the 1840s, born in Charleston, South Carolina, and this is her husband Robert, the original Robert Albright."

"I can see that you look like him," said Stephanie.

"Thank you. Flattery will get you nowhere."

"He's only kidding," said Michael, unsure whether he was right.

"What about the priest?" asked Stephanie.

"He's a great-great-uncle of mine. I'm not sure how many 'greats' go in front of the 'uncle.' He was a Lutheran minister and one of the earliest Albrechts to come to the States. How and why he came here is a mystery."

"My family has no interesting history," said Clare, "at least that I know of. I really should look into that. What about your family, your roots?" Clare looked at

Stephanie expectantly and took a sip of her martini.

Stephanie felt embarrassed. Should she tell them all she knew, all the misery of alcoholism and poverty? She didn't want to appear as if she was evading the topic.

"I don't know anything about my ancestry beyond my grandparents. I do know that they had a really tough time in life. And"—Stephanie laughed—"my grandparents' names are Smith and Jones. There are a couple of those in the world."

"This is true," said Clare.

Michael gave Stephanie a one-armed hug, putting an arm around her shoulder with an encouraging squeeze.

It was time for dinner and they entered the dining room. It had a long mahogany table with high-backed chairs. With one chair at each end and one at each side, the atmosphere compared to the warmth of the living room was almost inhospitable. The room called for a larger gathering, something to fill the space.

Stephanie looked around. In contrast to the portraits in the living room, the dining room's walls were covered with still lifes of fruit and flowers, and some paintings of hunting scenes with birddogs retrieving the kill, each work of art illuminated by a picture light.

"I didn't know if you like snails," said Clare, placing on the table a hot round dish with its tiny indentations filled with dark, amorphous forms. "If you don't, and I know a lot of people don't like them, you don't have to eat them. I'll get you something else. The three of us absolutely love them." Stephanie looked at Michael, who showed a perfect poker face.

"I've never had them, but I will try," said Stephanie and cautiously had a taste. "These are fabulous!" she declared and ate every single snail on her special porcelain escargot plate.

The salad with homemade dressing was fresh and delicious. By the time the main meal arrived, Stephanie had decided that Clare was a better cook than Kaisa, and that was almost an impossibility. They savored the herbs and spices of the chicken and rice entrée as they ate, conversing between bites.

"This is all excellent, Mrs. Albright!" said Stephanie. I will never be able to cook for you. I'll be too nervous."

"Nonsense," said Clare. "And can we agree that you call us Clare and Robert?"

"Thank you," said Stephanie, wondering if she really could do it.

"After all," continued Clare, "it makes sense if you're going to get married."

Michael dropped his fork onto his plate with a loud clang. Stephanie's head snapped up from her forkful of chicken on its way to her mouth. Looks were exchanged from Stephanie to Michael, Clare to Robert, Michael to Robert and Clare, Stephanie to her plate.

"Well." Michael wiped his mouth with a white linen napkin. "We weren't thinking of getting married, at least not yet. We thought maybe later, with the baby a little older, when we can have a real wedding. We don't want you to spend your money on that when we are already costing you loads."

"I didn't mean right now. Notice that I said 'if,' " said Clare. "Please, relax." Clare looked at Robert. Michael looked across the table at Stephanie.

"This dessert server has been in the family since Theresa Albright's days," said Clare out of nowhere. "I always think of what it was like in Charleston on a warm summer night, sitting out in the garden, enjoying peach cobbler like this. This is her recipe, you know, served with this delicate server. Just look at the silversmith's handiwork. There's nothing like this made any more, and, from what I hear, today's kids don't want any of this silver. Too much work, I guess, to polish it and wash it by hand."

"I like it," said Stephanie. "My family never had anything old and valuable like that."

"I'm glad to hear that," said Clare, obviously pleased.

On the way back to the farm, Michael detoured to the park on the lake.

"So, how do you think it went?" he asked.

"Your parents are great people. I was surprised that your dad spoke so little and that expenses—you know, our utilities, food, clothing—weren't brought up at all. I still don't know how it all will work."

"Well, this was like the first time we all got together. There'll be a time soon to talk about finances."

"I guess so." Stephanie hesitated. "One thing bothers me a little. When your mom mentioned marriage, I thought she really meant that they expected us to get married right now, you know, before the baby is born."

"Yeah, I thought so, too, but they had said we could make our own decisions when we are eighteen, and now we're almost there. Even without thinking of that, they wanted us to make up our minds about everything, don't you think?"

"I know, but I still think they secretly hoped we'd get married now, at least your mom did."

"Probably. When I said no, she kind of dropped the subject like a hot potato. But it's our lives. They trusted us to deal with everything our own way."

"Right," said Stephanie. "It must be hard, in a way, to give up control. I bet your ancestors were used to telling people what to do. Being that they lived in the South, do you suppose they had slaves, even?"

"Geez, I hope not! I never thought of that. Dad said they were from Charleston, from a big city. They didn't have a plantation."

"Be real. Not all slaves picked cotton in the fields. They worked in the kitchens, took care of the horses and the carriages, cared and even nursed the babies. They weren't all field hands. Besides, Charleston could've been their city residence. They may easily have had a plantation, too. Did you listen at all in Cougar's class when we were sophomores?" Stephanie punched Michael in the arm.

"Ouch," said Michael. "I must have. I got an A in the course. I refuse to believe my ancestors were so despicable as to own another human being."

"Those were different times, but I do hope you're right."

Chapter 41

Magnus wiped sweat off his brow. It was a huge job to remove the wall-to-wall carpet from the master bedroom, a light beige shag now showing dark, matted paths leading from the bed to the bathroom, from the dresser to the closet. The installation of the new hardwood floor was tricky with the less-than-perfect subfloor under it, but the final result was worth the strife, Magnus felt.

As each project in the house restoration was completed, Magnus rewarded himself with a dinner at a first-class restaurant. What connoted first class to him was sometimes different from most people's choices. He preferred ethnic food, regardless of the place of origin. He loved spicy Thai dishes, equally hot Cuban fare, or true Italian homemade sauce cooked all day by Luigi in the Italian restaurant by the lake.

Magnus grabbed a glass of water and checked his messages. An email from the DNA testing outfit! *That was rather fast!* thought Magnus. *Seems like only yesterday DeeDee and I split our sides spitting globs of saliva into the test vials!*

Apparently, the report was a preliminary one with the message: "We continue to calculate your data."

Magnus had hoped for a more complete and wide-ranging coverage of his characteristics and qualities. He already had a vague idea of what the distribution of countries of origin would look like. The report confirmed his presumption: fifty percent Scandinavian, forty-one percent British and Irish, seven percent Russian, and two percent Polish. Russia and Poland were surprises, but those countries, so close together, have changed their borders often, in the course of history, as well as doing business back and forth between them. Maybe an old-time traveling salesman had paid a visit to one of the Swedish maidens just across the Baltic Sea eons ago.

The report also indicated that he was two-point-seven percent Neanderthal and a shirttail relative of a certain charitable musician with a heart for the needy. *That's all right! Better than being related to a heavy metal druggie!*

Magnus called DeeDee. He never disturbed her during working hours, but this called for unusual measures.

"Hey, I won't keep you, but did you get your report?"

"What report?"

"The DNA results."

"No, I haven't looked at my personal email. I take it you got yours. What does it say? You're a descendent of a serial killer?"

"It doesn't say too much yet. They're still studying the results. Hey, I finished the floor in the master bedroom. Time to celebrate. Can you go out to dinner tonight?"

"Congratulations! I could, but if I got my results, too, I don't want to discuss them out in public. Why don't you come over to my place? We'll order pizza."

"Sounds good."

"Seven okay?"

"Sure. See you then."

It will have to be the best pizza around here to match the occasion! And Magnus knew where to get the best.

Sitting at DeeDee's kitchen table, she and Magnus deciphered percentages in the DNA reports.

"This is so neat. We are both fifty percent Scandinavian," said DeeDee. I know you are Swedish. Why doesn't it say that on your report?"

"From what I gathered, the Swedes, the Norwegians and the Danes are considered Scandinavians geographically. Sometimes, when people talk about Scandinavia, they mean all the Nordic countries including Finland and Iceland."

"So I could be Finnish like Alice. Well, I guess she's only half Finnish, right?"

"No, you're not Finnish. The Finns have their own gene. The rest of the Nordic nations are lumped together as Northern European."

"How do you know this stuff?" asked DeeDee wiping greasy pizza sauce off her chin.

"My original cobbler immigrant ancestor has interested me for a long time, so I dug up some information a while ago."

"Look at the rest of my report. I'm a lot of different things. Thirty-nine percent Sub-Saharan African. That really narrows it down, huh?"

"They're still calculating. There are more detailed reports to come. Hopefully, it's not like the Northern European 'all-in-one' deal."

"I know it. I have these huge groups. Six percent Native American. There are so many tribes."

"Wouldn't it be great if you were part Haudenosaunee?"

"And four-point-five percent East Asian. Who are these people?"

"That includes countries like China, Japan, Korea, et cetera."

"Well, it looks like I have covered almost the whole globe."

"Don't forget your point-five percent British/Irish blood. There's the connection that makes us both related to that musician."

"Wow! I wonder how far back that goes."

"Pretty far, I would guess. Was that all? I guess that makes a hundred percent." Magnus turned DeeDee's report to look at it closer. "I see I have more Neanderthal in me than you do."

"I hate to say this," said DeeDee, "but it's a derogatory term, isn't it, to call someone Neanderthal? I wouldn't boast about those genes."

"Not really. They found Neanderthal bones in the Neander Valley in Germany in 1926. For some reason, the British termed them stupid. That's where that comes from, but the joke's on the British. Recent data show that the Neanderthal were as intelligent—or more so—than the homo sapiens."

'You're such a scientist!" DeeDee exclaimed. "I can't wait to see more info. Even if it doesn't pinpoint my origins more precisely, I hope I get data on what illnesses I am susceptible to. If I have thirty-nine percent African in me, it means a slew of illnesses they may have that other races don't."

"I guess we'll just have to wait and see."

"I hate waiting," said DeeDee and crushed the already flat delivery box. They had eaten a whole large pepperoni pizza with extra cheese.

Chapter 42

By the time the last week of August arrived with its warm days and chilly nights, Lisa had made major decisions in her life. She had grown increasingly more attracted to Abdul, his gentle ways, his sweet, wide smile and black eyes, and his calming, low voice. They had spent all available hours together, sometimes alone sharing their life stories and memories with each other, talking long into the night and falling asleep on the sofa wrapped in each other's arms. At other times, they spent busy days playing with the children—hiking, bicycling, or swimming. After exhausting days, they invariably found a couple of the children nodding at the dinner table or falling asleep during a movie. The school-aged children spoke English most of the time, although their father made sure he exposed them to the native language of both their father and their mother. He knew now how difficult it was to continue to speak both languages, once the children were in school.

Lisa had felt awkward at first, hearing Farsi again. She also experienced a hollow, self -conscious sense of being talked about behind her back, although she knew that was not the case.

Somewhere along the way, Lisa realized she had pretty much moved into Abdul's house. She was familiar with every child, every room, and acted as a mother and the woman of the house, a progression she had never anticipated. Although her relationship with Abdul was warm and full of mutual admiration, Lisa was looking for more commitment. She knew enough about the Afghani culture to leave it alone, to let things develop on Abdul's terms.

Lisa had grown up as an only child, adored by her parents. The lack of siblings had pushed her to make friends in school, especially with children who shared her interests of music and animals. When the Chrysalis quartet was established, Lisa was elated. Not only did the group consist of talented singers, but they were all her best friends as well as friends with each other— Christine, Crystal, and Alice. Twenty some years later, they were still close.

Christine was divorced and, from what Lisa could gather, shy about dating again. Alice had been married for years, and Crystal was practically a newlywed, having married only a couple of years ago.

Lisa had had serious romantic relationships along the way, but none had been a deep enough connection to consider a permanent union of any kind, until now. Lisa knew she was truly in love. She sensed that Abdul felt the same, and that he was uncomfortable about the less than binding nature of their relationship.

The uncertainty with her job situation had started to bother Lisa as well. She wasn't sure she would be able to do surgery quite yet. She steeled herself and walked into the hospital administrator's office to discuss the issue. She wanted to keep the admitting privilege to the hospital. It was made clear to her that, should she return, she would need to be able to fulfill all duties of the obstetrician/gynecologist's job. Lisa felt she had improved in her physical reactions to loud sounds and noises, although she still felt anxious at times, particularly if she let herself think of the day of the attack. At least she had stopped having nightmares about the gruesome event.

She negotiated an arrangement to return to her job on a part-time basis, a compromise that was suitable for all parties, including her associate, with whom she shared her practice and office space on Main Street.

On a balmy night with tree frogs chirping in the locust trees and crickets competing with them in the grass, Lisa and Abdul sat in the gazebo, their favorite spot in the garden. Abdul seemed nervous and Lisa sensed that either something wonderful or something horrific was about to happen.

Abdul opened his mouth and, although his lips moved, no sound came out. He cleared his throat.

"Lisa, I've been thinking. You seem to be so comfortable with the children…" He paused and swallowed hard. "…and with me. What do you think about, how do you say, tying the knot?"

"Tying the knot? Do you know what that saying means? Are you proposing to me?"

"Yes. I do know what it means, and yes, I am proposing to you. I know I am not on my knees, but I mean it."

Lisa couldn't help it, and burst out in good-natured laughter. She pictured Abdul on all fours on the planks of the gazebo.

"It's 'on my knee,' on one knee, not both of them unless, in Afghanistan, you assume a different position when proposing marriage."

"Indeed, one knee. Do you have an answer?"

"I have a question. Are you doing this out of guilt?

I know that in Afghanistan you date with the intention of getting married, and you often still date only with a chaperone present at all times. Do you feel guilty that I'm here so much? That I haven't really lived in my own house for weeks? That I even moved my cat here?"

"I don't feel guilty. I don't regret falling in love with you. From the moment we met, I knew I had to have you. Will you have me?"

Lisa looked at him and said, "I definitely will."

"Wonderful! Tomorrow, we will get the marriage license and make an appointment for a ceremony. I am sorry. I want this to happen as soon as possible. Did you want a more formal wedding? A big reception?"

"No, not at all. You just started a semester, I just started my job, we have the kids and their school, so who has time for a party to please others? It doesn't make sense, looking at it from any angle."

Two mature adults making reasonable and reality-based decisions. Two people secretly thinking of a large reception with Afghani foods and music, a joyous occasion shared by all close to them.

"It doesn't make sense for us to own two large houses, either," Lisa continued. I will talk to Tom and have him put my house on the market," Lisa said matter-of-factly, and thought of the enormity of her statement a second later. She thought about what the house meant to her. It had been an anchor to her through the difficult time of her parents' death. It was a beautiful place, always on the Haudenosaunee Hills annual Garden Tour, the place people walking by slowed down to look at, admire and take pictures of. But it was, after all, only a building. Someone who appreciates period houses would love to have the Victorian gem.

"You mean it?" asked Abdul.

"I have all that I need in you," said Lisa and leaned against him. They walked into the house hand-in-hand. "Tomorrow, we'll tell the children," said Abdul, stopping in the middle of the kitchen.

"Children," said Lisa, confused, then continued, "Oh, definitely, and they need to be at the wedding ceremony, of course. Abdul, what are your thoughts of more children?"

Abdul's eyes became large.

"I have not really thought about it. I had always thought, even when my wife was alive, that the youngest was the last one, but…"

Lisa put her arms around Abdul's neck. "It's okay. It's fine. I'm fine. Your children will be my children. They are wonderful. I am fine not having a biological child of my own. I get my baby fix at my job every day I'm there. Don't worry. I'm good. Really."

Lisa was convincing herself more than she was reassuring Abdul.

Chapter 43

The skies opened up in the early morning hours of Stephanie and Michael's moving day. Stephanie woke up to an even drumming of raindrops on the porch roof. *The gutter above must be full of debris from the countless trees on the farm. It wouldn't make sense to clean gutters now, with fall so near, when the trees will shed their thousands of leaves and make the problem a great deal worse.* Stephanie shook her head. What seventeen-year-old girl thinks about cleaning gutters, unless, of course she wanted to avoid thinking of what was at hand.

To Stephanie, the issue of gutters was familiar and comfortable. Each fall, her father insisted on climbing the tall ladder to clean the gutters all around the substantial house. Her mother found it a ludicrous effort at saving a few pennies while risking your life. Each year, Stephanie listened to the raindrops heralding the time of her father's upcoming "suicide attempt," as her mother called it.

I'm glad Lola's house is very low. Even if you fall from a ladder's highest rung, it most likely won't kill you. Stephanie laughed. She was starting to act like an old worrywart!

Crystal and Gavin were having breakfast when Stephanie descended from upstairs.

"Good morning! What a yucky day!" Stephanie stretched, leaning backwards.

"It is. Luckily, you don't have to move furniture. It's all there, even if it's a bit dated. My mom didn't much pay attention to interior décor. All you need to take is your clothing and toiletries. Yor parents will bring the rest," said Crystal.

"That's true. I can't believe my mom saved everything from the time I was a baby. My parents have always been penny-pinchers. You haven't bought anything new, either, Crystal."

"You're right. I prefer recycling everything I can, as you well know." Ever since Stephanie arrived at the farm, she had admired Crystal's handiwork of refurbished pieces of furniture, sofa pillows made of an old crazy quilt, and a porcelain teapot that served as a container for a spider plant. Crystal was the daughter of an artist, after all.

"I like the idea of recycling in every way," said Stephanie.

****

Michael looked out the window. "Oh, shit!" he said out loud. Of course, it had to rain the day he was taking his things to the house—to *their* house, Stephanie's and his. He looked forward to living with Stephanie. Fatherhood scared him, but he knew that, should he need support, he had great men to talk to, with both their dads and Gavin. Especially Gavin, who was also going to be a new father, although he was old. Michael wondered about a man his father's age becoming a father for the first time. Being over forty seemed to him an age where all important things to look forward to in life were over, and life would be rather boring. Maybe a baby would keep Gavin from aging fast.

Michael packed his clothes from his chest of

drawers into suitcases, duffel bags, and boxes, and put one suit and a couple of dress shirts and a pair of slacks in a garment bag. The rest he could get later in better weather.

He looked around in his room—the shelves filled with trophies from football games, tennis matches, and swim meets, as well as ribbons on the wall from debate team competitions. Posters of his favorite bands and sports idols, books, and an old computer, now retired because he used a laptop and a tablet instead. The space reminded him of a dormitory room, a type of room he would not have, a carefree college life he would not experience. Had he made a wrong decision, after all? The classes he'd signed up for were challenging, and the schedule demanding.

What happens when the baby comes? It'll be tough, if I can't sleep at night. What if Stephanie needs more help than she thinks she will?

Both sets of parents could be relied on, but it would be embarrassing to ask for more help than all their parents had already committed to. As requested, Stephanie and he had made their decisions. Their parents had promised to stand behind them, to give emotional support in addition to financial aid. Stephanie and he were strong. It was up to them to show they were not letting their parents down.

"Dad, can I drive your SUV to take my stuff over?" Micheal looked sheepish. "Sorry I didn't ask earlier."

"Of course." Robert looked at Michael over the half lenses of his reading glasses. "Have you given thought to a real vehicle instead of the sports car? First of all, commuting a distance of sixty miles a day with a two-seater in a snowstorm probably won't be the best.

Besides, you'll have to get a car with a back seat for the baby and all the paraphernalia that goes with having one."

"Right." Michael's brain was on overload. He was making a mental list of all that needed to be done, all that had to be bought. A usable car was important. A family car. "Dad, can you help me pick a safe and large enough car? We don't need a new one or anything special. It just has to meet the needs of the baby. I think I have enough money saved from my summer jobs to buy a used vehicle."

"We'll see," said Robert. Michael felt like what his grandfather used to say: "Sitting on air and holding onto nothing."

"Son, you have a few weeks to get settled before the baby comes. It won't be easy to adjust to so many new things all at once. Your biggest job will be to take care of your studies. Consider them your full-time job. You'll be preparing the foundation for your little family's future. From what I see, Stephanie is a capable young lady who will do her part. In a couple of weeks, we'll look at cars." Robert handed Michael the keys to his SUV. "Here, the keys to your moving van. Your mom and I will stop by later."

"Thanks, Dad."

****

Tom lifted several bins of Stephanie's clothes into Alice's car. Items were arriving from numerous directions to Lola's place on the lake. *Two sets of parents, Crystal and Gavin, Alice and me,"* Tom counted, *"I wonder if these two have the slightest clue of how lucky they are.*

****

The Smiths had cleaned, repaired, and refurbished the old baby furniture from storage in the attic— Stephanie's old crib, changing table, and chest of drawers, all now bright white with new paint. A high chair, a swing, a playpen, a brand-new car seat. Stephanie's old car seat no longer met safety standards and Melinda had discarded it. *Such a shame, how it has become a death trap in just seventeen years or so. Somehow, Stephanie miraculously survived it.* With the van Craig borrowed from his business, they headed out to the little house on the lake.

****

The five couples arrived almost all at the same time. The rain had paused for a while, and everybody carried items into the house at an unusually efficient pace. Alice had brought baskets of small sandwiches, homemade cookies, and lemonade for all to enjoy as they sat around admiring the fabulous view after their task was done.

"Well, that wasn't so bad," said Alice, now free of her crutches. "Look at all the stuff! You'll be busy for a while." Stephanie smiled and Michael nodded. "Just think what it's like to move a whole household, years of accumulation." She looked at Tom, as if looking for permission for something.

Tom helped himself to more lemonade and said, "Can you imagine what it's like to move out of a big house like yours?" Tom took turns looking at the Albrights and the Smiths. "Or the Hughes house, for example? You probably didn't know that Dr. Hughes is selling her old place—she's marrying Dr. Naziri." Everyone expressed surprise, thinking the two hadn't known each other for long.

"Well, she got to know him before she went to

Afghanistan, and we don't know how frequent their communication was while she was there. You know, she's rather private." Alice looked at Tom. "I'm also wondering what it's like to move into all those rooms, but we'll soon find out." Tom took Alice's hand.

"You won't believe this, but we've decided to buy Lisa's house," said Tom, observing with a smile the reactions on the faces before him. "Some people downsize when they get older. We're doing the opposite!" Tom shook his head as if even he thought the move an insane idea.

Chapter 44

Magnus was angry, disappointed, and confused.

He'd been in the paint section of the large hardware store, trying to pick out colors for the guest bedroom walls. He wanted to keep the color scheme neutral, use a color that would suit a child's room from birth on and still be true to the colonial style of the home. He was scrutinizing samples of small cardboard slips when he heard a *ping*, the sound of a new email on his phone. He was excited—this could be the answer to the question he had posed to a wallpaper company representative.

Nope, no answer yet. Instead, it was a message from the DNA testing company indicating that more information had been gleaned from his sample. Magnus read that according to his DNA he was likely to have straight hair and liquid earwax. He burst out laughing and received several odd looks from his fellow shoppers and a few store clerks. In the upper corner of the email was a symbol showing that the test had matched him with relatives who might want to get in touch.

What a thrill! Maybe he could trace his family back even farther than the 1700s with the help of relatives in Sweden or England or Ireland. He had a lot to study. He picked up the paint called Serious Sage and left for home, ready to paint, leaving further investigation of his relatives for after the work hours he'd set for himself.

That evening, Magnus poured himself a glass of

wine and reclined in an old chaise longue on the lawn in the back yard. Once the inside of the house was finished, he would tackle the outside. It would take a great deal of research to create a yard in the style of the colonial days, but he would enjoy it all when the time came.

He glanced at the list of relatives who had indicated their willingness to be contacted. There was no guarantee the person he decided to write to would actually write back to him, but if he made his message interesting enough, it could be the start of unraveling the web of relatives in a serious way. He first paid attention to people who had included their full names and cities of residence, among them:

Johan Stenros, ninth cousin twice removed, Uppsala, Sweden

Kerstin Hussein, seventh cousin, Aachen, Germany

Liam Connor, third cousin, Dublin, Ireland

Ninth cousin, twice removed. Magnus wrinkled his brow. He'd have to google the twice-removed part. *That goes back at least nine generations. Johan Stenros might know something about the old cobbler who left Sweden and came across the Atlantic. Maybe my ancestor and Johan's ancestor were brothers.*

So Johan is in Sweden, Liam is in Dublin—both locations rather expected—but Kerstin Hussein is in Aachen, Germany. How did a Swedish girl married to a Middle Easterner—or at least I think a man with the last name of Hussein is her husband—end up in Aachen? This stuff is fascinating!

Magnus would definitely take the time to contact these relatives as soon as he had a little free time to concentrate on what to say in each case. There was still no information about possible diseases or susceptibility to them.

He was about to put the email aside when he noticed a relative with just initials. "D.D., half-sibling, Haudenosaunee, NY USA" jumped at him.

What the hell! This can't be DeeDee, or could it? If not her, who else could it be? It's just not possible. Of course, on the surface anything is possible, but how? Half-sibling? My mother certainly didn't have another baby thirty years ago. That I know for a fact. Dad? Really? No way!

He called DeeDee, his heart pounding.

Without greeting Magnus on the phone, DeeDee said, "Tell me it isn't true! Tell me there was a mistake in the testing procedure. They screwed up something, didn't they? This is not possible, is it? Tell me it isn't." DeeDee had received Magnus's half-sibling designation as well, indicating he was willing to be in touch—as if it were needed!

"I suppose a testing mistake is possible. We'll look into this, but you realize what this means if it really is true? This is the end of our parent-partnering effort."

"I know! How can we find out fast? Would Christine know?"

"I doubt it. We've never been close, but she would have told me about something this huge. I'll give her a call in a couple of hours when she's home from work and we can talk freely."

Magnus restlessly considered the variables. If the company made a mistake in testing, the procedure could be repeated. If the company was in the clear, he faced thinking of his dad in a new light.

He remembered his father as an academic, the head of the political science department at the university. He even dressed the part, wearing corduroy slacks and jackets with suede patches on the elbows. When he left the house, he'd always carried a black leather briefcase. In later years, he went back to his 1970s hairstyle—longer in the back, his slightly wavy gray hair touching the collar of the jacket at the neck. He was often gone on lecture tours a few days at a time, which to Christine and Magnus meant a slight loosening of healthy food rules. Their mother allowed them to have potato chips, candy, and those puffy orange snack foods usually reserved for the parents' cocktail hour.

If it was true that John Lindqvist had fathered another child, he certainly had had plenty of opportunities for it. Angry at the thought, Magnus tried not to judge his father precipitously, but if the DNA testing wasn't the culprit, their father was. How disappointing that would be. He felt sorry for his mother, wondering if she knew. Did his father even know? He may have gone to his grave thinking he only had two children. That didn't solve the issue in any way. Magnus hoped that, had his father known about the baby, he would have acknowledged her.

Christine was equally shocked. "Are you kidding?" she said, accentuating every word. "There's no way! Dad was devoted to Mom. They did everything together."

"Yeah, when he was around," Magnus reminded her.

That left a huge hole for Christine to fill in all possible doubts she had. "I just can't believe it. They must have messed up in the lab. Maybe…" She paused for a second and then declared in her confident-CEO-fashion, "I know what I can do. I have a friend—I've told you about her, Dr. Laura Kwan. She's a biochemist who does genetic studies. I'll see if I can have myself tested and matched. That would be quick. Laura will do it as a favor. She's the one with a son who has muscular dystrophy. I've helped her a lot with his adaptive equipment needs. Let me call her right now."

Christine, his older sister, always there with an answer. A call back from her confirmed her ability to have the test run the next day.

"By the way," said Christine, "I was going to call you with my big news. Of course, it has now shriveled to nothing compared to yours—I sold my business."

"You what?"

I sold the whole kit and caboodle."

"Really? What made you do that? I hope you got a good price."

"Oh, yes, I was very well compensated. Remember how I wanted to buy your house before you bought it? Already, then, I was ready for a change. But I didn't realize then that to have a real change I needed to unload my business, the only thing in my life causing me stress, with sleepless nights and nightmares, alternatingly. I am tired of the boardroom, the regulations, the tax issues. I'm coming home."

"You're coming back to Haudenosaunee Hills? For real this time?"

"I am. It'll take me a couple of months to find a place. If I can't find one, I'll have a house built. Do you mind if I bunk in with you till it's done? Or maybe I'll find an old wreck my handy brother can help me renovate." Magnus could hear the gentle needling in her voice.

"That's possible. You're more that welcome to stay with me. As you know, I have loads of room. What's your plan when you get here? You're way too young to retire."

"I'll take some time to recuperate from the rat race. Maybe I'll do some consulting. Occupational therapy has never left my bloodstream. Anyway, I'll give Tom a call tomorrow. What do you know about the housing situation in the Hills?"

"Not a whole lot. The last news was that people from New York City who could work online from home were moving upstate. The Finger Lakes seems to be a particularly popular choice for a country house. But Tom has his finger on the real estate pulse, for sure."

Magnus walked into the living room. He picked up the large photo of his parents from the mantelpiece: Carol, the stylish woman with her hair in a careful chignon, and John, the handsome Norseman, both with Mona Lisa smiles that perhaps hid secrets and lies, a tangled web of deceit.

He touched the back of a wingback chair by the fireplace, the chair his mother had taken from the house into her assisted living quarters, a chair that had been his father's favorite. Magnus sat in it, looked around, and grabbed his father's letter opener from the cherry side table. It was a long ivory knife, an ornately carved item obviously brought into the country before ivory trade became illegal. Or maybe it was a clever replica, a complete fake. A complete fake, like his father. Magnus couldn't tell. He knew metals. He was at a loss with bones, and even more so with synthetic materials.

Chapter 45

Kaisa arrived at Alice and Tom's house, immediately looking around the rooms and eyeing the furniture.

"Now that you'll be moving, I suppose you can still keep my piano. I will pay for the extra moving expenses and the tuning after it's been settled in its new spot."

"Sure, Mom. Lisa has a grand piano in her music room. Your baby can go right into its place. That house is so much bigger than this one that we can take all the furniture with us. Lisa and I are actually talking about having her sell some of hers to us, too. She's moving into a house that's fully furnished, as you know."

"It is. May not be her taste, though. Lisa has a lot of family treasures with memories attached."

"I know. I wouldn't dream of trying to have her sell me things she loves or is attached to, but I sense that after her Afghanistan assignment, she now values different things, things that are less tangible."

"That's actually not a bad thing," said Kaisa. "I sometimes wonder why I hauled some of my stuff here from Finland. You know, books that nobody else can read, well, except you, woven things very few appreciate. Only weavers understand the complexities of things that come off a loom. Do you have coffee?"

"I'll make some," said Alice and disappeared into the kitchen.

Kaisa looked at some of the furniture pieces that had found their way into Alice's house at the time of her own downsizing. Now they'd get a new home again.

What on earth are they thinking? They have a perfectly fine house, built at a time when construction work was still solid with quality materials, and now with both children gone in a few years, ideal for two people. Heavens, they could live in this house till the end of their days, especially since it's all on one floor. It's Alice, of course. With these impulsive decisions and whims, it's always Alice. She gets something in her head and won't let go, and somehow Tom goes along with her. Too late for him to grow a spine. Lisa's house is way too big for them. Alice already has an overflowing plate, and to add a big house to take care of is too much. Plus, she's even talking about a garden. It's total craziness. Maybe Pam will be able to help, living at home, but that's another thing: It's great that Pam's trying to save money, but what she really should do is fly out of the nest. It would only do her good. She's too serious. But far be it from me to try talking some sense to Alice. She doesn't listen anyway!

Alice handed Kaisa a mug with the text on the side: 'Exhale!' How suitable for Alice. Tom probably gave the mug to her on a day she was whirling about, unable to catch her breath.

Alice called to Tom in the office, "What time did Magnus say he was coming over?"

"After dinner some time. Does the time matter?"

"No, not really." Alice turned to Kaisa. "Why don't we take a sauna before dinner, then?"

"Works for me," said Kaisa. The sauna. In the move, they would lose the sauna. Of course, the Hughes house was big enough to build one in it with no trouble. "Is Pam joining us?"

"No. She went to see Stephanie at the lake after her classes. Now that Pam is in college full time and Stephanie is playing house in Lola's cottage, the contrast in their lives is really accentuated. I can only hope the two can appreciate what each is going through in their chosen lives."

"I'm surprised the parents came around to help the kids," said Kaisa. "Of course, who knows what goes on behind closed doors in each household. I have to hand it to you. You had a big part in getting everyone involved. I hope you're done with these rescue missions for a while."

"Don't worry, Mom. The new house will keep me busy."

Magnus arrived and handed a large bottle of expensive vodka to Tom. Responding to Tom's raised eyebrows, Magnus said, "We can all use some fortification today."

Clear as mud, thought Tom.

Tom and Magnus settled to a game of chess with vodka martinis, straight up. Alice had given in to her mother's wish to have a white Russian and opted for one with her. Alice was concerned about the medications Kaisa was on: one for the tremors and one for the hallucinations. There could be serious interactions with alcohol.

"Of course, everybody knows you're not supposed to mix alcohol and prescription drugs, but it's not like I'm a lush," Kaisa said. Little did Alice know she had hidden the medication meant for addressing the hallucinations. Kaisa knew she wasn't hallucinating. It would be irresponsible to medicate herself for it! She would take the drug to the annual event for disposing of medications when the police department next scheduled it.

The drinks tasted good. The women continued their talk about the upcoming move, seated in the comfortable sofa and armchair by the fireplace.

The chess game was over sooner than expected, and Tom was surprised that he had won. That never happened with Magnus across the chessboard. Magnus fixed a second round of drinks for everyone. Kaisa put hers on the side without making a number of it.

"I can't believe I beat you," said Tom, while the men walked over to join the ladies.

"I just can't concentrate. I have some pretty big news. It has to do with DeeDee and me."

"She's pregnant!" Alice burst out.

"No, she isn't, and she won't be. Not by my sperm anyway."

Magnus related the whole experience of finding DeeDee as a possible parent partner, the tale Alice and Tom had heard before but listened to dutifully as Magnus seemed to have a need to relive the story himself. He described the excitement they had felt realizing how much they appreciated various qualities in each other, how they would be perfect in complementing each other as parents of a child.

Kaisa took a sip of her drink. "Tell me, I'm old and only know how to make babies the old-fashioned way. How does this actually work? I take it you wouldn't have sex with her."

"Mom!" Alice interrupted. "You're getting too personal."

"Well..." said Kaisa.

Magnus smiled. "I don't mind talking about it. It's actually the same principle as artificial insemination in the farm animal world."

"Eww," said Alice, her eyes riveted to Magnus.

"You know, the veterinarian does the job, and the poor animal misses out on all the pleasure. With people, I actually like to call it artificial intercourse."

Kaisa leaned forward toward Magnus. Alice looked away, yet stayed glued to her seat. Tom wondered what was coming next. Kaisa had asked the question he himself had felt too apprehensive to ask.

"You know," Magnus continued, "I would go into a bathroom or another private place and do my thing. Then DeeDee would go in and actually empty the filled syringe into her vagina. Then we would light a cigarette." Magnus waited for a reaction. It looked like his attempt at humor had failed miserably, or his audience hadn't even heard what he'd said at the end, still trying to digest the entire description.

"That's interesting," said Kaisa.

"I don't know..." said Alice.

"So, anyway, this is not going to happen."

"It isn't?" asked Alice.

Everybody took a sip of their drink, Kaisa dipping into the second one in spite of Alice's warning hand on her arm.

"No, it isn't. Here's why. We were curious about qualities and quirks we both have, and wanted to know more about where they come from. Also, we were interested in possible inherited diseases, and DeeDee was curious about her ancestry. She doesn't even know who her biological parents were or are. So, we had DNA tests done, and—let me just put it this way—we are so happy we did. Turns out DeeDee is my half-sister."

"What?" exclaimed Alice, as if she were unable to process the message.

Tom had a look of disbelief. "There must be a mistake."

Kaisa took another drink and remembered a moment very close to this when she was sitting with Lola on a bench outside the seaside sauna on the Baltic. Lola had confessed to her that she had had a years-long serious love affair with John Lindqvist and that John was Crystal's father.

"Well, I must say I'm not that shocked. First Crystal and now DeeDee."

"Crystal?" Alice was confused and now worried. In addition to hallucinations, was her mother making up stories as she went along? "Is there a connection?"

"Is there a connection? You're damned right there is."

Alice thought hard. She recalled how, years ago in their Chrysalis days, Crystal and Magnus had both commented on a slight tic by their eye, a strange little quirk. Crystal had said hers had been checked and it was nothing to worry about. Magnus told everybody his was inherited from his father. Alice started to see the connection and the enormity of the finding.

Kaisa now regretted opening her mouth. She felt like a traitor. She had promised Lola she would keep the secret that only Lola, Crystal, and she knew.

"Crystal? What are you talking about?" asked Magnus.

"What? Oh, nothing at all. I must be confused," said Kaisa trying to save the situation.

"Mom, I think I know what you are talking about. This is serious stuff. I think you should tell Magnus what you know, and he can determine what he does with the information."

"What exactly do you know, Kaisa?" Magnus was about to implode.

"Well, first of all…" Kaisa swallowed hard. "I'm sorry I let that frog out of my mouth. I should know better. Maybe it's the White Russians talking." Kaisa pushed the almost empty second glass away from her toward Alice. "When Lola and I were in Finland, she confided in me. She had never told anyone about Crystal's paternity, but she had a great need to confess to someone, and I happened to be the lucky one."

"Does Crystal know, herself?"

"She does. The truth came out when Lola and Crystal were sorting out Lola's friend Margaret's things after her death. Crystal figured out the tic connection from a picture, and Lola told her the truth. But that's a whole other story you don't need to worry about."

"The tic connection?" Magnus was confused.

"You know, your father's tic, the one you and Crystal both have."

Magnus started to pace the floor back and forth, holding his head with both hands. First DeeDee and now Crystal. How many others were there? Who was this man? He loved his father, but he had just lost all respect for him.

"This is really too much! I had hoped beyond hope that the laboratory had made a mistake, but when Christine's friend verified the results of the test, I knew it was true. But this! Crystal is my sister? This is hard to take." Magnus headed for the kitchen for more drinks.

"No more for the women," Alice called out to him. "By the way, Mom, with Stephanie no longer in the guest room, you'll stay here for the night. Magnus can crash on the sofa or call an Uber. Nobody is driving tonight."

Tom was quiet. Now that he thought about it, he knew that small tic was shared by John Lindqvist, Magnus, and Crystal. They all seemed to wink from time to time. An innocuous but sexy little feature that would probably encourage a potential romantic partner, just like the cute dimples on Alice's cheeks had influenced him a long time ago.

Chapter 46

"You're up early," said Kaisa entering the kitchen where Tom and Magnus were having a breakfast of oatmeal and blueberries.

"Six is not early for me," said Tom. "Good morning! How did you sleep?"

"I slept well once I was actually able to fall asleep after a bombshell like you delivered, Magnus! It was tough. Even the vodka didn't help. I can just imagine how you feel, and then I had to add to it." Kaisa sat down beside Magnus. "I should've kept my big mouth shut."

"No, no. My world view has been altered a bit. My own life is still the same. I'm the same actor. Only the stage has been revamped. I just have to get used to it. Christine's return to the Hills will help a lot. She'll probably be staying with me until she can find a place of her own."

"Is that what you want?" asked Tom. "There aren't too many houses available. I think Alice and I grabbed the last great house that isn't a new-built. If we didn't have to sell ours to buy the Hughes house, she could move right in. Or, we could sell it to her, but her standards are probably a lot higher that what this house has to give."

"She said she would be calling you soon. She did say that she'd be looking for a small ranch, or build one."

"This house is definitely small and a ranch, but it's

somewhat dated. Also, would Christine want to live this far away, in the outskirts of town?"

Magnus wasn't sure. "Right now, she lives in a condominium in one of the high rises in the middle of Seattle. You can see the Space Needle from her place."

"Well, we can't offer that," said Tom. "Maybe she would settle for the tall monument commemorating a meeting place of several of the local Native American tribes. You can see it from the back deck in winter time with no leaves in the trees, if you know where to look, that is."

"Christine is used to living such a busy life, I'm wondering if she'll adjust to a quiet life with nothing happening. Well, I take that back. Things are definitely happening in individual people's lives, but outsiders don't necessarily know about it. Christine's divorce changed her. After she left her husband, she dove right into developing and running her company. I don't think she even took weekends off most times."

"Haudenosaunee Hills will make her slow down. Her childhood friends are still here, so the foursome can go back to where they left off at high school graduation," said Kaisa. "You know, this place really is like a small village, even if it's called a city. Just think of the people moving around in a small circle: Crystal moved to the farm and I bought her condominium. Lisa has now moved into my old place, and"—Kaisa nodded into Tom's direction—"now you're moving into hers. If Christine moved into your house, the game of musical chairs would be perfect with everybody a winner, no one left without a chair, er, I mean a house. Ridiculous, isn't it?"

"Unusual, anyway," said Tom.

"So." Kaisa turned to Magnus. "What happens now with the DNA-study results?"

"We'll go on as good friends. The idea of being related brings on a whole new dimension. Is that what you meant?" Magnus saw an expression on Kaisa's face telling him that he hadn't quite hit the nail on the head.

"No, I mean, did the results say anything about DeeDee's mother?"

"Not yet. She'll have to investigate all the names that come through as relatives. It only works if the other person is in the company's data base also, if they have had the DNA test completed. So far, all we know is that she's thirty-nine percent Sub-Saharan African. I think she said that area encompasses forty-eight countries. DeeDee said she counted. Like I said, she hasn't concentrated on her mother yet. The identity of her father was such a jolt, she'll be recovering from it for a while. We both will, as will Christine."

"No doubt," said Kaisa.

"What do you think Crystal's reaction would be, if I contact her?" Magnus asked.

Kaisa thought for a minute. "I think she would be supportive. She's an innocent party in this. She kept the secret, unlike blabbermouth me! I think Lola's opinion of your father will go down two more steps when she finds out."

"I wouldn't blame her. My opinion certainly changed, as did my sister's. You think you know someone well all your life, and you really only know the superficial or maybe what they want you to know or what you want to accept knowing."

Alice walked into the room, rubbing her eyes. "What? Nobody made coffee?" she said and set out to grind some coffee beans.

"How are you feeling, Mom? I really worried about those drinks and your medications."

"And I really worried about the two pieces of pie you ate for dessert."

"Then why did you bring it?"

"You aren't the only one here. Tom has two hollow legs. He could eat a whole pie and not gain weight."

"This is true," said Alice and felt guilt-ridden for having broken her promise to herself once again. The pie was not going to help in her weight loss efforts, but she hadn't been able to resist it.

Pam appeared in the doorway.

"When did you get in last night?" Alice wanted to know.

"Around midnight, I guess. Michael was studying, and Stephanie and I spent a long time talking about, you know, stuff. I wondered what happened here. Grandma and Magnus spent the night? I mean..." Pam blushed. "Yeah, how come you guys are here? Sorry to be so blunt."

"Just a coincidence." said Alice.

"Coincidence that we were here at the same time. No accident that we had too much to drink and had to stay over," confessed Kaisa.

"Mom!" Alice looked at her mother with disapproval.

"What? I'm telling the truth."

"Maybe I don't need to know," said Pam. I'm going back to Stephanie's on the lake. Crystal is coming over this morning to do class number two in the abridged childbirth course she's doing for Stephanie and Michael. I'm 'auditing the class for no credit.' Pam added air quotes to her statement.

"At this hour?" Kaisa was surprised.

"It has to be this early. Michael's first class is at eleven. He's excited about participating, though. He wants them to have a fulfilling birth experience as a couple."

"Will you also be there when it happens?" Kaisa was curious. "In my day, you just had your husband there, or not even him. Some women did it alone with just the medical staff helping them. I heard there were too many men who almost fainted at the sight of blood, and they became extra patients for the staff to take care of. Of course, this was in the day when just a few couples took Lamaze classes."

"Times have changed," said Pam politely. "I won't be part of it when the time comes. Just curious. I've studied childbirth a lot because of Stephanie, and I'd like to see what the real deal is about. Crystal will tell it like it is. They're just letting me listen and observe."

"That's good." said Alice. "Isn't that good, Mom?"

"Knowledge is always good," said Kaisa. "Is that coffee ready yet?"

Chapter 47

September mornings in New York State are sometimes stifling. Hot air trapped in the valleys creates an oppressive feel of being closed in, a feel of having to breathe air that doesn't move.

Stephanie had had a difficult night. With no air conditioning in the small house, and Michael's warm body next to her in bed, she was sweaty and uncomfortable. Being unable to sleep on her stomach, her preferred sleeping position, made her wake up several times during the night. Sleep's intended impact of returning a person to the previous energy and mental awareness level was interrupted. Stephanie woke up groggy, wiping matted wet hair off her forehead.

Crystal was coming over to review the first stage of labor and to introduce the second, the actual birth. Stephanie had secretly laughed at Pam, who had rushed to the library after finding out about Stephanie's pregnancy and devoured all the information she could in the books as well as online. Stephanie found it odd. Pam wasn't even pregnant. Stephanie herself had strangely pretended the pregnancy wasn't real...or if it was, it meant a protruding belly and discomforts of all sorts. She hadn't thought of there being baby in the picture, an actual human being, until she felt the first kick. The support group of her contemporaries had been a great help in bringing her to acknowledge that pregnancy was not a scientific experiment but truly a human endeavor, an event that changes your whole life.

Stephanie got out of bed and walked outside into Lola's flower garden. Crystal had had a difficult time tending it due to the demands of her job at the hospital and her dedication to helping Gavin with some of the farm tasks. Stephanie would pay attention to the garden in the spring, when she again was able to bend over successfully.

Michael was sleeping. Stephanie let him. He was organized to the point of annoying those around him. He had made sure his regular studies were completed before he went to bed the night before. Already he realized that the two long term papers during the semester were due two weeks after the baby's projected birth. He wanted to write the papers before the birth. He had been told by all mother figures around him that having a newborn who doesn't sleep much will not mesh with writing and even less with thinking.

Stephanie made herself a cup of decaffeinated tea, let it steep strong, and plopped numerous ice cubes in the glass pitcher. Kaisa had taught in the nutrition class that making your own iced tea is much more economical than buying bottled tea and avoided the excess sugar that most brands added.

The lake was mirror-smooth. In the distance, Stephanie saw an old man sitting quietly in his little rowboat, fishing. Crystal said he had appeared there for years, every morning in the same spot, except for a period of several months a few years ago when his wife was dying and he didn't leave her for a moment. The whole community knew it, and when he returned with his old familiar baseball cap, they knew his wife had passed and he wanted to continue living the life he had known. Same boat, same yellow bucket for the fish. He was a symbol of continuity.

Stephanie walked to the dock, sat down with some awkwardness, and dangled her feet into the water. The water was almost as warm as the air, and she wiggled her toes in it.

****

Stephanie, Michael, and Pam sat on the floor of the living room cross-legged, their eyes riveted on the chart Crystal had made. On it were the three stages of labor: effacement and dilation, birth, and delivery of the placenta. Crystal had covered the first stage. To Michael's horror, the first stage takes about twelve to sixteen hours, on the average, and as labor progresses, contractions become longer and stronger, sometimes almost unbearable. Crystal stressed Michael's part in the process as support to Stephanie. When he realized what was expected of him, he delved into the issue with great interest, often getting up in the middle of the night to google this or that unfamiliar term, until he felt comfortable. He had gotten lost on the pages of information about all stages and phases of childbirth. He even started studying possible complications. When he found himself starting to tense up and worry, he decided to leave complications alone.

Michael was able to ask intelligent questions of Crystal and impressed Stephanie and Pam no end. Michael came to a conclusion that if Stephanie and he made it through the long labor, the worst was over.

"So, it's the labor that's really the most difficult part, isn't it?" he said to Crystal. "The birth doesn't take much time at all, really."

"No two labors and births are alike. The information out there, including what I tell you, can give you a general idea, but there's really no way of knowing. I have some movies I recommend you watch. They aren't sugar-coated. They're made to be realistic, using good taste. Let's practice the breathing and relaxation techniques. Some people call them hoohaa when their labor progresses and the contractions get really strong. At that point, if they doubt the efficacy of the breathing and conscious relaxation techniques, I tell them to try a contraction without using them—and let me tell you, they quickly go back to them! Relaxation is especially important. You want to let your uterine muscle contract without the rest of the body interfering with it. Did you know the uterine muscle is the strongest muscle in the female body?"

"Wow!" All three said simultaneously.

"I feel kind of proud, you know," said Michael.

"About what?" asked Stephanie.

"I'm going to be thinking of all this stuff on my way to my first class today. All other students will be thinking of, you know, fast cars, the football game, the girl they met at the bar last night, the hiking trip they're planning..." As Michael spoke, he began to doubt his declaration of pride. Why was he thinking about what was in the minds of other college kids?

Michael left the driveway in his convertible, and Stephanie watched him go. *At least he will feel a breeze on his way to the university.*

Pam was just about to leave when Crystal said, "Stephanie, would you get me a large bath towel? My water just broke."

Both girls froze into statues.

"You know, a towel. A big towel to absorb the amniotic fluid. Even if some came out, it will keep generating more and it will keep coming. We just covered this. Sometimes the amniotic sac breaks as the first sign that labor is starting. Sometimes it's a little early, like in my case. The towel, please."

Stephanie ran to the linen closet.

"We have to get you to the hospital as soon as we can, don't we?" Pam was ready with her car keys.

"First, let's get me to the farm. I don't want to drive myself. If contractions start, they may be a little stronger than usual, with the water having broken."

Pam drove Crystal. She felt a great responsibility on her shoulders. The trip to the Pure Earth Farm had never been this long. Stephanie followed, driving Crystal's car. Her heart was pounding. She wasn't used to driving and found it difficult to concentrate. Arriving on the farm, she drove the car half into a dahlia bed. Gavin walked by the car and shook his head.

Crystal was a picture of calmness. She announced that the contractions had started.

"Gavin," she said, "you should probably change if you plan on taking me to the hospital."

"Oh?" said Gavin looking down at his dirty denim overalls covering a plaid shirt. "I'll do a quick change."

Crystal had packed her small bag a couple of weeks earlier, and now she called her obstetrician. As she had guessed, he advised her to go to the hospital. Crystal explained to the girls that the amniotic fluid was going to be looked at for presence of meconium.

"What's that?" asked Stephanie.

"It's the baby's poop," said Pam proud of her knowledge of this tidbit.

"Technically the first stool, yes," said Crystal. "Sometimes, meconium can be a sign of fetal stress, so we need to check for it."

"Fetal stress!" Stephanie was alarmed. "Shouldn't you get going? Why is Gavin taking so long?"

"Relax. It's okay. Everything will be fine. The water braking before labor starts only happens in about ten percent of pregnancies. And now, the contractions have started. Just think, I have three less weeks to be pregnant in this beastly heat."

Stephanie put her hands on her abdomen. "Tell me about it! I hope the weather changes for the next few weeks."

Crystal breathed slowly and deliberately. "That was a little stronger! I hope it'll go fast. Wish me luck."

"Good luck, Crystal!" said Pam and hugged Crystal. Stephanie followed, "Yeah, good luck. I know you'll be great. Have Gavin call us when you've had her. It's a girl, right?"

"I don't know. I don't want to know."

Stephanie knew her baby was a boy, but she wanted to keep it a secret from Michael, so she had told no one.

****

Crystal giggled at the thought of going into her place of employment through the official large main entry doors. An orderly met them with a wheelchair at Gavin's truck, and Crystal slid down from the cabin seat. Only a gurney would have made her feel sicker and more disabled, a woman who was a picture of health other than the mode of transport into the hospital! But she was familiar with the regulations and obeyed dutifully by sitting in the wheelchair.

It was as if Crystal had arrived home. All the staff

were familiar to her. As she was settled in the birthing room bed with Gavin at her side, the nurse announced that the doctor would be arriving momentarily.

A few minutes later, the door swung open. "Hi, cookie!" said Lisa.

Chapter 48

"Let's take a look at you," said Lisa after Crystal stopped crying for joy. Crystal had never stopped hoping beyond hope that somehow Lisa would deliver her baby.

"Your fluid is clear, by the way," Lisa mentioned as a casual comment.

"You knew I was a little worried about that, didn't you? Are you on duty?"

"I made a deal with your obstetrician that he would notify me immediately when he heard of your being in labor. All looks good. Labor on! You're in good hands. I'll check on you later." Lisa winked at Gavin, who had found himself an uncomfortable straight chair and dragged it to Crystal's bedside.

Crystal looked around after breathing through another contraction. The room looked different from the laboring mother's point of view. The fetal monitor was beeping with an even rhythm. The birthing bed was actually much more comfortable that she had imagined. She tried hard to be a patient rather than a nurse who needed to pay attention to all aspects of the proceedings and routines of the room. Crystal had had contractions, but now she was finding out what made the mother's face turn into a grotesque grimace. She concentrated on breathing while Gavin wiped her forehead with a cold washcloth and comforted her by massaging her back until the moment Crystal could no longer tolerate anyone's touch, including Gavin's.

The day turned into evening. Crystal attempted to catnap between the contractions, which were now coming fast and furious. Lisa checked in periodically. According to her, Crystal was dilating satisfactorily.

A new crew of nurses arrived at shift change, surprised to see Crystal. The atmosphere was low key and quiet.

Morning arrived and, after what seemed endless hours, noon. With no windows in the room, Crystal started to feel claustrophobic, something that would never have occurred to her when working in the same room. She was tired. She was discouraged. She was teary-eyed.

With another examination, Lisa gave Crystal permission to push. She felt relieved that now she could actively do something. She pushed with each contraction for what seemed to be a long time. Gavin was in awe of the extreme strength it took to bring a new person into the world.

"I have to hand it to you. I don't think I could do it." Gavin's respect for his wife and all women grew with every push.

"Yeah," said Colleen, the nurse attending to Crystal, "just think of pushing a grapefruit through your penis! That gives you an idea." Gavin made a face too indescribable for words. Although Crystal was exhausted, she laughed out loud. *Leave it to Colleen!*

"Here we go!" said Lisa. Gavin saw Lisa as a football player ready to receive the ball. Crystal pushed two more times and her daughter was placed on her chest.

"Hello, Anna!" Crystal said gently. How could

anyone so tiny, so bloody and covered with cheesy vernix, so loud and scratchy-voiced, be so beautiful!

The whole birthing room staff sang the Happy Birthday song while Anna was cleaned, checked, and weighed. Five pounds, three ounces, a perfect baby.

By the time Crystal walked into her hospital room, with Lisa's encouragement, it was late afternoon. She would go home the following day. Crystal was starving. The hospital dinner of baked chicken, mashed potatoes, and green beans tasted heavenly to her. Crystal handed the chocolate mousse to Gavin. She hadn't noticed whether or not Gavin had eaten anything. She had packed protein bars for him. Crystal took Gavin's hand.

"It's been a long time." She stopped to count. "How many hours? You need to go home and get some rest, Daddy!" Gavin beamed.

"I'll just wait till they bring Anna in. I can't leave before I see her again."

After Gavin said goodbye to his little family, Crystal called her mother. She would probably still be awake.

"Hi," Lola answered Crystal's greeting. "I'm glad you called. Mauno and I were just looking at tickets for when the baby comes. How are you?"

"I'm great, Grandma, pack your bags. Anna is here. Anna Loretta."

Lola started to cry. "A girl! Are you all right? Is the baby okay? She came early, didn't she?"

"She did, but she's a perfect five-pounder. Babies gain about a pound a week in the last month of pregnancy. I can't imagine a baby weighing a lot more than she did. I've seen some big babies, but their moms were big, too."

"I'm so happy for you all—we both are. When

would be a good time for us to come?"

"Anytime is fine. If you come right now, you'll probably be put to work. I may need some help."

"I can't wait. Get some rest. We can talk about details later. Oh, and I don't want to be called Grandma. It makes me feel old. I'll think about a name I want."

"Mom, you're so vain!"

Crystal rested her head on the pillow, remembering the roller coaster of emotions and sensations of the last thirty-or-so hours. The phone rang.

"Crystal, hi, this is Magnus. How are you?"

"I'm fine, thanks." What she wanted to say was that she was out-of-this-world exhausted, her bottom was sore, and her breasts were tender.

"I don't know how to tell you this, but I'll just say it right out: I was told that you, Christine and I are siblings—or, well, you are a half sibling to us."

A bolt of lightning! Crystal immediately felt bad for her mother. Lola had confided in Kaisa, who was the only one in addition to Lola and Crystal who knew the identity of Crystal's father. Kaisa had let Lola down in a serious way.

"I think I know, but who told you?" Crystal couldn't believe she had just given birth and here she was talking to Magnus about old secrets. Yet the topic was intriguing, and she listened carefully.

"Well, it came out in a conversation at Tom and Alice's house. Kaisa seemed to know. She said this wouldn't be a surprise to you. She'd had a couple of drinks."

"I'm sorry. I think I have kept it a secret to preserve my mother's and your fa— I mean, *our* father's reputations, not that it really matters what anybody thinks of how you live your life. Don't get me wrong. I have nothing against having you and Christine as my brother and sister. In fact, I can't think of better people to be related to." Crystal thought this might be a good time to end the conversation for now.

"There's another thing," Magnus continued with momentum. You know my friend DeeDee, right?"

"Yes, through Alice. We got to know her while we were dealing with Stephanie's issues."

"Okay, right. DeeDee and I were going to enter into a parent-partnering deal. Are you familiar with the concept?"

"Yes, we've had a couple of births with that scenario."

"We decided to do a DNA test for possible helpful information about our families. Also, DeeDee was hoping to find out who her parents were. She's adopted. Well, are you sitting down? Turns out she's my half-sister, which means she's yours as well."

"Holy shit! Sorry. Are you sure? But she's black, isn't she?" Crystal immediately felt ashamed of her simplistic statement.

"According to her DNA, she's thirty-nine percent Sub-Saharan African, fifty percent Scandinavian, like us."

"I actually never had my DNA tested. I guess it never seemed necessary. My mother knew for sure who my father was."

"I believe it. And Dad and you and I have the tic. Kaisa and Alice reminded me."

"Right."

The nurse wheeled Anna into the room.

"Magnus, I need to go. My daughter is hungry."

"What did you say?"

"You heard me correctly. I just had a baby a couple of hours ago. I should go."

"I am so sorry! Why did you let me blab on? Congratulations! You must be so happy. I'm really sorry I disturbed you at a time like this."

"My choice to talk. And thanks. We'll talk more later."

Crystal would have spent some time trying to figure out how the African-American girl ended up as her sister, but she had more important things to do, such as looking closely at the intricate little fingernails of her beautiful daughter, admiring her thick black hair and intense brown eyes, and smelling the amazing new baby scent emanating from the bundle in her arms.

Chapter 49

Tom, Magnus, Gavin, and Bobby wore heavy-lifting back supports to move furniture. Alice had insisted on making sure the men didn't injure themselves hauling the heavy pieces out of the ranch and into the Victorian. They used rented trucks and Gavin's pickup. Lisa had hired a moving service for her move. Today, half way through the day, Lisa's method started to look like a brilliant idea to Alice. The only paid service they had hired was a piano-moving company, which charged by the number of steps the movers had to negotiate. The piano was the heaviest item in the household, and required knowledge of how to handle such a monstrosity. There were two steps out of the ranch, two steps on the pathways into the new house, and another four to get it inside the house. There it stood already, having been the first thing to be moved, a day earlier. Kaisa's beloved baby grand, which Alice had promised to store in her house, to love and to cherish, in good times and bad, now had a perfect spot to live without crowding a living room.

Alice had brought in a large box that now sat in a corner of the dining room. On it, she had written DO NOT OPEN OR ELSE!

Pam had been a great help organizing the move. Each room in the Victorian had a designated number written prominently on a slip of paper on the door frame. Each packed box and piece of furniture had a number matching the room. Pam had first thought of using colors, but with the great number of rooms in the house, she quickly ran out of primary and secondary colors. She felt it was unfair to have the guys try to decipher between magenta, mauve, and fuchsia. Pam had double-checked the numbers on each box, making sure the fours were not too similar to the sevens and that there was a line under the nines to differentiate them from the sixes. No box would need to be moved twice.

Alice and Pam drove from one house to the other and back again, bringing clothing still on hangers, large houseplants, and the most delicate glassware received from Finnish relatives on major life events such as birthdays. Alice never used it, afraid she would break it, so what good was it? She'd made a decision now to bring it out and have people enjoy it. *If it breaks, it breaks!*

Lisa had used a professional cleaning service to get the house ready for its new residents. Alice appreciated it and felt guilty when one of the men brought in clumped grass or street dust on work boots as they tromped onto the foyer's shiny black-and-white-checkered tile floor.

Alice also felt strange for not having hired anyone to clean the ranch they were leaving behind. It wasn't too late for that, but in negotiations with Christine, they'd decided it made little sense to clean the house thoroughly, since Christine was renovating the kitchen and the bathrooms before moving in. She would store her belongings for the time being. Christine had taken no time at all to decide on Alice and Tom's house. The other choices available were houses either too large for one person or requiring too much work inside and out. She knew the ranch, liked its floor plan and size, and made an offer on the basis of a video tour and the fact that she knew the house had been well taken care of.

Alice opened boxes in the kitchen. There were what seemed to be hundreds of spices, only used for a special recipe once or twice. *I wonder what I made with sumac, juniper berries, or saffron?* she thought. Those with expiration dates still months in the future had made the move with Alice.

Alice gave Tom an hour's warning. "Kaisa will be here with lasagna and salad at one. Just so you know."

"Sorry I'll miss all that good cooking!" Gavin had made a half-day commitment and said his goodbyes before returning to Crystal and Anna, who had been alone for the first time since Anna's birth.

They ate from floral paper plates, a phenomenon never seen in Kaisa's house. "Irresponsible waste! Besides, food never tastes good off paper. Next thing you'll tell me is that you serve wine in paper cups!"

"Don't worry. I'll never serve alcohol to you again in anything," Alice huffed and looked at Magnus. "So sorry."

"No worries," Magnus concentrated on piercing a cherry tomato with his fork.

"Did you talk to Crystal?" Kaisa was not deterred.

"I did. I actually goofed up big time. I called her when she was in the hospital and had just had her baby like two hours earlier. I was embarrassed. There she was, on top of the world, and I announce her father had had a thing with yet another woman. She was okay about it, though. A classy lady."

"Yes, she is. I still haven't seen the baby. With school and the move, you know. I had planned on throwing Crystal a baby shower, but the baby came early. I also heard from someone that she didn't want a shower."

"I wouldn't give it a second thought. Crystal is not materialistic. That type of thing is not her style." Kaisa herself disapproved of anything she considered unnecessary hoopla.

"Man, I feel tired. Digesting food is hard work." Tom rubbed his belly. "But we should keep going to get all the stuff unloaded. There are only boxes, and then the bikes and kayaks, et cetera, left at the old house." With three additional truck runs, the job was finished.

Kaisa had made coffee and managed to find real coffee mugs. The entire crew sat on the porch, tired and dirty.

"I need to run an errand." Alice got up. "I'll be right back."

When Alice returned, she was beaming. She opened the door to the back seat of her car, and out jumped a dog, a mix with large paws, long gray-and-white hair, and what looked like bangs in need of cutting.

"This is Barney. He's almost two."

Tom was baffled. "Whose dog is that?"

"He's ours. He can be yours, but I hear that male dogs attach to a place—you know, they guard the house. Female dogs are more apt to get attached to one person."

"He's adorable!" Pam gave her approval with Bobby in full agreement.

"Alice," Tom's voice sounded authoritarian and not entirely convinced of the idea of a new family member. "The question is who will take care of the dog? Where did you find him?"

"He belonged to an elderly couple wo had to move to an assisted living situation where no pets are allowed. Their family couldn't take him either, so I said I would take him. I can even take him to visit the couple somewhere in a park or something."

Tom was frustrated. "And how did you find out about this couple?"

"One of my fellow teachers knows them. He was talking about it in the teachers' lounge."

"Too bad school isn't conducted online anymore," Tom murmured. "Again, who will take care of him? You're at school, I'm at work, Bobby's at school and at his ball practices, and Pam's in college."

"Well, it's not like he's a puppy. He doesn't have to go out all that often," Alice tried.

"Dad, some days my classes don't start until late, and a lot of them are at night. That's the beauty of a community college. I can help. How can you say 'no' to this face?" Pam squeezed Barney's cheeks.

"Yes," Alice was appreciative of Pam's support, "and check this out!"

Alice took Barney to the middle of the porch as if on stage. "Sit!" she said. Barney sat beside her and looked up at her for additional directives. "Lay down!" Barney did as he was told and put his chin on his paws. Alice walked the length of the porch with Barney on the leash after the command of "Heel!" and Barney followed without a flaw. "See?" said Alice. "This is not just any dog. This is a brilliant specimen."

"I have to agree with Tom to a point." Kaisa sat up straighter. "Alice, when Stephanie left and Lisa picked up her cat, you promised you wouldn't look for another cause, another person, or another animal to help."

"I said that, Mom, I know, but I can't help myself. Besides, if we're not on this earth to help those in need, why are we here?"

The silence was interrupted by a songbird's trill. It appeared to be in agreement with Alice.

"She has a point," said Magnus. "None of my business, but if this causes a big problem, I can take Barney."

"We'll be all right," said Pam, now apparently in charge of the issue at hand. She gave Barney a big hug.

"There's a box in the dining room with a threat not to open it written on it. Bobby, would you bring it here, please?"

Out of the box came toys, a bed, food, everything a dog would need. Tom looked at the happy dog, now playing with what looked like the skin of a squirrel. He looked at his family's happy faces. He looked from Kaisa to Alice and said, "Not only are we here on this earth to help, we are here to make each other happy."

Kaisa gave a nod, but her mind went further. *You aren't responsible for making others happy. That's way too much to ask of anyone. You can only make yourself happy. Like they say in Finland, 'You are the smith of your own happiness.'* This argument had been given out so many times by people who majored in aphorisms, Kaisa felt it had been completely worn out, and decided to rethink it.

Tom sat down after petting the supposed new family member.

"There's no way to win, with three generations of women as your opponents," he lamented to Magnus.

"You're most likely right. You gave it a valiant effort, though."

Chapter 50

DeeDee had hardly slept for over a week. She had sent a message to all the people on the DNA site who had indicated their willingness to be contacted. At last count, it amounted to seventy-two. DeeDee was elated. She had biological relatives all over the world. Some names and places were identical with names on Magnus's list. Logical. Although she was curious about her Northern European relatives she shared with Magnus, she desperately wanted information about her mother.

Messages with requests for information came from Sweden, Norway, Austria and Japan, all with either the first or the last name clearly Swedish from Agnes to Arvid, Andersson to Svensson. She apologetically put them aside.

Then one morning, the world opened up to her. A message arrived stating: *I am your second cousin. I live in London, but my family is originally from Nigeria. I'd like to tell you what I know of the person whom I believe to be your mother. Please, send me your email address. If, after what I have to tell you, you are interested in establishing a close contact, perhaps we can Skype.*

DeeDee felt faint. She immediately called Magnus. He wasn't at his most alert at five o'clock in the morning and made no sense of her chatter. Asked to repeat, DeeDee slowed down and told him the hopeful news. Magnus was happy for her, but gave a few words of warning about a possible disappointment. After all, he had experienced a devastating let-down about his father's character.

DeeDee went about her day in a fog. She had thought she knew herself in minute detail, but chances were she could be a totally different individual in a few days. She wondered if knowing where you come from actually changes you. She imagined it would, to a degree. Knowing her father's identity wasn't the same as having intimate information about both of your parents and the circumstances that brought them together.

Her day was full of meetings, individual conferences, and enormous amounts of paperwork. DeeDee kept checking her phone for a possible email, until she realized her message including her email address was still in the draft box. *Damn, a whole day wasted!* At least now her second cousin G.M. in London had what she needed to change her American cousin's life forever.

Another excruciating week went by with no news. New third, fourth, and fifth cousins popped up regularly on the DNA site. No email.

DeeDee couldn't sleep. It was affecting her ability to carry on a normal life.

At three o'clock in the middle of the night, with a full moon shining in DeeDee's bedroom window adding to her sleeplessness, there was an eerie *ping* on her tablet—an email from G.M. *Maybe she can't sleep either?* No, it was already eight a.m. in London.

DeeDee shivered when she saw it was a lengthy email. She needed to concentrate fully to receive what could be devastating news, so she prepared herself by stopping in the bathroom, making herself a cup of tea, and wrapping herself in the tartan throw blanket from the corner of the sofa. She closed and opened her eyes, crossed her fingers, and started reading.

Hello, Denise,

I can only surmise from your name that you were adopted by a French couple, but I'm ahead of myself.

Let me start with ancient history. Back in the late sixties, there was a civil war in Nigeria. Our great-grandparents decided to move to England at that time, to escape the war, I assume. Their two daughters, both in their early twenties, moved with them, your grandmother, of course, being one of them. She had four children: three sons and a daughter. Your mother is that daughter, Sade Odita.

DeeDee tested the name for a fit. *My mother, Sade Odita!* She was familiar with Sade, the singer, and knew the correct pronunciation. This meant she would probably have to correct people for the rest of her life—*No, not Sadie!*

When Sade was growing up, she had a great desire to see the world. She used the Eurail system to see all of Europe. While in secondary school, she was an exchange student to Brazil. She offered to work as a nanny for British and French families on their summer vacations in exotic locations. Early on, she was interested in what made the local government work and her interest led her to study political science and world politics. In 1991, she received a scholarship from the University in your city, Haudenosaunee Hills, New York.

"Bingo!" muttered DeeDee. Sade was a student of John Lindqvist's, the head of the political science department at the university.

There was talk that she left the university and moved

to Binghamton, New York, where she had a baby and gave it up for adoption. In later years, she regretted her decision and looked for you, but there were too many strict adoption laws in New York, so she gave up. It is not clear to me whether Sade ever told your father about you or the pregnancy. Have you located him?

Sade does not know I am contacting you. If you would like to pursue building a relationship with her, I will talk to her. She is now in Belgium, working for the European Union in Brussels. She is there as a representative of France. Her father is French with Nigerian ancestry as well, and Sade has a dual citizenship. She never married and she has no other children.

Please, let me know if I should make contact with Sade regarding you.

Sincerely,

Grace Madder

DeeDee was crying large tears that dropped on the screen of the tablet on her lap. Her effort to have a child had failed for now, but it had brought her something equally treasured—her parents. She was a product of an adventurous, trusting girl and a bright college professor with a roving eye.

A rather old college professor! He must have had something to make women swoon over him! I have a brother and two sisters. Who knows, maybe more will appear when I get a chance to study the Lindqvist side of the family tree!

DeeDee let her imagination and wishful thinking get the best of her. *Now that I know who my mother is, I can get my biological and my adoptive mothers together. Or, maybe not. Mom DuBois would not approve of the whole thing, since she doesn't even know about my quest for having a child. I need to be patient, not like Alice, who jumps headfirst into a body of water without checking on the depth first.*

"Guess what!" DeeDee said to Magnus on the phone. "I found my mother!"

"Wow! I'm so glad! Who is she and where is she?"

"She's Sade Odita, who works at the European Union Headquarters in Brussels. I'm Nigerian!"

"Nigeria isn't part of the European Union, unless I am seriously misinformed."

"No!" DeeDee laughed. "I mean my ancestry is Nigerian. This is so exciting! I got a long email from my second cousin in London, you know, the one I told you about, G.M.? G.M. is Grace Madder. She's very willing to help me get together with my mom."

"That's wonderful! Now you can sleep."

"Probably not until I know she's willing to meet me."

"Okay. Have positive thoughts and go back to bed."

DeeDee had awakened Magnus in the middle of the night again for the umpteenth time. It had become an unfortunate habit of hers, which she would need to watch or she would be in danger of losing a good friend. Now that she had a breakthrough in her search, she could relax a little. However, the night at hand was a lost cause. She picked out a movie to stream, carefully choosing one with a happy ending, the sappier the better.

Chapter 51

There was an air of anticipation among the pregnant teens before Kaisa's final lecture, a quiet momentum that could only be seen in the girls' periodic glances toward the door and low-level whispers among the young mothers-to-be.

The series of classes was ending after the weeks of combined lecture and hands-on-practice sessions on cooking and nutrition.

Kaisa walked in the door with her heavy canvas bag. The girls welcomed her by clapping their hands and whistling. Kaisa was alarmed for a second. She still wasn't used to thinking of whistling as a sign of admiration and approval. In the Finland of her youth, it was extremely rude to whistle after a performance of any kind. It connoted total failure that often caused the performer to leave the stage in a huff or in tears. Needless to say, it was an infrequent phenomenon. Now recognizing the intended purpose, Kaisa smiled widely.

"Thank you, thank you. You have been great students. I believe most of you can take something valuable from the class with you. Anyone care to share?"

Stephanie spoke up. "I think the most valuable lesson from the class is something you said almost in passing one time. You said that the best nutrition for the newborn is breast milk."

Some girls nodded, others looked away, still others

had a smirk on their faces open to interpretation.

"I'm glad. Of course, breast feeding is not my area of expertise. I don't want to guilt those who choose to bottle-feed their babies. My opinion may have come through, but just remember it's only an opinion. *The best one at that,* she added under her breath. Diplomacy was so hard for Kaisa.

Another girl offered a topic that was important to her. She remembered the good advice from the "Stretch It" lesson, a lecture where Kaisa demonstrated how one whole chicken can yield numerous meals from the original oven-baked version to chicken salad to soup, utilizing even the bones for stock. In this way, the chicken was stretched as well as the pennies.

Someone made a side comment declaring their mother to be a wasteful person by throwing out the leftover turkey carcass with lots of meat on it after the Thanksgiving meal. Kaisa was thankful for her ability to keep a poker face.

"I'll remember that you didn't yell at us when we screwed up making something. My mom has no patience with me in the kitchen," said a shy girl who hardly ever opened her mouth.

"I hope I made cooking and even shopping for food fun and interesting. I'm happy that most of you attended the classes, especially since this is all voluntary."

"Now you tell us!" called out the girl with numerous tattoos and piercings. Kaisa understood the girl's sarcastic humor, which had come through in earlier weeks as well.

"Even if you took nothing else from these classes, I hope you'll attempt to stay away from fast foods, sugary and fatty things, and remember that meals can be put together from all sorts of ingredients. There is no rule that spaghetti has to be eaten with spaghetti sauce, that sandwiches have to have a top, middle and bottom. Try them without the top and eat them with a fork and a knife if you want to. Who says dinner consists of meat and potatoes and a vegetable and salad?"

"My dad says that. Well, take away the salad," said a rather plump girl. This sentiment was familiar to most.

"Well," Kaisa continued, "today, we are going to go against everything I have taught you during these weeks. We're going to make a cake. How many of you think it's hard?"

"It's not hard. You just have to open a box, add a couple of things like water and eggs, and bake it."

The statement earned a lot of laughter.

"Did you ever read the ingredients on the side panel of those boxes? Rule of thumb: if you can't pronounce the ingredient, don't use it. We'll make cupcakes out of three ingredients today. They aren't completely healthy, but even I'm not so controlled that a little slip here and there isn't allowed."

"Can we eat the cupcakes when we're done?"

"Certainly. This is an occasion for celebration. But, before we go into the kitchen, I have something for you." Kaisa took cookbooks out of her bag with KW embroidered on the side.

"Do the letters on your bag mean Kitchen Witch?" asked the girl with tattoos.

"Yes, they do," said Kaisa, laughing.

"This is a cookbook for beginners." Kaisa held up a thin book for all to see. It's called 'No-Nonsense Cooking.' The recipes are economical, with simple ingredients, and they are not time-consuming."

Moving into the kitchen, Kaisa asked, "Now, as we are going to bake something, what's the first thing you do?"

"Wash your hands," said someone.

"Excellent! What about the second thing?"

"Warm up the oven."

"Yes. You don't want to have your batter ready, waiting and going flat, while the oven heats up." Kaisa clapped her hand together. "Okay, for this batter, you need only one measuring device: a cup. It can also be a half a cup or a coffee cup. You measure three ingredients with it, whatever it is, and you'll have equal measures. First you mix a cup of eggs and a cup of sugar. You beat them up and gradually add a cup of flour. That's it. Today we pour the batter into cupcake molds, but you can also make a large cake with the recipe. Much better for you than boxed cakes."

The girls were enthusiastic as they went through the process of measuring, mixing, and baking. Once the cupcakes were out of the oven, Kaisa said, "Now, we're done. Why would you want to slab a greasy frosting on these and add even more sugar? Not necessary."

"I've never had a cake without frosting!" said Stephanie.

"Try it—you'll like it." Kaisa winked at her.

As Kaisa said her goodbyes, some of the girls got teary-eyed.

"You've been great!' said the girl with tattoos and gave her a bouquet of gigantic dahlias of various colors. "These are from all of us. They are from the garden of a friend of my mom's."

Kaisa hugged her and got her sweater sleeve caught on a metal chain leading from the girl's ear lobe to the front pocket of her leather vest. Once released, Kaisa wished the girls good luck with their deliveries, their babies, and the rest of their lives.

Kaisa got the most accolades from Stephanie on her way to deliver Stephanie to the lake.

"Mrs. Weston," Stephanie said, "I just want to thank you again for agreeing to do this class. If it had been someone our mothers' age, the girls wouldn't have taken her seriously. And our moms are not great in the kitchen like you are."

"Thank you, and you can call me Kaisa. I know kids your age try not to address old people at all, as they're not sure what to call them. 'Mrs. Weston' to me is my husband's mother. Now that you are about to be a mother yourself, we can be on a first-name basis."

"Thank you. That will be super hard, but I'll try."

With the dahlia bouquet leading the way, Kaisa walked up the steps of Alice's new home, the Hughes house. She wondered if she would ever be able to call it anything else. The steps to the house were rather high, as she had noted on moving day, now realizing her new hip didn't react in any way. Alice could stop worrying and loosen her stipulations on where Kaisa could walk, what steps she could take, and so on. Kaisa observed that Alice had worked tirelessly to get the house settled. There was nothing to renovate or repair. Therefore, each piece of furniture could be placed in its permanent spot. Kaisa did remember, however, that Alice had a habit of getting tired of one furniture arrangement or another and switching things around from time to time for no particular reason.

Barney met her at the door with Alice. He sat dutifully by Alice's side, hair covering his eyes almost completely.

"He's so goofy-looking, he makes me laugh," said Kaisa.

"I thought you didn't like the idea of a dog."

"I love dogs. It's you I'm worried about, but let's not go there again. I got these from the girls." Kaisa turned the dahlias around left and right to reveal all sides of the bouquet. "Can I put them in water for the time being?"

"Sure," said Alice and opened and closed several kitchen cupboards, "If I only could remember where I put the vases."

"A bucket or a pitcher will do," said Kaisa and pulled out a water pitcher from the dishwasher.

"Coffee?" asked Alice.

"You bet. Thanks."

Looking into the back yard from the kitchen window, Kaisa could see the faint line in the grass separating the lawn and what used to be a vegetable garden. She remembered Lisa's parents, mostly her father, toiling in the garden most summer evenings. Kaisa pointed out the demarcations to Alice, who brought out a drawing she had made of her future garden. She had consulted with Lisa, who remembered precisely what bed had had carrots and beets, and which corner had a supportive construction made of sticks in a teepee fashion for climbing green beans or cucumbers. Planned for the areas in between were beds of marigolds to discourage harmful bugs.

"You know," Alice enthused, "I've never been able to have a garden, living out of town like we did. The deer ate everything. In town, I can get to work and enjoy the fruits of my labor. I'll even share the overage!"

"How is Lisa doing?"

"I think she really loves her life now. She's obviously head over heels in love with her husband, and she has taken on the role of a mother very naturally. We'll see what happens when the kids reach puberty. It'll be a little more hectic."

"Well, I think you said it. She loves the role of a mother. Maybe that's what Abdul was looking for: a mother for his children, and Lisa was looking for a father figure, which she gets in the professor. Being an only child, how could she know what she was getting into?"

"Says one only child to another, don't forget! What difference does it make? Lisa loves kids. Come on, Mom, Lisa is an obstetrician dealing with babies all the time!"

"I could buy that argument if she were a pediatrician, otherwise no."

"What's your problem, Mom? Why are you such a killjoy? Why can't Lisa just love the man without bringing the father idea into it? And why can't Lisa just love the kids as well? You don't need a degree to like children."

"I suppose you don't. You know, we always talked about this type of stuff in the sauna."

"You mean we gossiped."

"I guess. What are you going to do about a sauna? Where are the drawings for that?"

"Mom, leave me alone."

Chapter 52

Christine was disoriented. Instead of hearing the honks of cars and the sirens of emergency vehicles seventeen floors down, she heard an indeterminate rumble. She got out of bed jet-lagged and perplexed. The reality of new surroundings quickly became clear to her. Looking out the window, she was back in her childhood. The age-old maple tree was still grasping the soil by its thick roots. A piece of slate, with the name "Amy" printed on it, stuck up from the ground by the fence, where her beloved dachshund was buried. The birdhouse Magnus had made in shop class in high school was still nailed to the garage wall.

A view out of the other window revealed the source of the rumble—two farm vehicles involved in harvesting corn now crept toward town with a line of impatient drivers behind them, their job finished already, before eight in the morning! A true contrast with Seattle.

For many years, Christine had convinced herself that she was happy in the corporate world, making big decisions, moving in circles of money and status. Yet she had been restless. When her mother was still alive, Christine visited Haudenosaunee Hills as often as she could get away which, to her chagrin, wasn't often enough. Carol never made her feel guilty about her infrequent visits. The feeling was there, nevertheless. Christine had always had a secret yen to move back home, to rejoin the friends she still had in town, in particular the Chrysalis sisters who had all stayed put or returned after completing their education.

Christine yawned and stretched her arms, reaching for the ceiling, the ceiling where the once fashionable popcorn surface had now been removed. The new ceiling had to wait until Christine was able to move out and into her own house. She was tired from selling her business, from the process of selling her condominium and buying the new house, the decisions about what to move with her, what to trash, and what to do with things in between those two choices. She was also weary from the recent shock of returning home, and not only to a brother but a brother and two sisters, a good friend of hers being one of them—her mind in turmoil about Magnus's disappointment regarding having a child, DeeDee's relationship to her and Magnus, Crystal being her sister. No wonder she had felt a special bond to Crystal all her life. They were a year apart, which meant that when her mother was at home dealing with a baby, her father was who knows where doing a lot more than lecturing about the Middle East situation. Her parents had seemed happy. Christine had started to doubt her abilities to judge character. Of course, when all this took place, she was too young to realize it. Her mother had never mentioned anything, but that did not surprise her. Could it be that she didn't know, either? If she knew, it was no wonder that Carol was not friends with Lola, unlike her relationship with Lisa and Alice's moms. She must have known. Too late now to know for certain. There was Lola and there was someone else who had a child with John Lindqvist. From what Magnus told her, DeeDee now knew the identity of her mother, and was close to finding out whether her mother wanted contact with her. A foreign student in Dad's class! My God! Christine had mixed feelings about a man who obviously had enjoyed his family and appreciated them and yet was a philanderer and a womanizer, a total jerk! She could only feel sorry for the man whose self-esteem needed bolstering through conquests.

I'm glad they're both dead! Christine shocked herself by her thought that would be judged most inappropriate if uttered in public. Was she so selfish her ego wouldn't be able to stand public knowledge about her parents? She knew that eventually everyone would know the Lindqvists' dirty laundry. People loved tabloid material, and her father had produced a good dose of it. She was glad she was back in town to provide emotional support to her brother. Being gay in Haudenosaunee Hills was difficult enough, even if attitudes had changed considerably in recent years. To have a scandal in the family in addition added a heavy burden on him and now on her. "A shared sorrow is half a sorrow," as Carol used to say. Christine wondered if there was a saying about anger, about disgust, about hate. She and Magnus faced a long winter with serious talks and introspection. They were starting from scratch. Most people had changes foreseen in the future. The two of them had a newly changed past, an oxymoron if there ever was one.

Christine took a shower and spent several hours on the phone, calling the Chrysalis girls. Although Saturday mornings were busy, she caught all of them: Crystal over-the-moon happy with her new daughter, Anna. *I'm an aunt! I have a niece!* The idea of aunthood came to Christine as an unexpected newsflash. Crystal and Christine had a great deal to talk about, conversations that needed face-to-face contact.

Lisa now lived in the old Weston house, Alice's childhood home. How odd! Lisa, the girl who was always "together," always excelling in everything she did, everything she touched, had now conjured up a family for herself without the required pregnancies. Lisa also claimed on the phone that as Abdul was a widower and had been trained in household duties by his first wife, her task in that department was easy. It was also unique that a woman from a different culture had taken it upon herself to act unexpectedly "western."

Christine caught Alice grocery shopping. As usual, Alice had left her carefully prepared list at home.

"Well," Alice said, "I'm safe getting pretty much everything. We used up most of our food before the move. I've got to hand it to you for buying a house practically over the phone."

"I know the house, having been there so many times. It's a perfect place for me."

"You'll make it greater with the new kitchen and bathrooms."

"It's not that they're not usable the way they are. I just want to put my own mark on them, make them look like me."

"I get it. I'm all carved wood, cookie jars and rag rugs. You're shiny, clear surfaces and everything geared toward unencumbered living. Am I right or am I right?"

"You are right. Your style is cozy. Mine has developed into a 'function first' approach. In fact, I'm going to the house today. Tom gave Magnus the key."

It was afternoon by the time Christine drove her rental car to the ranch. She sat in the car for a few minutes thinking of the location of the house. *This is a perfect compromise between Seattle's downtown and a place in the country. No neighbors next to me, but several within viewing distance across the meadow, now yellow with goldenrod...*

Christine walked around the house through Alice's ferns and lavender. Alice had told her not to bother planting flowers, except maybe marigolds. Chistine heard a rustle in the woods. Ther reason for the ban on flowers ran out of the woods—a herd of six, seven, eight white-tailed deer bounding through the back yard.

The tour of the house was a snap. All looked to be in order. The renovation crew would be on-site starting Monday morning. One place in the house Christine hadn't remembered seeing was the basement. It was unfinished except for the sauna. Christine had forgotten about it. How wonderful! As teenagers, Lisa, Crystal, Alice, and she had taken saunas at the Weston house, competing over who could stand the highest heat. Alice always won, but she had an unfair Finnish genetic advantage. Now that they were all in town, they could do it again. As Christine walked up the stairs, she noted a little mouse scooting across the floor. Deer and mice! What other creatures might her new place be hosting? She was enamored with the pseudo-country setting, but was this still too country for her?

Christine stopped at a hardware store to make the final decision on the toilets. She spotted a beautiful young black woman looking at vanities. They smiled at each other.

As Christine was driving home, she caught herself wondering. To see a black woman in a Seattle hardware store was nothing unusual, but to see one in Haudenosaunee Hills was another. The city itself had few black people apart from the university students. She came to a conclusion that the young woman must have been DeeDee. *Is this place really that bigoted and lacking in races other than Caucasian that I could recognize a person I have never met only by the color of her skin? Or is it me?*

Christine knew she and her friends had grown up in a very beige life, void of anything complex or colorful in all senses of the word, without exposure to a wider range of humanity. She considered it a great loss. Yet, here she was, coming back to her roots. It had been a compulsion for her to return. After marriage to a narcissist, a divorce within a few months thereafter, and after owning and running a multimillion-dollar company, she had put an end to what she now called self-abuse. Here she was in a small city, hers to use as a stage for whatever she wanted her life to be. She wouldn't be satisfied with anything half-baked, including her relationships.

Chapter 53

The wind was cool and there was a discernable feel of autumn in the air. Gavin had thought twice before suggesting a sailing excursion up the lake, concluding that if it didn't happen now, it would have to wait till next summer. His guests, Lola and Mauno, were serious sailors, especially Mauno. Gavin had a childlike wish to show his skills to Mauno, a man who had lived his whole life on the Baltic Sea, sailing around the hundreds of islands in the Finnish archipelago said to be the second most beautiful in the world after the Greek islands.

Lola and Mauno had flown over to meet Anna, of course, but also for Mauno to be introduced to the family he had inherited by marrying Lola. He was equally enthused to meet other people in Lola's life and to get the feel of the Finger Lakes region. Mauno had traveled to the United States in his banker days, but he had been exposed only to the banking meccas like New York, Boston, Dallas, and Chicago, metropolises, far different from the little towns on the Finger Lakes whose banks had cozy names like Your Community Bank and Neighborhood Bank.

Although a skillful sailor, Gavin felt inferior to Mauno in his ability at the helm of a boat. The rugged Finn had experienced storms in an area where you could not see the shore in any direction and navigated his boat through narrows straits in shallow waters. Their outing would be purely for leisure, and on a small lake.

The breeze was perfect for a sail and the October colors on the hillsides were breathtaking bright reds, yellows, and oranges. Mauno was in awe. He had seen pictures of the area's fall colors, but he'd secretly thought the colors had been enhanced or photoshopped in other ways.

"You're lucky to hit the colors just right with your timing. Had you not arrived, I too, would have missed them from this vantage point. I've sailed very little this year. Too busy, I guess, although I know you need to make time for things you love, and I do love sailing."

Gavin tacked and jibbed up the lake for a while. They passed Lola's cottage on the shore. Tapping on the tiller, Gavin offered Mauno his captain's hat, which he readily accepted and tested the wind.

Lola lifted her face toward the sun, now milder and gentler than in the hot New York days of summer. She was luxuriously happier than ever before. Her new granddaughter was perfect, and she herself was in a happy, successful relationship. She had had a difficult discussion with Crystal a couple of nights ago. She had let her temper flare when she heard about Kaisa's breaking her trust by letting the cat out of the bag regarding John Lindqvist in front of his son. John's real character was being revealed, one indiscretion after another. Somehow, in her twisted thinking, she had considered it to be acceptable for John to love her and father a child with her. Hypocritically, it was not okay for John to have a child with someone else. Learning that John had had numerous affairs evoked in her a jealousy she found irrational. When she found Mauno and moved to Finland, she had hoped to be able to leave John in her previous life. She had succeeded, to a degree. However, now that Christine and Magnus knew the truth, Crystal had a natural connection that bound them. And little Anna Loretta was John's granddaughter, too.

How was it that she allowed a dead man to unhinge her thoughts periodically? Maybe that was just it! It was impossible for her to face him and let him know what she really thought. She couldn't call him every name in the book, let him know how devastated she was. She couldn't tell him about her traveling the world to avoid him in later years. By dying, he had cheated her one last time, cheated her out of the opportunity to have him hear her feelings. Lola sighed. She knew she needed to forgive and forget, as difficult as it might be.

They sailed half way up the lake, turned around, and on the way back, docked the boat at Lola's old home. Gavin had arranged for them to meet the "renters."

Lola was getting her sea legs and walked like a duck to greet Stephanie on the shore, a fresh-faced young girl with obvious physical awkwardness caused by her full pregnancy.

"Hello," said Stephanie. "I'm sorry Michael isn't here. When I talked to Gavin, I was reading his schedule wrong. Please, come in." She giggled. "Funny that I'm inviting you into your own house."

"It's your house now," said Lola. She looked around.

Before stepping in, Lola noticed the saved twigs. "I see you kept the branches. Planning on a bonfire?"

"I remembered the Solstice celebration, and Michael and I decided to host one next June. You're invited."

"Thank you." Lola was touched. *This girl has only a loose connection to Finland through Pam and Alice, yet she remembered. That shows she's a caring person.*

"I made some coffee. I know in Finland they drink a lot of it."

"Wonderful. Yes, indeed, they do, over twenty-eight pounds per capita a year, if you can imagine! More than any other country in the world."

Lola sat in what still was her couch with her decorative pillows. She felt strange.

As if Stephanie had read Lola's mind, she said, "I want to thank you so much for offering us this house to live in. We are so grateful, and we try to live up to what your expectations are."

"I'm glad to help. It works both ways. It's not good for a house to sit empty for months on end. When is the baby coming?" Lola asked, having already heard that Stephanie was due any time in the next couple of weeks.

"Not soon enough," said Stephanie. "I'm ready— oh, boy, am I ready! When Crystal's water broke right there," Stephanie pointed to a corner of the couch, "I was so jealous. Nine months is such a long time to wait."

The men walked in. Stephanie offered coffee and, to everyone's surprise, *pulla*, Finnish coffee bread.

"I made it myself with Pam's help." Stephanie beamed.

They spoke of the house, and Mauno studied Lola's map of her world travels.

"I am so happy here," announced Stephanie. "Do you have any wishes for the garden? I will attack it in the spring."

"You just take care of your little family. The plants either grow or they don't. Not the end of the world."

Gavin wasn't sure this was the same Lola who just a few years ago had kept Crystal in a stranglehold to make sure her beloved plants did not perish while she was in the Tibetan mountains or the Pompeian ruins.

Gavin moored his boat in the marina. He would store it in a couple more weeks. On the way back to the farm, Gavin gave them a tour of the small city and its immediate surroundings. Lola laughed at the "musical houses caper" now completed by her friendship circle. It appeared Christine's move to Alice and Tom's house was the last maneuver in the game. They passed Kaisa's condominium by the lake. The meeting between them would be interesting. Although Lola had been angry at Kaisa, she was not about to chastise her friend for having had a slip of the tongue. The woman had enough to deal with, from what Alice had told Crystal. Parkinson's disease isn't easy, especially if you also have to suffer hallucinations.

Lola had made a lunch date with Kaisa and looked forward to it. Kaisa, after all, was the reason for her newfound happiness. Without Kaisa, she wouldn't have Mauno.

Crystal and Anna greeted them at the door.

"I hope you don't mind, but I just ordered pizza. I did make a salad, also," said Crystal, handing the baby to Lola.

"Good. I told you not to fuss. Take-out of any kind is great. It's all new to Mauno. Watch him eat pizza with a fork and a knife. A lot of Finns even eat hamburgers that way. They looked at me in horror when I tried to take a bite out of a double-layered cheeseburger, holding the dripping monstrosity with both of my hands!"

Lola sat in a rocking chair snuggling Anna to her chest. She buried her nose in the crook of the baby's neck.

"There really isn't a better smell in the world than that of the neck of a new baby," Lola cooed.

Crystal smiled.

"I've decided," said Lola.

"Decided what?"

"I want to be called Grandma."

"Really? I thought you said the word makes you feel old."

"You say a lot of things when you're young and foolish."

"Mom, you said that just a couple of weeks ago!"

"That was before I met Anna. I had to wait and see how it felt to have a grandchild, and I must say, I feel grand!"

Lola kissed Anna's headful of thick, black curls. Anna hiccupped as if in agreement.

"Stephanie seems to be a rather level-headed young lady." Lola laid the sleeping Anna on the blanket on the couch.

"She's grown up a whole lot in the last few months. Responsibility has hit her hard, and she's dealing with it. The poor thing is so ready to have that baby, but you know how babies are. They come when they feel like it. If she doesn't go into labor soon, they will induce her."

"She is so young," said Lola. "What did you say, eighteen?"

"Not even. Her birthday, as well as Michael's, is in early November."

"Aah," sighed Lola, "to be that young again."

"Do you really feel that way? You'd want to be eighteen again?"

"Only if I knew then what I know now. As they say, 'youth is wasted on the young!'"

"Any other cliches you know?"

Chapter 54

It doesn't take long to internalize new customs and habits. Lola realized she had just made the driver behind her irate by sitting calmly at a red light with her right turn signal blinking. It had taken her a few months and a couple of traffic tickets to learn Finland's law: No turning right on a red traffic signal under any circumstances, a rule Kaisa had warned her about and she had blissfully forgotten until the tickets served as good reminders.

Lola was on her way to pick Kaisa up for their lunch engagement. Although she and Kaisa had not been particularly close through the years, a special connection had developed between them during their time at Kaisa's cottage on the Baltic.

Lola entered the long hallway of Kaisa's building. As Crystal's old condominium, Kaisa's home was familiar to Lola, though she remembered Kaisa had renovated the apartment to suit her if she were to have mobility issues in the future. Lola hoped Kaisa would feel comfortable enough to share with her the true state of her health, both physical and mental.

Once they'd arrived at their lunch destination, the view of the lake from the winery restaurant at its high elevation was amazing. The bright colors Lola had admired from the sailboat a couple of days ago were downhill from them, in the forest sloping to the lake below.

The atmosphere between the two women was strained. Instead of wine, which they expected each other to order, they asked for iced tea, a guarantee for maintaining control.

"So, how are you really?" Lola started the part of the conversation both of them had dreaded and both of them wanted over with as soon as possible.

"What do you mean 'really'? You already asked me on the way here in the car."

"I did, but you didn't answer."

"I thought I did." To Kaisa it sounded like Lola had already been filled in on her status by her daughter.

"I just mean that I know you to be a master at hiding your symptoms and won't accept help, even if needed."

"I'm pretty stubborn, I have to admit. And no, I am not hiding anything. I still have a tremor. At times it's worse than at others, and I know I have to take my medications religiously to keep it in check. As far as other ailments, I really don't have any. My hip is back to normal, and I try to eat correctly and move enough in order to keep my bones strong, and..." Kaisa hesitated before continuing, "contrary to popular belief, there's nothing wrong with my mind."

Lola listened intently.

"Alice is under the impression that I'm hallucinating. She even did her best to convince my doctor to prescribe psychotropic medications for me. I'm not taking them, of course."

"You're not?"

"Hell, no. I know I'm not hallucinating. The only so-called hallucination of mine is the woman living in the condo next to me. I've never seen her. She seems to keep to herself pretty much all the time. And," Kaisa lowered her voice to a whisper, "this is really disturbing—I'm sure she's a murderer or at least she abetted in a murder some time ago."

Lola wrinkled her brow. "What on earth makes you believe that?"

"She had receipts of thing she had bought, suspicious things, like a large canvas, rope, an anchor."

"Why would that prove anything? You haven't seen the person. How do you know it's a woman?"

"Well…" Kaisa now spoke almost inaudibly. "She had a bloody mink coat airing out on the balcony."

Lola now believed Alice was correct. Kaisa had gone off the deep end with her incredible story. *If Kaisa isn't taking her medication, no wonder the woman is so real to her.*

"Have you called the police?"

"Yes, but they won't do anything. They say they investigated, and there's nobody living in that apartment. Tom says the same thing."

"Well, I hope it gets solved soon." Lola was at a loss for what to say. She now realized Kaisa was on shaky footing and decided to tread lightly when it came to Kaisa's telling Magnus about John.

"I do, too. Secrets are never good for anything." Kaisa sighed deeply.

"You're right. I was so upset with you when I heard you had betrayed my trust. I remember that August evening when I told you about John being Crystal's father. You shocked me by being nonchalant about it. You seemed to know him better that I did."

"Are you insinuating something? Are you kidding? I had enough to do dealing with one man. Why would I want another?"

"No, Kaisa, I don't mean that," said Lola and touched Kaisa's arm.

Both women smiled at the strange scenario Lola had presented. Kaisa continued, "Your eyes were blinded. You were in love. I just mean that the man had a reputation, you know."

"I was in New York City in those days, unaware of his double or triple lives. Anyway, when I told you my secret, I assumed it would stay with you."

"I know. I truly apologize. I had had a couple of White Russians. Alice was so upset with me for many reasons and probably still is."

"Although it stings, I'm willing to let it go. You and I are close enough to get over this. Truth should never hurt anybody."

"It shouldn't, but there's always collateral damage somehow. Christine and Magnus have had to thoroughly reformulate their idea of their father. That is most likely a mind-boggling exercise. I'm glad they were friends with Crystal already."

"Yes," Lola agreed, "it would be twice as difficult if there were a stranger in town claiming to be your sister."

"But there is. You didn't hear about DeeDee?"

"Of course I did. How could I not mention her? But she's not really a stranger any more either, is she?"

"She's been in the picture for a while and is as baffled about all of this as the rest of the kids, and they'll always be kids to us, right? But they are all strong people, able to deal with this."

Lola nodded her head, thinking back to the time she was an impressionable kid easily swept off her feet by a charmer experienced in seduction.

"So, we're good?" asked Kaisa to cleanse her conscience one last time.

"We're good," said Lola.

On the way back, they stopped at Crystal and Gavin's farm to pick up a few decorative pumpkins for Kaisa's balcony already decorated by cornstalks and orange lights. The balcony looked festive, matching all the other balconies except for the one next to Kaisa's. It was bare.

"I have something for you," said Lola and brought in a large, flat package from her car. "Here, with a great big thank you!" said Lola and handed Kaisa what obviously was a painting.

"My cottage!" exclaimed Kaisa. "I have just the place for it." She took another painting off the wall above the dining table and replaced it with the painting of a small red cottage with white trim. The crevasses among the rocks and boulders had heather and bilberries growing in them. Beyond the white-trunked birches, you could see the shimmering Baltic Sea with a small sauna on the shoreline.

"My childhood," said Kaisa, the tears running down her carefully made-up face leaving visible wide marks. Lola hugged Kaisa.

"It doesn't seem so long ago, does it?"

"I know. I shock myself every time I look at my hands." Kaisa put her left hand on the table. "Check this out." The women studied Kaisa's old hand, a topographical map of tendon mountain ranges with rivers of veins on the slopes, oddly exaggerated dark gray-blue waterways, large brown age spots merging into each other, and translucent skin so thin it seemed to float on top without being attached to the tissues below.

"When you look at little Anna's plump hand, it's hard to imagine this hand was like that once upon a time, isn't it?" Kaisa asked.

"Your hand is beautiful, too. It tells a million stories."

Lola promised to get together with Kaisa before she flew back to what she now called home. Driving to Crystal's, Lola had a strange feeling. She was sure she had heard a sound of conversation from the unit next to Kaisa's. Of course, it could have come from the apartment above just as well. Lola put it out of her mind.

As Lola was getting closer to the farm, she thought about the conversations between Kaisa and herself. They were two grandmothers whose grandchildren were years apart in age, grandchildren who were wonderful sources of pride—Anna, the innocent newborn, a perfect miracle, and Pam and Bobby, accomplished and sweet, with their distinct personalities. All this to talk about, but what had they discussed? Their past sins and indiscretions, their lapses in judgment—well, mostly hers. Lola wondered if it was even normal for two women not to brag about their families. Were the two of them so selfish, so wrapped up in their own issues that they couldn't soften up a little and be like women who gush about their offspring? Kaisa had always said that Finns didn't necessarily show affection easily. They certainly don't gush. Lola could now verify Kaisa's statement, after having lived with the stoic people for a year and a half.

Kaisa has an excuse. What is mine? she wondered.

Chapter 55

DeeDee had cleaned her apartment from top to bottom, including all closets and cupboards, expending the nervous energy bottled up in her.

It appeared she was a daughter of a cosmopolitan powerhouse of a woman who moved in professional and social circles DeeDee had only read about in ladies' magazines. This high society lady wanted to meet her, first via FaceTime and later in person. It wasn't clear to DeeDee whether the FaceTime contact was a trial run, an interview to determine DeeDee's qualifications for "daughterhood," or an authentic gesture of inviting DeeDee into the world of Sade Odita.

DeeDee felt intimidated. The days were crawling slowly between the notice of a possible contact and the actual date. DeeDee struggled with a possibility of being rejected for one reason or another, not so much by a blunt statement of disapproval but by her mother's gradual fading into oblivion. DeeDee tried to comfort herself. If her mother didn't want anything to do with her, she most likely wouldn't have agreed to the meeting online.

When DeeDee had found Sade Odita, she had hesitantly called her parents in Binghamton. As usual, her father had few words to say, only that DeeDee was an adult who could make her own decisions. Her mother was surprised, not that DeeDee was able to track down her birth mother, but that she had wanted to find her in the first place. She took it as a personal afront. Through sobs, she wondered why she and her husband were not enough, and that often finding your biological mother causes a great deal of heartache. John Lindqvist and Sade Odita were no news to the DuBois couple. They had known the story of the foreign student and her professor. To dig all this up again seemed useless at best and harmful at worst. DeeDee decided to give her parents time. She had dealt with issues of adoption in her job numerous times and knew that emotions won over practicality, at least initially.

Emotions ran high in DeeDee. In addition to cleaning her apartment, she spent countless hours working out in the gym of the apartment building. She kayaked with Magnus and ran with Christine until what she called a day of reckoning.

DeeDee set up her computer in the best possible position away from disturbing lights of any kind. She waited for the signal from Brussels. When she finally heard the ring, she jumped on her seat. She clicked on the green circle with the word "Accept." Her heart was pounding.

"Hello, Denise," said the beautiful woman on the screen in a distinct British accent. She was dressed in a fuchsia suit of an exquisite fit. Her face was perfectly symmetrical and her hair was pulled back revealing a high forehead and large eyes. She looked stunning and stylish.

"Hello," said DeeDee, not knowing how to address the majestic being, and continued, "Ms. Odita."

"I don't expect you to call me Mum, Mother, or Mom. What about Sade?"

"That's fine, Sade." DeeDee was seldom tongue-tied, but this situation was difficult. There was an uncomfortable silence that DeeDee felt an urge to fill, wondering if Sade was testing her communication skills. With that in mind, she continued, "Thank you for agreeing to talk to me. I know this may be uncomfortable for you. If you'd rather keep things the way they have been for thirty years, I'm fine with it. I now know who I am."

"Denise…"

"People close to me call me DeeDee," DeeDee interrupted. "I couldn't pronounce my name when I first learned to talk, so I called myself DeeDee."

"DeeDee, I made a decision to meet you, not out of curiosity about what happened to you, but out of genuine caring. When you share a body for nine months, it's not for naught. I was young and impressionable. Your father was everything a young girl admired: a handsome man with impeccable taste in everything, a brilliant scholar, and he was witty—oh, how witty! He also was older, well, quite a bit older, with distinguished gray at the temples. I found his maturity more attractive than the foolhardiness of the young college boys who surrounded me."

"Did you love him?"

"I was infatuated with him and definitely in lust with him. Maybe you can call it love, I don't know."

"Sade, I need to tell you that I have met his children. His son Magnus looks just like him, judging by photographs. His daughter Christine just moved back into town from Seattle, and then there's Crystal. She's another daughter of John's by another mother. There was another affair."

Sade was hesitant.

"DeeDee, I think I'd like to concentrate on you. Tell me about yourself."

DeeDee told her story from beginning to end, making Sade laugh at some parts and shake her head at others.

Hours later, they were still talking. Sade finally said, "Listen, we don't have to catch up with thirty years' worth of history in one sitting. Let's agree to do this again and I can tell you about myself."

DeeDee felt aghast and embarrassed. She wondered if that was an intended dig. The conversation truly had concentrated solely on her, although DeeDee felt that Sade had invited it. DeeDee wondered how she could be so dense. Any conversation should be a flowing give-and-take, with each party expressing interest in the other. She had monopolized the discussion in telling her mother about herself. Not once had DeeDee asked about Sade's life. *What happened to her after she left the United States after DeeDee's birth? What did she study later and where? Who is she now as a person? What exactly does she do in Brussels for France and the European Union?*

"I'm so sorry. I hogged the conversation. Do you know this rather primitive expression?"

"I've heard it. Don't worry. I do have a dinner engagement at my favorite restaurant, a five-star establishment I don't visit very often. Someday, maybe you and I can enjoy a meal there."

DeeDee had no idea what Sade was talking about, of course. She assumed it was a high-class restaurant in Brussels. If she could have a meal with her mother, she could have it at a greasy spoon up the street and feel equally privileged for it.

"That would be lovely," said DeeDee, "and thank

you for accepting me into your life."

"Thank you for taking the steps to get in touch with me. We'll do this again soon, all right?"

"All right," said DeeDee quietly.

DeeDee leaned back in the office chair and closed her eyes. Her mother was amazing, living in another world both figuratively and literally, with thirty-seven hundred miles between them. A woman of substance! DeeDee continued to chastise herself for not asking Sade anything about herself. Was she so anxious to sell herself, to be accepted, that she acted like a self-centered teenager? Hopefully Sade realized how important this was to DeeDee and would be willing to overlook her childish overindulgence.

DeeDee needed to call her parents, but she decided to wait a couple of days. It was important to be truthful about Sade's welcoming her, but to give her parents a glowing report would be rubbing salt into the already festering sore DeeDee had reopened. It would be insensitive to list fascinating facts about Sade to the DuBoises. It served no purpose, and would put her parents in the position of comparing themselves to Sade, two styles of life that could not and should not be compared. Maybe, if she ever went to Brussels or wherever her mother was in Europe at the time, she could take the DuBoises with her. After all, Sade owed them a debt of gratitude.

DeeDee googled the restaurant Sade had mentioned, and its menu of sophisticated platefuls of culinary masterpieces. *Sade is eating well. When I go there, I'll definitely ask for outdoor seating.*

Awake in bed, DeeDee realized that not once had she or Sade shed tears during their conversation. Sade had said all the right things, but she hadn't come across as a warm person. Nice enough, but oddly distant when talking to your flesh and blood. Maybe that was just it. She was flesh and blood to her, but not heart and soul. Sade needed time. DeeDee needed to be understanding. The world needed to slow down for both of them.

Chapter 56

It was Halloween. Appropriately for the occasion, the wind was howling, with gusts causing the old ash trees on the shore to lose their branches on the ground, another sign that the poor tree was living its last years. Lola had tried her best in years past to save it from the destruction of the ash bore, but she knew she was fighting a losing battle.

Stephanie was oddly calm. She had finally gone into labor earlier in the morning, with infrequent contractions stronger than the Braxton-Hicks "practice" ones. The doctor had told her to wait until the contractions were stronger, longer, and more frequent before leaving for the hospital. She had talked on the phone with her mother, Crystal, Alice, and Michael's mother, who was at the JFK airport awaiting departure. A flight scheduled for arrival in Rochester in the morning had been delayed due to a mechanical problem, and the Albrights were now being rerouted. Clare was upset that she had chosen to accompany her husband to a medical conference in New York City. Her shopping on Fifth Avenue was certainly secondary to her grandchild's birth! Stephanie had offers for help from Crystal and Alice, but she turned them down politely. "Thank you, but I'm good." She was impressed by her own resolve to be as adult-like as possible. She did give her mother permission to come to the hospital when she had settled. She had no idea how

Clare would react in the birthing room. Alice would immediately try to take over the proceedings. To have a distraction like Alice's likely behavior next to you would stress her beyond belief. She hadn't practiced relaxation techniques only to have Alice destroy the peace. Crystal would be wonderful, in fact too perfect. Stephanie was afraid she would lose control, and she didn't want to give Crystal a chance for comparison. Stephanie knew her thinking was childish. Her mother would be all right. She would sit demurely by her bedside and allow Michael to be the main support in all aspects of the experience.

Poor Michael. He and Dr. Albright had found a suitable used SUV a few days ago. *High time*, thought Stephanie, as the hospital wouldn't allow a newborn to go home in anything but a legally approved infant seat. Now, as Stephanie counted seconds of her contractions, Michael labored with changing a tire on his new vehicle. Great luck for him to have found a large nail in the tire, possibly from the construction site up the road where a couple from New York City was renovating an old wreck of a cottage into a year-round home. The temporary "donut" would take them to the hospital, and Michael would deal with the issue later.

On the way to Haudenosaunee Hills Central Hospital, Stephanie's contractions became stronger and uncomfortable enough for her to switch from the slower breathing to the next level.

At the door, they were met by Melinda Smith with her most worrisome mother-look on her face. She was trying her best to hide her fears by smiling a lot and fussing, first over the throw covering Stephanie's legs in the wheelchair and later the sheets on the bed.

"Mom, relax. It doesn't help me that you fidget and

fret," Stephanie touched her mother's arm, and almost screamed out the last words with the strong uterine spasm.

Stephanie labored on, Michael alternated between rubbing a tennis ball up and down Stephanie's back and studying the fetal monitor. Melinda talked incessantly, wrung her hands, offered Stephanie a bottle of water from her handbag, and then drank it herself. Melinda got so many calls on her cell Stephanie told Micheal to confiscate her phone.

"Oh, sorry. I told some of my friends I was going to be here. They're just curious."

"I'm in no mood for your curious friends. I have a job to do here."

Heavy labor had gone on for hours. Stephanie was exhausted. The monitor indicated fetal stress. A conference of sorts ensued in the nurses' station with lowered voices. The obstetrician returned and announced he was going to do a Caesarean section. They needed to get the baby out quickly.

To Stephanie's disappointment, the situation called for general anesthesia. All at once, Michael and Melinda were ousted from the room after quick kisses, and the room took on an air of urgency. The activity level increased as Stephanie was prepared for surgery and wheeled into the operating room.

In the hallway, Michael and Melinda used each other as a sounding board, contemplating the situation, until they realized making assumptions and guessing was not helpful. They switched to talking about proper PH levels for garden soil, the proposed several-stories-high condominium building by the lake, the recent high school homecoming game where, for the first time,

Michael wasn't the star. They talked about anything that kept their minds off what was going on in the operating suite.

Craig Smith walked in, baffled about his inability to reach his wife on the phone. He sat quietly with his elbows resting on his knees, chin on his hands. He and Michael discussed the tire versus the "donut." Melinda paced the long hallway. She looked out the window and saw an inflatable pumpkin and a witch on the lawn of the house across the street. It was dark and still stormy. *All the little goblins and princesses could forget about trick-or-treating in this weather!*

Just then the doctor appeared. He was well aware of the anxieties of the family members, as he walked over to Michael and said, "Congratulations! You have healthy son."

Michael teared up. "Thank you. How's Stephanie?"

"She's fine. She'll be in recovery for a while."

Melinda hugged Michael and her husband. Forgetting all formalities, she hugged the doctor as well. Michael talked to his parents, who were now driving home from the Syracuse airport. Clare was crying with joy. Robert was seriously concerned after hearing the words "fetal stress."

"He's okay now, right? No complications?"

Michael convinced him that everything was fine and that they could see and hold their grandson the next day.

Soon the Smiths were driving home, Craig intent on avoiding debris the wind spun around in the street, Melinda on her cell phone telling everyone Stephanie's baby had been born. It was almost midnight, and she woke up half the people on her list of contacts.

Stephanie spent some time shedding the effects of

anesthesia. The incision had come to life as the medications wore off, but she was surprised at being allowed to nurse the baby, with all the drugs still in her system.

The next day, Stephanie got a roommate.

"Hey it's you," said the tattooed girl settling into her bed. "Did you have a Halloween baby? I hoped to have mine on Halloween, but I missed by a day."

Stephanie hadn't even thought about it. "I guess my baby's birthday cakes will always have orange candles!"

"What did you have?"

"I had a boy, C-section. And you?"

"I had a boy, too."

Stephanie had seen the girl's arms and legs with numerous tattoos. Now she saw a snake, the length of her spine, peeking out of the opening of the girl's hospital gown. She obviously hadn't had a Caesarian, judging by her quick ferret-like movements.

"I named him Rex. My name is Colly, by the way." Stephanie was sure there had been introductions at the nutrition class, but the name did not sound familiar.

"Neat," answered Stephanie. "Like a king. I'm Stephanie. You mean your name is like the dog breed?"

"No, with a Y, comes from Colleen. What did you name your son?"

"Robert Michael. Michael's dad's name is Robert. It comes from an old ancestor of his in the South."

"Tradition, huh?"

"Yeah. I like the name, though. Michael's dad is always called Robert, not Bob, Rob, Bobby or Robby. I think calling a two-year-old Robert is a bit formal."

"No kidding! Pompous, if you ask me. Who are these people anyway?"

"Well, they are super-nice people. Dr. Albright and his wife. I'm just happy Michael's father's name isn't Reginald or Archibald or something."

"You're kidding! So now they have a grandson whose blood isn't blue."

"You're nuts! Nothing uppity about them when you get to know them. What's blue blood anyway? You know everybody's blood is blue until it's oxygenated."

"That's actually not true. Blood is red no matter where it is. The veins look blue, but it's misleading. There's a good study on that. You should read it." Colly gathered the long hair on one side of her head into a bun with a rubber band.

"Where did you learn about this study?" Stephanie caught herself trapped in a web of preconceived notions.

"Oh, I just get interested in something and dig a little deeper. You know, like Mark Twain said, 'I never let schooling interfere with my education.' "

Stephanie was about to ask Colly what type of schooling she'd had, but thought it might be gauche. Her eyes were closing.

"You know, I've got to take a nap."

"Sure. Sweet dreams."

Colly and Rex were released to go home the next day. It never became clear to Stephanie where home was for the two of them. During their time in the hospital, no one had come to visit Colly. When she left, Stephanie looked out the window and watched Colly and Rex get into a taxi.

Chapter 57

The nutrition class over, Kaisa contemplated what she could do next. She had been inspired and energized by her involvement with young people. That experience provided one of the reasons she would give a resounding "No!" to any suggested move into an assisted living setting or senior housing of any kind. She couldn't even see herself in Florida, where some of her friends had moved to escape the cold, snowy winters. Kaisa needed it all—four seasons with the good and bad aspects of them all, people of all ages around her, the richness of life! She regretted settling in a small city with no diversity to speak of. The university brought in people of varying backgrounds and cultures. Carol and John Lindqvist had been part of that scene. It showed in the parties they gave, the friends they had. Kaisa's life had been mostly void of exotic influences, full of rather boring characters from her husband's legal world.

Weighing her choices, the college scene became more and more captivating. She could audit a course in a topic she wanted to learn more about, or why not take a course for credit? That would force her to take the work more seriously. The fine arts department offered courses in silk printing, watercolors, and weaving, among a litany of art forms. *Weaving!* Kaisa had always been a weaver, from childhood on. The course description was alluring. She could enhance her current skills and further develop her artistic abilities by incorporating today's abstract forms. Alice had stored her loom, now in pieces after Alice's move. Tom could put it together again in no time, in the basement of the new house. Kaisa felt good about herself and decided to get a head start by googling sources for yarn.

After her midmorning walk, she entered her building, exchanging pleasantries with a stylish older woman, who seemed to follow her. As Kaisa unlocked her door, the woman fumbled with the key ring and tried a key in the door of the apartment next to Kaisa's.

Kaisa's heart made a somersault. This was proof she was not hallucinating.

"Excuse me," she said to the woman, "do you live here?"

"I actually live downtown, but I'm here part of the time."

Kaisa didn't want to appear overly zealous, but she couldn't help herself.

"I'm so glad you exist…that you live here…I mean, that you are here sometimes! You have no idea! I am Kaisa Weston, by the way."

The woman wrinkled her forehead slightly. "I guess I'm glad I exist, too," she said with a smile. "My name is Mary Johnson."

"Will you be around for a while right now? I mean, can you stay put? I need to do something." Kaisa realized how idiotic she must appear to this woman.

"I will be here for the next few hours. Why do you want me to stay put?"

"I have to prove to my family that you are a living, breathing human being. They think I've been hallucinating."

"I believe I am real," said Mary Johnson, happily humoring this obviously well-meaning neighbor of hers before she stepped into her condominium.

Kaisa was beside herself. If Mary Johnson was good for her word and would stick around, Kaisa could settle the hallucination nonsense once and for all. She was shaking, looking for her phone in her purse. Kaisa remembered that she was, most likely, dealing with a criminal and reminded herself to be careful.

Kaisa called Alice. Of course, no answer.

Tom was probably at a closing or a meeting. She didn't even bother to leave a message.

Pam was in class. She had probably walked to class and couldn't get to Kaisa's anyway.

Lola answered on the fifth or sixth ring, right before Kaisa was about to get desperate.

"You need to get here right away!" Kaisa blurted out.

"Is everything all right? You sound panicked. Are you at home?"

"I'm fine. And yes, I'm at home. I just need you to come, so you can be a witness."

"A witness? What on earth?"

"Remember I told you about a suspicious woman living next door? I met her. She's here right now. I actually talked to her, and she said she would be here for a while."

"She's in your apartment?"

"No, in her own. You need to come right now, please!"

The idea of a murderer behind the wall was secondary to the fact that the woman existed, and Kaisa was about to prove her sanity to the world.

Lola arrived covered in dirt. "Hi, Sorry I look like this. Gavin and I were digging up the last of the beets and carr—"

"You're fine," Kaisa interrupted. "Listen. She's there. She's next-door right now. Her name is Mary Johnson. You need to see her, that's all. We don't need to be chummy with her."

"Okay, so we just go to her door and you say, 'I need to show you to my filthy dirty friend.' That's smooth."

"Maybe I should invite her for coffee in my place?"

"Probably a better idea. We'll be on home turf that way."

Kaisa took a deep breath. "Let's roll," she said.

Both women rapped on the neighboring door, two small, elderly women, one sweaty from her inner turmoil, the other dressed in dirty overalls.

A tall woman in leggings and a long Chinese tunic answered the door. Her bobbed hair was gray with purple overtones either intentional or the result of bad shampoo or treatments for silver hair.

"Hello again," she said.

"Hello," responded the duo. Lola tried to peek behind the woman into the apartment. She saw a sparsely furnished room with a large desk, a computer, and a chair. Almost a prison-like atmosphere. The drapes were closed.

"I am Lola Kuusinen," Lola introduced herself. "Somehow, you look familiar to me."

Kaisa was surprised at the statement and wondered how Lola could in any way be familiar with a murderer.

"Mary Johnson," said Mary, waiting to see why she had been asked to stay put. "I've been around a while, off and on, for about two years."

"I've been in Finland most of that time, so I couldn't know you from around here."

"In Finland. That's interesting," said Mary and Kaisa grabbed her opportunity.

"Why don't you come over to my place? We'll have some coffee and chat. I'm from Finland originally."

"Thank you, but I can't stay long. I have a deadline."

She would have to have a 'dead' something. Kaisa made coffee and brought out a braid of *pulla*.

"Oh, you must be the one! Thank you for leaving me some of this delicious bread. I'm sorry I've been so antisocial after moving into town."

"You're very quiet. I wouldn't even know you existed if it weren't for the bloody mink. I don't mean a live animal. You had a mink coat on the balcony in the spring. It had blood on at least one lapel." Kaisa swallowed hard. She wondered if she'd left the bread knife anywhere within reach, should things develop in a wrong direction.

"Oh, that," remembered Mary. "That wasn't blood. It was red spray paint. I inherited the mink, an almost floor-length fifties-style coat from my mother and had it stored for years. After a while, I felt that since I had nothing to do with killing the minks decades ago, I should be able to wear it without guilt. When I was walking to my car after a concert at the Eastman School of Music one night, two hoodlums attacked me with spray paint. I'll probably never get the stains out. I would never buy a new mink coat, but it is a shame not to use something that is so warm, even if politically incorrect."

One mystery solved! Kaisa smiled.

"The other thing cluing me into someone's being in the apartment was the stack of papers on the balcony.

They flew to the yard during a wind storm. I gathered them up in hopes of finding at least a name, but couldn't."

"Thanks for returning them to me, although there was really no need."

Kaisa kept thinking of innocuous ways to bring up the strange purchases, but failed. She decided to present the issue as a joke.

"I could see they were just some old receipts of different sorts—canvas, rope, an anchor, you know, basic stuff you need to dump a body into the ocean." Kaisa carefully observed Mary's face for any sign of being caught, any sign showing admiration for Kaisa's way of having figured it all out, but Mary laughed raucously, a laugh incongruous with her sophisticated presence. Kaisa grew increasingly more alarmed.

"They were from that long ago? I had taken care of a boat for a friend on Cape Cod for a year. I think it was 2014. He had me buy some things for his boat for when he returned from his sabbatical."

This woman thinks on her feet! The story sounds believable!

"So, somehow, these receipts were so important that you saved them for all these years?"

Lola sat quietly sipping her coffee, chewing on her *pulla* and admiring her friend's courage to forge on recklessly.

Mary laughed again, the kind of happy, high-pitched laughter that makes those who hear it feel better.

"Well, I am an author. You may know me by the name of Gunilla Brooks."

Lola dropped her coffee cup and it shattered on the floor.

Paying no attention to Lola's mishap, Kaisa said, "You wrote *Hemlines* and *Tiaras and Crowns* and...and...and...I can't remember. I love your books!"

"Me too," chimed in Lola, on her hands and knees picking up pieces of porcelain.

"With a name like Mary Johnson, I decided to use a *nom de plume*. The papers you found tell a lot about me. First of all, I always write my first draft longhand. There is something special about the flow of ideas from the brain to the arm to the fingers to the pen and paper. It's been studied and published. Take a look online. Secondly, I'm a tightwad who recycles everything. I save every piece of paper that's mailed to me if it has a clean back side. I write on the backs of doctors' reports, insurance documents, begging letters from charities. Why throw out perfectly good paper? We need to save our trees. They're our lungs, after all!"

"I have to agree. So, you sort of go into hiding when you are working on a book? Away from people completely?"

Lola was worried that Kaisa's questioning was going to get too personal, so she jumped in.

"Kaisa's just wondering, since she knew you were around and yet she never saw you."

"I'm actually living downtown with a friend who escaped New York City last year. I use this apartment to write. My schedule tends to be very erratic, always depending on who and what inspires me. I need a quiet place for my escape to the world of my characters."

Kaisa was dying to ask whether the friend was male or female but thought better of it. It was information only a busybody would want to know.

"Well, I do need to get back to my routine and my

book. Thank you for the coffee and the bread. We'll talk about Finland another time. I spent a semester at the University of Turku in my younger days."

Kaisa and Lola hated it when someone threw out bait and prevented reeling it in. They were always ready to discuss Finland and couldn't for the life of them understand why everyone didn't share their passion. By leaving with all the answers to Kaisa's questions, Mary had left a void. The mystery of the woman next door was now solved, but there was so much more to know about her.

"Thank you, Lola, for coming over. I now feel victorious!" Kaisa gave Lola a big hug.

"Victorious for not losing your mind? Or victorious for having proven your family wrong?"

"I must admit, a little bit of both. When I was first diagnosed, there was a time I doubted myself, wanted to withdraw, almost stopped driving, et cetera. Then you and I went to Finland together. You are a big part of my deciding to fight this disease. The mystery woman made me feel like I was on a downward slope again, but I feel like a winner now!"

"Thank you, dear," said Lola. "And without you I wouldn't be as shamelessly happy as I am.'

Chapter 58

Kaisa checked the time, alternating between her cell phone, the range, and the microwave. Time had never gone by this slowly. She calculated Alice was usually home around four o'clock unless she needed to stop at a grocery store on the way. She often ran out of things in the middle of the week or even in the middle of preparing a dish. She did a lot of impulse cooking often requiring ingredients not readily available in an average kitchen. Through the years, Kaisa had come to the conclusion that the impulsivity, the overindulgence, and the overflowing need to help others were characteristics of her own mother. Not only did Alice look like her grandmother, she acted like her, which made it easy for Kaisa to predict Alice's reactions to life's twists and turns.

Kaisa attempted to read a book, but her concentration was disturbed. She cleaned the bathroom medicine cabinet. She decided to bake Karelian pies, labor intensive enough to eat up the time from now until when she could do her victory lap at four.

With freshly made rye baked goods in her basket, Kaisa drove toward Alice's house. She was turning into the driveway of the ranch when it occurred to her that Alice didn't live there anymore. Kaisa laughed out loud. *Alice Doesn't Live Here Any More* had been one of her favorite movies in the seventies. Kaisa's preoccupation with Mary/Gunilla had caused her to follow an old, established routine without thinking. She had driven to the spot remembering nothing she saw along the way.

Kaisa turned the car around, observing that Christine's work crew were just the type she would appreciate. There were no signs, outside, of the huge chaos and untidiness going on inside the house. Kaisa looked forward to the metamorphosis from Alice's informal, inelegant style to Christine's worldly, modern, refined approach to interior design.

Driving astray was unusual for Kaisa. She was "well-oriented to her surroundings," as she had read in her last doctor's report. Driving toward the old Hughes house, she wondered if she could blame the blunder wholly on being preoccupied with Mary or was it possibly a sign of overall failing? She decided on the former option.

"Wow! You made Karelian pies! You don't make these every day. What's the occasion?" Alice was pleased to see her favorite pastries in Kaisa's basket. "Did you make egg butter to go with them?"

"Of course." Kaisa lifted a small plastic container onto the table. "And," she said, "we do have cause for a celebration: I met my neighbor—you know, the woman next door."

Alice's level of concern shot up instantly. The hallucinations had now taken another step up. *Maybe the medication really should have been increased.*

"You'll never guess who she is!"

Most certainly not. Alice said, "Who is she, pray tell?"

"She's Gunilla Brooks!"

"Yeah, right! You wish!"

"No, really. She sometimes uses the condo next to

me as a place to write, away from everything. Her real name is Mary Johnson. Gunilla Brooks is her pen name. She came to my place to have a cup of coffee with us."

"You said she sometimes uses the place for writing. Where is she the rest of the time? She doesn't sleep there?"

"She's living with a friend downtown and comes over whenever she wants to write. I don't think she sleeps there. I've never seen lights in the condo later at night."

"Is she from this area originally? I never... Wait a minute. You said she had coffee with 'us.' Who's 'us'?"

"Oh, Lola was there. I called her over when I met Mary. I knew you wouldn't take my word for anything. I needed a witness. The three of us had a lovely chat. Mary has spent some time in Finland, you know!"

"Lola can verify your story?"

"It's not a story. It's true," said Kaisa proudly, punching Lola's name on her speed dial. "Here." She handed the phone to Alice. Lola readily repeated the events of the morning to Alice.

"I'll be damned," said Alice, giving the phone back to Kaisa, "Wait, what about the blood on the coat, and the suspicious papers you told me about? I must admit, I actually didn't really pay close attention to all that."

Kaisa explained the facts and blamed her overactive imagination for letting her conjure up the criminal scenario in her mind. "So now you can relax. I'm not losing it totally, like you thought."

"I'm really sorry, Mom." Alice was thoughtful for a moment. "You should probably have a checkup. You know, having taken all those pills for months for hallucinations. And that's my fault. Geez, I insisted you be put on them! I'm really sorry!"

"Don't even think about it. I never took them. I knew I wasn't hallucinating. I still have the unopened prescription bottles, two bottles, a ninety-day supply each. I didn't want to let you think I wasn't taking them, so I even got the refill." Kaisa winked at her daughter.

"Mom, you are incorrigible!"

Bobby walked in with Barney.

"Have a good walk?" asked Kaisa.

"Hi, Grandma. Barney is a good runner, except that when I try to run with him, all these people want to stop and pet him."

"Oh, yes, especially the female kind." Alice looked at her mother with a knowing glance. With Bobby out of earshot, Kaisa asked, "Has Tom had a talk with him? You know, 'that talk'?"

"Oh, yes, a few years ago. Stephanie's living with us brought some issues to light for him. I don't think the boy will be stupid any time soon."

"Good. How's Stephanie doing, by the way?"

"She's home now. To take care of a newborn and recover from major abdominal surgery at the same time is tough. I hear both grandmothers are involved and a big help. I wanted to go over to help, but she has her own mom, and Michael's mom, plus Crystal. I wish those kids all the luck in the world."

"They'll need it!" agreed Kaisa with a slight "I told you so" message directed to the absent young couple.

Pam came in through the kitchen door, out of breath.

"I found a shortcut to the college through the woods. It's great not to have to walk in traffic. It reminds me of our old place out of town."

Kaisa was curious. "Do you miss your old house?"

"No, I love this house, its history and style. I just have to find my woods every now and then. Oh, man, Karelian pies! Can I have one?" Without waiting for an okay, Pam spread egg butter on a piece and enjoyed the unique taste experience.

"A true Finn with Karelian pies and the woods," said Kaisa, obviously pleased.

"Mom," said Pam, "remember when you asked me to think about something special you and I could do together? I've been thinking and I've got it—I'd like to go to the Dickens Christmas in Skaneateles. What do you think?"

"I've never been. It's so close and somehow we just haven't gotten around to it. Sounds great." Alice was happy with Pam's choice. She could have wanted tickets to a loud concert or planned an expensive trip far away.

"Check this out." Pam pulled out her tablet and scrolled pictures of the last time the event took place, so Alice and Kaisa could see. There were theater productions, sing-alongs, bands, and chestnuts being roasted on an open fire, which was in reality a grill on the sidewalk. There were also pictures of first-class restaurants, great old places to stay, and a busy Main Street on the lake with boutiques galore.

"And look at the outfits!" gushed Alice. "Visitors dress up in Dickensian garb also, not only the performers. Look at this shiny, purple taffeta dress with all the white silk roses and lace, and a fur coat to cover it." Kaisa looked closer and thought of Mary's inherited mink. "And this," Alice went on, "this one is amazing!" She was looking at a two-piece dress made of bright red velvet with a matching hat. "When is this?" she asked.

"It goes on for a while, starting right after

Thanksgiving. Let's pick a time closer to Christmas. Maybe there'll be snow and it'll feel more like Christmas."

"Great idea," said Alice. That'll give me more time for sewing."

"Sewing?" Pam looked at Alice quizzically. "You mean you would make outfits for us?"

"Well, of course, and also coats. It might be a really cold couple of days just then."

"Mom, this is already causing you stress. Can't we just go and enjoy the event in our regular clothes? Not everyone dresses up."

"I know, but to get the most out of it, wouldn't you want to be dressed according to the style of the day?"

"Only if you think you have time, Mom, which I know you don't. Also, outfits of this type cost a lot of money to make. Velvet and taffeta—are you kidding me? They're really expensive. You can't even use them later in your real life. I don't know about you, but I'm probably not going to traipse through the woods to the college to attend classes in taffeta, and I doubt that you'll be teaching in velvet. Why make these useless garments? I'll be happy with walking the streets and watching people and maybe eating in a good restaurant. As long as I'm with you, the rest doesn't matter."

Alice thought of her propensity to "go all out." It produced great results most of the time, but it also obligated her to raise the bar for herself each time, to strive for perfection. To have someone ask her to lower her expectations for herself was almost painful. However, this was something Pam had specifically asked for. The request already stemmed from Pam's opinion that Alice didn't devote enough time to her daughter. The least she could do now was to listen to Pam's wishes.

"I hear you," Alice said to Pam. "Instead of spending time and money on the outfits, maybe we can stay at one of the historic places."

"I'd like that," said Pam and hugged her mother.

Alice looked at Kaisa, who continued scrolling through the pictures. Alice was thankful to her mom for having said nothing. "Want to stay for dinner, Mom?"

Kaisa happily accepted. She now had another opportunity to tell her story of the amazing Mary, the mink, and the murder to Tom, Pam, and Bobby, and have yet another chance to gloat thoroughly and completely.

Chapter 59

Haudenosaunee Hills was home again to all four Chrysalis sisters. They had gone their separate ways to college. Although three of them had returned home with their diplomas under their arms, Christine had taken hers to the West Coast. Now, after twenty years, she too had returned to the place that held their hearts.

Alice wanted a reunion get-together, and she tested the waters with Crystal.

"Hey, I've got an idea. I'd really like the four of us to get together, and husbands, too, of course. What do you think about a progressive dinner? Thanksgiving is coming, and we'll all be involved with our extended families. We'll have time to do it before that, don't you think?"

"I like the idea. Especially when we would only need to prepare one part of the whole meal."

"I'm checking with you first, since you have a baby and are a little more tied up than the rest of us. Well, maybe Lisa…"

"I'm fine, especially if we do it while my mom is still here."

After checking with everyone, Alice set the date, assigned courses for each, and designed invitations using a time-consuming paper-cutting method she had learned watching a TV program she called educational fluff. She had felt guilty about it, but TV was one thing she had been able to engage in with her foot in a cast and elevated.

A four-course dinner was perfect for a quartet. Lisa would start with a soup, followed by Alice's entrée. Crystal was responsible for the salad, and the evening would wind up at Magnus's house for dessert, Christine's house being under renovations.

Magnus offered to foot the bill for a stretch limo for the afternoon and evening, an offer everyone gratefully accepted. A good meal called for stronger beverages, especially in the wine country.

"Are we dressing up?" asked Crystal, willing to do it to please the others. "I mean like formal wear?"

"No way!" said Alice. "Who does that these days?"

"I don't know. I've seen Christine's closet, so I just thought..."

"Nah, I don't even own anything fancy. Let's just go casual."

"Works for me." Crystal was relieved.

Alice decided to include "casual" under "attire required" in the invitations, but changed her mind. The invitations' content was cut back with every edit, and the final product was a simple threefold paper with cutouts you could see through.

Dressed informally, Christine surprisingly in designer jeans, the group gathered around the foyer in Lisa's house. They raised their glasses of sparkling wine. Alice was about to make a welcome speech, as the dinner was, after all, her idea, when Abdul Naziri spoke up.

"I want to welcome you all to our home, a house full of childhood memories for all of you. I thank you for your friendship and hope you will never forget your bond with each other. Thank you, Alice, for arranging this most unique way of dining. Please, enjoy some hors d'oeuvres. The first course will be ready soon." Abdul raised his glass. "Welcome!"

"To Chrysalis!" added Lisa.

"To Chrysalis!"

Alice wondered if Abdul always just took over in any situation. Of course, this was his house and he had a right to welcome everybody. She wondered what Emily Post would have to say about this scenario.

They sat down to Afghani ash soup of noodles, kidney beans, and chickpeas. Alice noticed there were no utensils. Maybe the children had set the table.

Lisa showed how the soup should be eaten by hand using naan bread as a spoon. A rather stiff atmosphere broke with everyone learning to fish out noodles with bread. All fought an urge to assist with their left hand. The room filled with laughter and some well-meaning jabs at Abdul and his customs. No one declined Abdul's offer of a second glass of white wine.

Two small children came from upstairs and whispered something to Lisa, who excused herself from the table. Alice looked at Lisa following the children up the stairs. She felt touched by the scene of children and a woman who clearly was happy in her role as a mother.

"Sorry about that. We had a slight mishap the sitter couldn't handle. She was too shy to come down."

Alice could see Niles in the kitchen. She was surprised to see the cat out and about with so many people around. Living with a large family must have influenced his basic reclusive Siamese psyche. The large family certainly seemed to agree with Lisa.

"Time for the entrée," said Alice and started to collect soup bowls from the table.

"Just leave them. I'll take care of them later, or we will." Lisa leaned on Abdul.

Magnus, who had been given a special invitation to join the Chrysalis group, opened and closed limo doors for all.

Walking into Alice's house, now furnished with larger sofas, wall hangings from Kaisa's loom, and antiques from Alice's childhood home, Lisa looked around. She had lived in this house most of her life, but the different décor had changed it to Alice's house. Lisa was at peace with that. Crystal and Gavin wanted a tour, while Christine studied Alice's wonderful new range and Tom talked to Magnus and Abdul about his idea of what to give Alice as a Christmas present she would love— blueprints for a sauna.

Alice served a Finnish stew of beef, pork, and lamb, rutabaga casserole, and sweet peas, a traditional wintertime meal of the old Finland. She also served a full-bodied red wine. As they finished, Pam appeared, an apron covering her jeans, and shooed away everyone attempting to assist.

She's such a good kid! Alice stole another sip of her wine from the kitchen counter.

At the Pure Earth farm, Lola greeted everybody at the door. "Hi, welcome!" she said. "I just brought the salads to the table. Please, enjoy." Lola disappeared.

"Did your mother make the salad?" asked Christine, now thinking of Lola in a slightly different light than before.

"No, I did. She's my helper in so many ways these days. I'll really miss her when she leaves in a couple of weeks. I need to find someone to care for Anna. A while ago, Stephanie and I had talked about maybe her babysitting for me. The babies could grow up together and she could have a small income, but now with her Caesarean, it's not going to happen for a while, and I'm looking at going back to work part-time in January."

"She'll be fine by then," said Lisa. "There were no complications, right?"

"No, but it shook her quite a bit. I'll have to see. Two babies are a bit more challenging than one."

"Yes, or five older ones all at once." Lisa laughed.

"True. How is that going? Motherhood is hard, isn't it?"

"It's hard, but it's wonderful. I have now realized how terribly lonely I was in my childhood. I look at our kids at night"—Crystal and Christine smiled at the "our kids"—"all saying goodnight to each other, and I almost cry. I always went to bed alone, from the time I was about ten, and read myself to sleep. I love the hustle and bustle and the love, even when they are having their skirmishes."

The salad was a Caesar salad with kale added for extra crunch. Crystal had made the croutons from her homemade bread, adding lots of garlic and spices. She served her favorite Finger Lakes Riesling, feeling cheated because she wouldn't have any of it. Mothers were known for sacrifices, and to give up alcohol was a small sacrifice for a nursing mother.

Magnus had made a cherry cheesecake that the women declared a caloric bomb but they cheerfully cleaned their plates.

No one but Tom and Alice had been in the house since Magnus started his restoration. All were in awe of the paint and wallpaper choices, as well as furniture pieces now in complete harmony with the style of the house—Colonial simplicity and splendor at the same time.

"I made some limoncello for an after-dinner drink. Anyone interested?" asked Magnus. Everyone but Crystal was ready to try it and little by little emptied the bottle.

Christine spoke up. "Do you girls remember the night we were in the den in the basement here and tried to come up with a name for our quartet?" The other three Chrysalis members nodded and rolled their eyes. "Well, I never told anyone this, but we emptied a couple of bottles from my father's wine cellar. When Mom and Dad came home from Dad's office party, you had already gone home. I quickly said goodnight to them and went to bed. The next morning, Dad invited me into the living room. We sat by the fireplace and he told me how disappointed he was in us. I played innocent, but it was impossible to fool the master of deceit, if you know what I mean." Everyone nodded. They knew. "He was disappointed that we had been drinking, but here's the rub—We had emptied two bottles from his collection of rare wines. They were worth twelve thousand dollars a bottle!"

"Oh, my God!" said Alice, and reflexively pushed away the tiny *digestif* glass.

"Really?" Lisa couldn't believe it. "Well, what did we know about wine? We were young and innocent."

"Not to mention stupid!" said Crystal and laughed. "That's really funny!"

"I know," said Christine. "It's funny now, but I was shaking in my shoes in front of my dad."

"So sorry," said Lisa.

"How did you then come up with the name Chrysalis

for your group?" asked Abdul, having never heard the story.

Lisa explained. "It's a composite of all our names: CHR in Christine, the YS from Crystal, AL in Alice, and the IS from Lisa."

"Very nice," said Abdul. "Are you going to sing again, now that you are all in Haudenosaunee Hills?"

Everyone looked at each other.

"Not out of the realm of possibility, right?" asked Alice.

"Sure," said Crystal.

"Why not?" said Lisa.

Tom looked at Alice. He already saw her planning a worldwide concert tour, acting as a performer in the group as well as the agent, the promoter, the marketing executive, and the historian for the quartet.

"Great! Why not? Why not now?" Christine hummed one starting note for each woman. They immediately knew which tune was going to follow and, to the men's delight, sang *a cappella* "Don't Sit under the Apple Tree" in perfect four-part harmony.

Chapter 60

Kaisa, forlorn, drove to the Pure Earth Farm. The gloomy scenery of leafless trees, muddy roadways, and cloudy skies served to keep her spirits low and melancholy.

Lola and Mauno were flying back to Finland in a couple of days. It was always bittersweet for Kaisa to witness someone going to Finland, whether it was their first trip or a return home as in Lola and Mauno's case. Kaisa wanted to go along. Homesickness was a devious friend. It enticed you, yet when it had you in its hold and you acted on it, it turned on you. Kaisa would travel to Finland and, each time, develop a homesickness for the Finger Lakes in just a few weeks' time.

"How's my primary witness?" asked Kaisa, hugging Lola.

"What a caper that was!" Lola invited Kaisa in to sit by the fire. Anna had her six-week checkup and both Crystal and Gavin had gone on the visit to the doctor. Lola and Kaisa had a lot of admiration for today's fathers, who "did their part."

Settled on the sofa with cups of steaming coffee, they replayed the hallucination scenario. To Lola's inquiry whether Kaisa had cleared the air with Alice, Kaisa shook her head.

"You know her. She flies off the handle and always makes more of an issue than is necessary. I've thought about this a lot. She's actually like me. We both have major control issues. I want to be in control of my own life, and yes, I still think of her as a child of mine, not as an adult equal to me. In my book, she shouldn't be telling me what to do. Yet, as a mother, I take the liberty to tell her when she is making a wrong decision. I know, I know, it's completely wrong, but, you know, she really does try to run my life. Haven't you noticed?"

"She has your best interest in mind. If you mean her suggestion for you to teach a nutrition class, there was nothing wrong with it. I think it did you a lot of good. And making sure you take your medications? What's wrong with that? The mother-daughter roles will reverse at some point in our old age. With some people, it will happen sooner than with others."

"I am fighting against it. When Alice just announced that she'll be in charge of Thanksgiving and Christmas, I resented it. It has always been my job, and hearing this from her is like a slap in the face. On one hand, my culinary skills are fantastic enough to teach others, on the other hand, I'm not capable of organizing a dinner."

"You've done it for decades. Be thankful Alice wants to step up. It's time for you to relax, let the younger ones take over."

"It means I'm old and I'm being set aside to sit in a rocking chair, knitting socks."

"What's wrong with knitting socks? I'd love to know how. I guess I never sat in one place long enough to learn."

"I could teach you, but it could be tough over social media. So tell me, how is it that you don't have these problems with Crystal?"

"Crystal and I have different problems. She's so

independent, she forgets to tell me about events in her life. She found no reason to tell me she's planning on going back to work in January, for instance. Not that I could do anything with the information except to fret about what will happen to little Anna."

"It's the need -to-know syndrome. Of course, when I know about something Alice is planning on doing, I tend to say what I think of it, and that doesn't always help in maintaining a good relationship."

"We're just lucky we have daughters who agree to have us in their lives no matter how much abuse we shell out."

"I wouldn't go that far, but I certainly could make some changes. I'm just hoping this blasted Parkinson's doesn't make changes in me whether I want them or not."

The doorbell rang. When Lola opened the door, looking straight at her was Magnus, a perfect replica of John Lindqvist in his younger years, the handsome Viking she had fallen in love with. Crystal's car pulled in and Crystal came up beside Magnus.

"Hi, Magnus. Mom, what's with you? Didn't you invite him in?"

"Well, I just...I...I wasn't thinking."

Crystal walked in, Gavin following with a baby car carrier. "Come in, Magnus."

Magnus stood by the door.

"I have something I want to give you," he said to Crystal, and went back to his car. Returning, he was carrying a heavy piece of furniture, a small bench of sorts. He put it down. "I discussed this with Christine and DeeDee." Magnus looked at Crystal and smiled. "You know, with the rest of our dad's children."

Lola moved slowly to sit by Kaisa as if looking for protection from the information that was attacking her.

"This is the cobbler's bench brought here by our ancestor, the first Lindqvist to immigrate to the Americas in the seventeen-hundreds, at the time when the country wasn't even the United States yet. I want you to have it. With what has happened, it's not at all a sure thing that I will ever have a child to carry on the family history. I do know that little Anna is John Lindqvist's full-fledged granddaughter and the bench belongs to her. This little bench was one thing Mom was always very protective of. Chirstine and I weren't allowed to sit on it. Our kids' minds couldn't figure out why you shouldn't sit on a bench. To us it was like you shouldn't sleep on a bed."

Lola listened to the son of her lover from eons ago and looked at two of John's four children—John's children they knew of. If there were more, that was now immaterial.

"Thank you, Magnus. I will treasure it, but I will most likely let Anna sit on it. It's so low, it will probably be the first piece of furniture she can climb onto."

"By all means," said Magnus and left wishing all a good day.

"So it goes," said Kaisa. "Time. Just like that." She snapped her fingers. "Well, I need to go as well. Crystal, my offer to drive Lola and Mauno to the airport is still on. Did you think about it?"

"I did. I like to say my goodbyes at home, right here, not in public. What do you think, Mom?"

"I like it. too. This way, you don't need to drag Anna out in this lousy weather."

****

Lola, Mauno and Kaisa were uncharacteristically

quiet on the way to the airport. Kaisa stayed with them until they got through the security checkpoint and gave their last wave from behind the body scanner. She walked to the large windows where people could sit in rocking chairs and view planes taking off and landing. She watched several planes disappear into the clouds.

Kaisa stood for a long time, until her legs were aching. She wiped her teary face and sat in a rocking chair.

This is okay. I'm okay in a rocking chair. All I need is knitting needles and yarn, and I'll show them. Not only can I knit, but I can also design my own patterns and, if needed, spin my own yarn! And, if absolutely necessary, I can raise my own sheep! Just watch me!

A word about the author...

Maija DeRoche is a weaver of stories as well as lace, cloth, and rugs. A native of Finland, mother of two and grandmother of three, she puts her pen and her loom into creative action in New York's beautiful Finger Lakes.

Always a Weaver is her second novel, a sequel to *Forever Chrysalis*.

Thank you for purchasing
this publication of The Wild Rose Press, Inc.

For questions or more information
contact us at
info@thewildrosepress.com.

The Wild Rose Press, Inc.

www.ingramcontent.com/pod-product-compliance
Lightning Source LLC
Chambersburg PA
CBHW060942030726
47503CB00003B/695